ALOHA LAGOON MYSTERIES

Ukulele Murder
Murder on the Aloha Express
Deadly Wipeout
Deadly Bubbles in the Wine
Mele Kalikimaka Murder
Death of the Big Kahuna
Ukulele Deadly
One Hawaiian Wedding and a Funeral
Photo Finished

BOOKS BY AIMEE GILCHRIST

Aloha Lagoon Mysteries:
Mele Kalikimaka Murder

Birdwell, Texas Mysteries:
Digging Up Bones

Rules of the Scam Mysteries:
The Tell-Tale Con

MELE KALIKIMAKA MURDER

an Aloha Lagoon mystery

Aimee Gilchrist

MELE KALIKIMAKA MURDER

CHAPTER ONE

———

Summer made up the bulk of my work for the entire year, but it also constituted the bulk of the money for any resort. For that, I was willing to work. However, right now, the second time this year that my current resort, Aloha Lagoon, had massive crowds, I wasn't so keen. Christmas at the Aloha Lagoon Resort was a big deal. Christmas for me was nothing but trouble, and I had the shirt to prove it. It said *Bride*. I'd crossed it out with a magic marker and put it through my paper shredder. I'd had to buy a new shredder.

"Charlotte, three of the lights are out on the big palm," my assistant, Mallory, said, hopping around like a bunny jacked up on speed.

It seemed like Mallory was the only other person, besides me, in the town of Aloha Lagoon—which I liked to call AL in my mind to avoid confusion with the resort with the same name—who wasn't caught up in the slow pace of Hawaiian living. Not shockingly, she was another corporate transfer from Chicago. We'd both rolled in smack in the middle of the high season, when the previous manager, Phillip Kealoha, had dropped dead, face first in a plate of *lomi lomi*. His heart attack probably wasn't from stress, given how infuriatingly low key these people were, but it might have been from the fact he'd weighed a startling five hundred pounds.

We were some of the first outsiders that Freemont Hospitality Inc. had sent into Aloha Lagoon. That had probably been a good move on their part, given how little we fit in on the island. It wasn't that we were the only nonnatives on the island, because we certainly weren't. We were just the only ones who hadn't learned to adapt yet to the casual vibe that moved everyone else along the lazy river of least resistance.

Actually, that wasn't completely true. Mallory was starting to learn. The prior week, she'd tried to come to work in shorts and tank tops, instead of her Aloha Lagoon uniform or acceptable office attire. I'd rather drop dead in *my lomi lomi* than come to a professional situation in shorts.

I followed her across the beach, my heels pitting in the sand. There was probably a good, practical reason these people lived in sandals, but I couldn't bring myself to do that either. I also couldn't find it in myself to wear my blonde hair in any style other than a tight bun, or seek out a tan, or any of the other things my employees did.

The big palm was in the middle of the resort's expansive driveway. It got a lot of attention from the staff and acted as a Christmas tree in lieu of an evergreen. Personally, I had little opinion about the big palm. It was big. And it was a palm. But saying so would have gotten me lynched.

Grateful to step onto the paved driveway, I shook off my shoes and approached the tree. In the small time it had taken Mallory to track me down, I'd gone through my list of Christmas chores, and seven lights were now out. It wasn't such an easy matter to switch them. They were the same lights Aloha Lagoon had been using for something like an absurd forty years.

Sighing, I added a notation to my planner to have the already overburdened handyman, Ikaika, deal with the lights before the tourists started rolling in for the first party of the Christmas season six days before the holiday. Unfortunately, that was a scant—I glanced at my watch—six hours and twenty-six minutes from now. Also unfortunately, much of the staff I really depended on to help run this place were out of town, either for the holidays or for other issues that had happened to coincide with the holiday. So, for us, we were operating with a skeleton staff compared to a normal Christmas rush.

I glanced back up to Mallory. "Thank you, Mallory. Could you send Alex to my office?"

Even asking the question was slightly painful. Alex Cho was both the bane of my existence and the only reason I was able to run Aloha Lagoon at all. He knew it too. That was half the problem. The other half was that the guy delighted in harassing me, and I delighted in looking at him, which was a problem all on its own.

As the Leisure Groups coordinator, Alex technically answered to me, but that was merely a front. We both had master's degrees in hospitality, but he had been working for Aloha Lagoon for ten years. This place was nothing like my previous experiences troubleshooting for hotels and resorts all over the world. Hawaii was a place unlike any other I'd been, and managing this resort was way above my head, because the people who worked here would simply watch me while I spoke, nod a lot, then leave and do whatever they wanted. It was the Hawaiian way, and it made me crazy. The only one who spoke their language, figuratively and sometimes literally, was Alex.

Though Aloha Lagoon was a smoothly run resort with many good employees, Alex had a way with this place. Without him the entire resort would have been in ruins in just the six months since I'd flown in. However, just because I knew it didn't mean I had to like it. Ours was a very precarious relationship. Neither of us spoke of the fact that all I had going for me here was organizational skills. Everything else was on him. He drove me crazy, but there was no getting rid of him. Not unless I was also interested in getting rid of my position at Freemont Hospitality, Aloha Lagoon's parent company.

On my way through the lobby, I paused for a moment, entranced by the shower of white lights the staff was hanging from the ceiling, and then I shuddered. Christmas and I had once been BFFs, but we'd broken things off between us. My reasons were legitimate, but no one would ever hear them. My ruined holly-jolly nuptials were not something I talked about. Instead, I always got the reputation as the local Scrooge. That was better than the truth any day.

I barely made it back to my office before Alex did. Gritting my teeth, I waved at the door, gesturing him inside. Alex always looked like he'd just woken up. I faulted him for not being professional, but at least he wore the look well, and the female guests couldn't get enough. His off-white linen shirt almost tried to look professional, with a collar and buttons, but he ruined it by not buttoning the majority of them. He might have even saved it by just wearing a shirt underneath, but he didn't bother with that either. Tanned skin and sleek muscles were the only thing he had underneath that shirt. He wore white board shorts and tan docksiders, and his black hair was mussed like he'd rolled out of bed and come right here.

I knew it wasn't true. I came to my office at five thirty in the morning, and he was always there at nearly the same time. If I didn't know it, though, I wouldn't have believed it. He flopped onto a chair, folding one leg over the top of his knee and slumping down. I took my seat behind the large cherrywood desk that dwarfed me, as it had been designed for the giant of a man who had preceded me, and getting a new desk would have been a tacit agreement that I was at least a semipermanent fixture.

Alex removed his sunglasses and winked.

"Morning, Charlie."

I flinched, begging my practical side not to rise to the bait. My greatly squelched passionate side always wanted to. Charlotte was a difficult name to shorten. Lottie was childish, Char sounded weird, and Charlie, well, Charlie was repulsive in every way. So I always insisted that everyone refer to me by my entire name. There was no shortening it. Not for most people anyway. Though I'd made it clear that no nickname was acceptable to me, Alex continued to use one. Somehow, without even asking, he'd zoomed in immediately on exactly the one I considered the absolute worst, and he insisted on calling me that. I would have preferred Char.

In the last six months, I'd given up on trying to get him to stop. Now it wasn't giving instructions to an employee. It was just rising to the bait. That was exactly what he wanted, and exactly what *I* wanted was to deny him any pleasure I could. I might have had to work with him, but I didn't have to enjoy it. Especially when he went out of his way to see that I didn't.

"Doors open at six thirty," I reminded him.

Technically, there were no doors to open, since there was no fence around the resort. And even if there had been, anyone could have walked up from the beach. Every other resort Freemont Hospitality ran had a fence and a gate and a security team stationed in a visible place. Aloha Lagoon had a security team, and normally they were a well-oiled machine. However, currently the head of security, a heavily muscled Hawaii native named Jimmy Toki, was away at some surfing competition. So we had a temporary team in place. It included a partially blind Haitian man named Si, and, occasionally, Detective Ray Kahoalani, or one of his officers, who showed up and pretended to do security checks in return for access to the buffet. We weren't exactly a bastion of safety. No one worried about it though. Except me. I worried about everything at Aloha Lagoon that wasn't by the book.

For a small town, Aloha Lagoon had an oddly high occurrence of crime, mostly during the high season. In my head that could be, partially at least, mitigated by proper security measures. But this town was not interested in the stuff in my head, and the resort only marginally more so. Corporate had been clear to me that I was to let the resort function as it had always done. I was here only to stop everything from grinding to a halt after Phillip had died and to wait for another assignment. As of yet, that assignment hadn't come, and I had no idea why. I called corporate once a week reminding them that I was trapped in the land of palm trees and dead ambition.

"Gotcha, *Boss*." Alex's grin was infuriating, only because he did it to mock me. Well, and because the smile was something he wore *really* well. Well enough that I concentrated on anything but him. He smiled at me to mock me—same way he said the word *boss*, like it was somehow a joke. To him, it probably was. It was too bad too. Alex had a smile that could easily have been weaponized and used against women the world over. He didn't have dimples so much as interesting creases that formed on each cheek. His teeth were perfect, ridiculously straight and white against his tanned Korean skin.

I slammed open my planner, and focused all of my attention there. "I printed a list of everything that still needs to be checked before guests start to arrive. Talk to the employees and make sure they've got their jobs under control. I'm going to drive into AL and check with the vendors—oh, and visit with the band to make sure they have everything in order and they're ready to take the stage at seven. And speaking of the stage, can you check to make sure it's completely sound? Ikaika is completely swamped, and now the lights are out on the big palm."

Normally, there was a rotating schedule of who got to go out of town when high season or Christmas rolled around. This year, everyone who was gone had a very legitimate reason, and we had a staff that was super overworked. Jimmy was competing, the assistant manager, Rachel, had gone home to New York City for a much-deserved family visit, and Juls, who was a powerhouse herself, had been temporarily transferred to Florida by corporate to take over for the manager of the resort in Palm Springs while she took maternity leave.

"Oh come on, Charlie. You can change the lights. I'll hold the ladder."

Everything was a joke to him. He probably would have found it hilarious if I toppled off the ladder while wrestling with that ancient string of lights. The whole thing looked like it belonged on Snoopy's doghouse. I wasn't risking a limb for that.

"Pass, thanks." I kept my voice even and dared looking up at him. One sharply arched eyebrow, the right, was slightly hitched, the smallest hint of a smile playing on his mouth.

He grabbed the list from my planner, without asking if it was the copy I wanted him to have, and stood. "Consider it done."

For all his faults, that part was actually true. If nothing else, I could trust Alex Cho to get the job done, even if I didn't always like the way he did it.

* * *

The band, Pacific Rim, was a popular local band that played covers when people wanted it, traditional Hawaiian music for the resort, and reggae for themselves. Tonight they would be playing long sets of traditional folk songs interspersed with holiday favorites. Of course, they'd be required by some kind of local ordinance to play Bing Crosby's "Mele Kalikimaka" at least every half an hour. They checked everything off my list with ease, and I headed away from the bandleader's house, satisfied that aspect was in hand.

The next stop was the bakery. The resort had its own kitchens, of course, but occasionally, like at Christmastime, the burden was too much for just us. The entire town would normally gather somewhere to celebrate at the big Christmas Eve luau. Over the years since the resort had been built, the town had slowly elected to move the festivities there. In just a few days every single person in AL would be up at the resort for some holiday fun. That's where the bakery came into play.

The place was run by Ellen and Aiden, who were makers of the world's best scones and also had a power in the kitchen that bordered on witchcraft. They assured me all was in hand and that their staff would be headed our way in less than a week. After that, I stopped at almost every restaurant in town, checking off the same. Much of our food was actually provided by locals for this particular event, but even with their help, it was too great a job for any one source.

That done, I climbed back into my car and rolled down the window, enjoying the breeze coming off the water, pulling in the sharp, tangy scent of the ocean mixed with the gentle smell of sun-warmed sand. If I were in Chicago, it would be snowing and bitterly cold. I didn't like to compare, or take any chances that might compromise my ability to leave Hawaii at the first given opportunity, but I had to admit, if I had to do Christmas, getting baked under a tropical sun wasn't a bad option. Especially since I was trying to shake the memories of Chicago's white Christmases. AL was small and quaint. A place that centered around the resort and offered mostly services that catered to tourists who flocked in year round or to the staff who worked and lived at the resort.

Driving its roads was a pleasure too. Little traffic, friendly drivers, and only the occasional wild animal standing on the road—it never felt like a chore to get around AL. It was when I started considering getting a convertible that I rolled up the windows and turned on the air. I had no plans of morphing into one of the locals. Nothing could stand in the way of leaving the moment an opportunity presented itself. I was very determined not to fall in love with anything or anyone in Hawaii. I jabbed the radio button until I found a station not playing holiday songs and headed back to the resort.

The resort was only a few miles out from downtown AL, and it was a short trip back. I remembered, suddenly, that I had no clue if I'd asked Alex to check on the linens. Shoot. These

were the little details that made me good at what I did. But if I
went to the staff and instructed them in how I wanted the linens
done, they'd merely nod a lot, and I'd come in with the guests to
find that everything had been arranged in some traditionally
Hawaiian manner and not in the Freemont way. Somehow I
lacked the ability to say the right words to motivate this staff.

I turned to the phone on my dash and instructed it to call
Mallory. It was immediately obedient and put the call through,
but in a few rings I was directed to voicemail. I left a detailed
message about the linens and sighed. I would not call Alex. Not
unless something was on fire. I'd check it myself when I got
back.

I called Mallory again from the parking lot, but there
was still no answer. Irritated, I went by the main resort building,
which housed the kitchen, conference rooms, stores, offices, and
check-in desks. It was the epicenter of the resort. The resort was
massive, and there were many different areas, places where
guests could either join in the fun or feel like they were in a
world all their own and sharing their paradise with only those
they elected to be with. Aloha Lagoon was, by far, Freemont's
largest resort, covering nearly sixteen acres of land. There were
multiple restaurants, bars, and stores on-site, and everyone had
an option for getting what they needed. In the middle of it all
was the main building.

A quick check in the dining room told me that all was
well in the land of linens. Alex, clearly. Mouth twisting, I
checked off the note in my planner and headed to the offices.

The administration offices were contained in a large
warren of small rooms located at the back of the main building. I
checked every one of those fifteen rooms for Mallory, but she
was nowhere to be seen. The resort was too large, and there
would be no way to find her if she was running some kind of
check on the outskirts of the property. It was a poor time for her
to go exploring though. We were down to a mere two hours
before the first guests would begin to pour in for the official
holiday kickoff party.

I sighed and snatched up the packet of papers that
needed to go back to my office. I had no idea why Mallory had
chosen to leave them on the desk in her office instead of

returning them to mine, but her lack of responsibility today was really annoying me when this was the second biggest day of the year. I slid the papers into my desk and grabbed up one of the handheld radios that the whole staff carried when we were on-site. I didn't carry one when I went into town, but now I was on the hunt for Mallory and, regrettably, Alex.

I scanned the property as I walked the perimeter of the main building, looking for anything out of place. It was sometimes hard to skirt this primary area, since there were buildings attached as well as others a short distance away. Walking around it meant dodging between shops and eateries. Turning on the plastic box in my hand, I flinched at the scratching howl of an angry radio. Pressing the button, I identified myself. There was a procedure for the use of these, but few people followed it. Of course I did. Procedure was my friend.

"This is Charlotte Conner. Silas Accius, please identify."

Eventually, Si's laconic, drawling voice came over the line. He was ancient, nearly blind, and I suspected he was an illegal Haitian immigrant. He'd been here before I'd ever come, and he was likely to be here long after I was gone. "This is Si."

"Could you do a check and tell me if buggy seventeen is missing?"

When I'd arrived, that was a change I *had* implemented—the following of emergency guidelines. One of them included checking out specific carts for important members of the staff, ensuring they could always be found in the event of an emergency. Most people ignored the rules, but Mallory wouldn't.

There was a long, loud pause while I waited for the call to come back. Finally, Si's voice came through. "No, ma'am. Seventeen is right where it ought."

"Thank you, Si." I turned down the speaker, sure I'd be able to hear it if someone really wanted to talk to me. Where the heck was Mallory?

* * *

The guests started arriving early, as guests were wont to do. If this had been one of my normal resorts, they'd have been kept out by the gate and entertained on the street by performers, redirected to the beach, or offered the option of being driven to the hottest local shows or shopping. There would have been no strange faces wandering around in the main building at fifteen till. Not that there were hot shows or shopping here, but still.

In the lobby, I spotted Jillian, the head concierge, Finn, the head bellboy, and Eve, the day clerk, along with all of our day staff and a few temps hired for the holiday festivities. Even Si and Ikaika were moving through the crowd, trying hard to be circumspect. Every member of the staff, even the night workers, would be present for the start of the festivities later. Alex was working a crowd of bikini-clad girls barely old enough to be legal. Who wore a bikini on December twenty-third? It was Hawaii, but jeez. *Draw the line somewhere.* I would have judged him—I kind of wanted to anyway—but I knew girls like that were part of the lifeblood of Aloha Lagoon. Both the resort and the town. If they were happy, the coffers would also be. Alex knew how to work a crowd, and that was exactly what he was doing.

Who I did not see was Mallory. I wouldn't fire her. She'd been my assistant for three years, and our parents were best friends, though my own relationship with Mallory, who was ten years my junior, was slight. However, this was a serious infraction, and if I found out she'd disappeared with some surfer, I'd have to give her some kind of reprimand. I needed an assistant who could be trusted on one of the most important business days of the year, even if it took a write-up to do that. I didn't make friends with employees. It wasn't appropriate, but it was difficult not to be fond of someone who had worked beside you for years. I didn't want to play the tough guy.

I radioed Alex, not the slightest bit guilty for scaring the girl who was already hanging off his chest. She'd only met him ten minutes ago! Once again, *draw the line somewhere.*

"This is Charlotte Conner. Alex Cho, please identify."

Alex looked straight at me, even though he hadn't so much as glanced my way since the crowd had started to arrive.

How had he even known where I was? "Looking right at you, Charlie," he said, ignoring the proper identification.

I sighed. He heard it, and his mouth curved up in one of those grins that was likely to be irresistible to every woman in the room, aside from me, of course. And only then because I spent all of my time very focused on ensuring it was not. Very slowly, in his low and openly flirtatious voice, he said, "This is Alex Cho. How can I service you, *Boss*?"

It took a minute to control the hot wash of irritation he always seemed to bring up inside of me. If only I could control the emotions he churned up in me as easily as I could control everything else in my life. I took a long, slow breath and carefully asked, "Have you seen Mallory?"

The expression changed, and he was all business suddenly. I could practically read the process his brain was going through. He was looking for a mental connection to the last time he'd seen her. Realizing it wasn't recently. Starting to wonder if he should be worried. I'd been through all of it already.

He shook his head, his tinny voice carrying through the wire. "No. I haven't seen her since this morning. When did you see her last?"

"Right before I spoke to you in my office. I'm a little concerned."

I watched his chest rise and fall with a harsh breath. "I'm sure it's fine. She's starting to relax a little. Maybe she found someone to hang with instead of working."

If she had learned to relax quite that much, she was on her way to a formal write-up, but there was no reason to say it. There was no question Alex already knew. He got away with things I'd never allow in another employee, but if he disappeared on the first day of high season, or Christmas, he would be out the door.

"I'm coming over. We'll look for her."

Before I could object, he dislodged the little brunette still clinging to his shirt and strode through the crowd, reaching my side so quickly that it made our radio conversation seem kind of ridiculous in retrospect.

"There are a lot of guests," I objected. "We need to be working."

He grabbed my arm and directed me to a much-quieter part of the lobby, near the hall to the administration offices. "Where were you guys when you saw her last?"

I pointed toward the front door. "She took me out to see the big palm. Remember, the lights weren't working? I asked her to have you meet me in my office. That was it. I haven't seen or heard from her since."

He rubbed his chin, lost in thought. He needed to shave. This was a business. I said nothing though. AL wasn't the type of town where people shaved, even when it was a business.

"That's the last I heard from her, too."

The sound of tinkling wind chimes, magnified loudly enough to be heard by the entire crowd, was our cue to return to the lobby. It was time, and Mallory would have to wait. I'd seen videos of the last manager, Phillip, from last Christmas and the six years before. I knew the drill. Because I didn't speak the language, I couldn't be quite as proactive as he was. I also didn't have a wife, so I couldn't lay a kiss on her underneath the mistletoe to commence the festivities. But I had public speaking skills, and I had Alex Cho, who did speak the language. We'd make do.

We made our way to the ballroom, the crowd we'd been battling filing into the room agitated, like hungry school children headed for lunch. The buzz of excitement in the crowd would have been heady if I wasn't still reeling from my breakup with Christmas. It would have been a few years ago. Before Jared ruined everything, I'd spent every Christmas seeking out the best decorations, the fullest trees, the brightest lights. If Christmas wasn't for everything sparkly and gorgeous, I couldn't imagine what was. My obsessive love of Christmas had been the only shred of whimsy I'd ever possessed, and I'd lost it. Only cold practicality remained. I pasted on a fake smile and followed Alex to the stage.

The resort was understated elegance in every way, as every Freemont resort was, but the Christmas bug had bitten everyone but me, and decorations made this room festive. Brightly colored lights and boughs of holly were festooned from one pillar to the next all along the room. A huge Christmas tree was set up in the corner, already decorated with silver and blue glass balls. Electricity moved through the small sea of guests, faces all turned my way. I waved to the assembled crowd.

"Hello. For those who come every Christmas to celebrate with us here at the Aloha Lagoon Resort and Spa, you might not recognize me. Earlier this year, the Aloha Lagoon family was saddened to lose our general manager, Phillip Kealoha. My name is Charlotte Conner, and I'm currently the general manager here. I hope I will start a new tradition of seeing you here every year. Merry Christmas to all of you, and we hope you enjoy the next week of festivities!"

I smiled, but they were empty words. The faster I could get out of Aloha Lagoon, the resort and the town, the happier I'd be. I could only hope some other poor shmuck from corporate would be standing here, suffering this celebration, by the time next year rolled around.

Alex took over for me, speaking the same message in Hawaiian. The likelihood that anyone in this crowd could even understand Hawaiian was slim, but they came for the atmosphere, and they loved it when the words were spoken. I couldn't help but be a little impressed, even though I knew he'd been raised in Hawaii. It was a difficult language, spoken by very few people, and there was little of it that I understood beyond *aloha* and *Mele Kalikimaka*, of course.

When he finished, he flashed a much more sincere smile to the crowd, and we started to move off the stage, waiting to give the cue to the band. It started small, the faint noise of someone chanting in the crowd. Within seconds the chorus of "kiss, kiss, kiss" was floating in the air. *Really?* We weren't Phillip and his wife here, people.

Alex glanced at me, then up at the mistletoe for a long second. Then he shrugged and pulled me forward. With the amount of force he used pulling me back to his side, I expected him to lay one on me with violence. I was ready for that. One kiss, and we could go away and do something actually useful. Only that wasn't what he did at all. For a second he just stared at me, dark eyes inscrutable. Then he lowered his head and pressed a butterfly-soft kiss to mostly my bottom lip.

It was barely a touch. My skin prickled. *Work.* This was for work. For the crowd. It was just a show. Nothing to it. I was just simply not going to think about it. One mindless little kiss. Not a problem. I would not concentrate on the fact that this was Alex, the man who embodied everything I didn't want to like about Aloha Lagoon. I was definitely not going to concentrate on the way he smelled, like something warm and exotic, or the texture of his threadbare shirt, the heat of his skin radiating from underneath. I was not going to zero in on his firm, warm lips. Not even a little.

I was also not going to respond to his mouth parting over mine, breathing in my breath, burning me with his heat. There was the smallest hint of a second where the searing sweep of his tongue burned across my bottom lip. I couldn't stop the harsh pull of my breath, struggling to remain removed from this charade.

There was a suspended second where we stood, lips open, barely touching, barely breathing, barely moving. As if we'd received some kind of silent message from a mysterious source, we sprung away from each other in unison. Trembling, I barely restrained the urge to wipe my hand over my mouth, destroying everything about the show we'd just put on. The applause from the guests was thunderous. All for that stupid kiss.

I walked calmly across the stage, giving one more wave and signaling for the band. No matter what, I wouldn't share my feelings with guests. That would be, above all, unprofessional. And that was the one thing I would never be.

I was going to kill Alexander Cho. I was going to go to his cabin, out there on the beach, and I was going to strangle him in his sleep. Then when I was finished, I would kick him a few dozen times, just to get it all out. I didn't like this resort. I didn't like Christmas. And I especially didn't like Alex, with his smug grins, and his lazy glances, and his tousled hair. I hated the sparks still dancing on the end of my tongue, and I hated my traitorous pulse that thumped at my throat.

The radio at my side sprang to life. "Hey, Boss, we got a problem." The disembodied voice belonged to Ikaika, a squat, middle-aged Polynesian man who refused to follow any of the rules I tried to create, but who could fix anything on the entire Aloha Lagoon property with only his box of tools and a small coterie of assistants.

I squeezed my fingers together to stop the trembling before picking up the radio. I felt Alex sidle up next to me, but I refused to even look at him. "What is it, Ikaika?"

"The waterfall is losing flow. I tried to send a guy in, but it's too slick to place the ladder. I need the crane."

The waterfall was manmade, but it was gorgeous. The focal point of the party area out behind the main hotel, the fifty-foot water feature was a major part of the festivities that would follow dinner. "I'll be right there."

I wasn't thrilled to encounter a problem of this magnitude, but I was happy to have an excuse to get away from Alex and away from the party. If we couldn't get the waterfall fixed, a good half of the after-dinner show would be ruined. This was no small issue. I cut through the crowd, all heading to their seats, and headed for the back door. To my chagrin, I eventually realized that Alex wasn't staying in the dining room. He also wasn't headed to his office or off into the night to check on the property. He was coming with me.

I decided to ignore him. It was better for all of us that way. I picked my way across the sand until I reached the large stonework patio where outdoor parties were held. In just two days, we'd be hosting a wedding right here. For the holiday shows, it was one of our most popular features, and there was no way we could go on without fixing it.

The twenty lights at the base of the waterfall typically made for an elegant light show. But for the moment they were merely distractions, shining on the sadly slimy back wall of the falls. Ikaika was right. Nothing was flowing but a rather pathetic drip of water right down the middle.

"Stanley, can you please bring the crane?" The question was spoken immediately next to me. Alex. Talking to a man in our vehicle department. Even he didn't follow the radio rules. How could I expect anyone else to?

It took Stanley, a balding white man who always looked like he was wearing white linen pajamas, approximately four minutes to work his way from the massive airplane hangar, which acted as our garage, across the sand and to the waterfall. He parked next to the falls and lowered the platform. Ikaika lumbered his way on, and to my surprise, Alex joined him.

Ikaika slapped the edge of the crane and yelled in Hawaiian. Really, I needed to learn some, but I kept thinking, *hoping*, I would be gone before it would be helpful.

I watched the men directing Stanley in how to position the crane and then flinched at the sight of Ikaika scaling the edge of the crane and disappearing into the mouth that would lead to the metal piping that was clearly blocked. "You're breaking OSHA rules," I shouted the reminder. Of course, they paid me no heed. They didn't want my opinions, and we had exactly half an hour in setting darkness to get this thing fixed before people started coming out.

Momentarily, I heard Ikaika yell. Water pushed him out of the mouth and spewed him off the side. A scream caught in my throat as Alex reached out and grabbed Ikaika, one hand on his arm, one on the hem of his shirt. I was so riveted to the horror of the impending accident that I couldn't even look at the falls finally pouring out again, just as engineering had intended. A combination of Alex's strength and Ikaika's monkey-like climbing abilities meant that Ikaika was back in the crane within seconds, but it felt like hours.

Letting out a slow breath, I finally moved my attention back to the waterfall, looking for evidence of what had caused the malfunction. There was a large pool at the bottom, a home for the lights, festively blinking red and green in honor of the holiday, and a filtering system to send the water back up the pipes.

Horror crept up on me as my brain finally connected the pieces of what I was seeing. It was apparent now what had been blocking the waterfall. White dress, pale twisted limbs, fans of brunette curls, sightless staring eyes. Mallory was not making time with a local surfer. She wasn't about to get a reprimand.

She wasn't even alive.

CHAPTER TWO

Completely numb, I couldn't react at all. The horror momentarily overwhelmed anything that might come later, like the realization of how this would impact the Christmas events. As manager, I needed to be worrying about that. But I couldn't even move on to the familiar security of work. I couldn't do anything but stare. Even my breath was partially frozen, working its way out on a thin wheeze.

"Breathe, Charlie." The whisper came from the right. Alex. The slightest hint of practicality remained and told me that he must have come down from the crane to see what was going on. He was probably right. I needed to breathe. But I couldn't find the air.

Suddenly Alex grabbed me by the shoulders and forcibly turned me away from Mallory's broken body. The action shocked another wheezing breath from my lungs. Then another. Without thinking, I struggled to turn back and get another look at Mallory. Alex pulled me into a tight embrace against his chest so I couldn't possibly move. Then he buried his face in the hair covering my ear and whispered, "Stop looking, and breathe."

It was shocking to be hugged by him. So much so that a part of my brain jogged and returned to reality. I was torn between fighting to get out of his arms and just using a handy, big, strong man to give some of the comfort I so desperately needed. I wasn't comfortable with Alex, for so many reasons. That couldn't be denied, but for a moment I was weak and took the comfort. The sight of Mallory's body was really sinking in, and I was racked with chills, completely overwhelmed. Alex was oddly comforting, warm and solid, with an embrace that was tight enough to make me feel a safety I desperately needed without making me feel trapped.

I closed my eyes tight and pressed my face against his chest, hoping that somehow the images burned behind my eyelids would disappear as easily as the night around us did. I could feel him turn his head. "Ikaika, can you please call Detective Ray and get Silas?"

Though he kept his voice calm and even, the mention of the police sent another unpleasant shock through my limp body. Mallory was only twenty-two. She had a whole life ahead of her. Her mother knew mine. How would I tell her? How would I explain broken Mallory, dead when her adult life had barely started? In a move so unprofessional it made me ill, I burst into tears. Alex stroked my hair, a gesture that would have enraged me at any other moment than this one, and made comforting noises.

It took me almost a minute to stop the hysterical sobbing and pull myself together. I decided to pretend it had never happened. If I wanted people to respect me, I had to remain responsible and professional all the time. No matter what happened. Even if a dead body of someone who had not deserved to die this way landed at my feet. I pushed out of Alex's arms, and I wondered if I was imagining his reluctance to let go. Well, if he thought I couldn't handle it, he was wrong. This was why managers should never break down.

He moved to stand between me and an easy view of Mallory, which I had to admit I appreciated. The urge to look again was overwhelming. I hurriedly wiped my face and composed my expression, squaring my shoulders. I could do this. I owed it to Mallory and to the corporate office. I wished Jimmy were here. The real head of security would have come in handy instead of Silas, who was too old to move quickly and not a paragon of security practices. When Silas arrived, I directed him to cordon off the area, because all he was doing was standing there staring at the body, not that I had done much more. I appreciated Alex's efforts to protect me, but I had pulled it together. It was time to get things done.

I stepped around him, staring for a long second at Stanley, who was off the crane and kneeling down next to

Mallory, pointlessly trying to find a pulse. I had never seen a body before, but even I could see it was far too late for any attempts at preserving Mallory's life.

"Why would she have gotten inside of the waterfall?"

I didn't even realize I'd spoken the words out loud until I saw Alex shift uncomfortably. "Charlie...I don't think she did."

I gestured in the direction of the waterfall. "Well, of course she did. You saw her come out of it, same as I did. How else would she..."

The words trailed off as it finally occurred to me that this was probably not an accident. That brought in a whole new dimension that I had never considered, and I had to work hard to control my breathing. Mallory might have been murdered. My assistant. My hotel. My responsibility. *How would I tell her mother?*

Once again, for the second time in just a few moments, Alex came to my rescue when I was on the verge of losing it, though this time perhaps inadvertently. "What do we do now, Boss? We have to keep the other guests from coming out here."

I snapped out of my fugue of horror and guilt. Of course. It was nearly time for the presentation to start. The band was likely already waiting just inside the performer's door for a cue from one of us. Within the next couple of minutes, guests were going to start wandering outside to enjoy the beginnings of another sweetly scented Hawaiian evening. That couldn't happen.

I pointed at Alex. "Please go inside and corral the guests. Find another activity to keep them still for a bit while we figure out something else for them to do tonight. The band will need to reposition themselves to perform in the grand ballroom. We need all hands on deck. Every single employee. I'll stay here and deal with the police and..." I swallowed hard. "And the coroner."

Alex rubbed a hand over his mouth, stilling for a second before finally speaking. "I think it might be better if we traded. You go inside and take care of the guests. I'll let everyone know we have an emergency on the radio, and stay here with...Mallory."

He was not making that choice because he wanted to be here. He was making it so that I didn't have to be. It was the first time I could recall that I was truly thankful to have Alex Cho as my second in command. For a moment, I wanted to throw my arms around him and hug him again. I pulled myself together.

"Thanks."

He nodded solemnly, all traces of the usually flippant man gone. "If you have no specific requests for who needs to do what, I'll just assign people to pick up the pieces. Call me with the new plan when you have it figured out."

I turned to leave and found a few guests were already coming, drawn by the noise and chaos near the waterfalls, especially when the sounds of sirens rent the air. I used all the no-nonsense command I could muster to herd them back inside. Heading immediately for the stage in the ballroom, I drew on my inner core, secretly some sort of take-charge general in a tweed skirt, and pulled everyone's eyes my way with loud, calm words.

"Excuse me. Could I have every eye up here? Yes, you guys by the door as well, thank you. We've had an accident, and we won't be able to move the festivities outside tonight as they're usually done. However, we do have the band on hand and the holiday vibe inside. If you'll just be patient for one more moment, we'll get started celebrating a very merry Christmas, island style."

I plastered on a smile and was super thankful when young Jillian, the day concierge who already should have gone home, appeared at the side of the stage, clipboard in one hand, radio in the other. "Alex said I'm supposed to keep the guests busy with some games while the others move out all the tables."

"Bless you, Jillian," I said, scrambling down the steps and ushering her up. There was the sound of confusion and dismay in the crowd, and that was a sound no resort manager ever wanted to hear.

Blessedly, Jillian used the interpersonal skills that had won her promotion to head concierge and was immediately able to charm the disgruntled crowd and had them singing the traditional Hawaiian Christmas song, "Kani Kani Pele," within seconds. Smiles started to reappear by the time I joined the waitstaff and all the free employees to move forty tables into the grand ballroom. There were smaller rooms, but they wouldn't fit this crowd. The only option for keeping them inside and happy was to set this place up. A few guests tried to stop me and ask for more info, but I brushed them off politely.

While the tables moved with efficiency, I could hear Alex's voice over the radio, of course not following protocol. I could forgive it though, since he was on top of every single detail that I couldn't cover from my place inside.

Together, we had the entire event moved inside within fifteen minutes, and I relieved an exhausted Jillian and left Ginger, a girl from the accounting department, who was Alex's sometimes assistant, inside to run the events for the moment, starting with a speech from the local Aloha Lagoon mayor, Haulani Kalama. By the time I went back outside, I left behind a bar serving piña coladas, the band playing "Mele Kalikimaka," and smiles all around. As much as I might disdain their laid-back attitudes, when it was all on the wire, this staff had come through like champs.

I hurried back outside to join the two police cars behind the hotel, probably every single car on the force. There were also two ambulances and a red car with an insignia that I assumed that belonged to the coroner, though I could have been wrong about that. I hadn't made a point of making friends, because that wasn't the reason I was here, and I was on my way out anyway at the first available opportunity. However, I did recognize Detective Ray Kahoalani and an officer milling in the crowd. By this time, Mallory's body was thankfully no longer in the open but moved on to an ambulance cart and covered with a sheet. I made a point of not looking in that direction, even though a part of me desperately wanted to.

Now that the emergency of getting the guests set up on a new course was over, the horror of the situation was starting to creep back in. Alex crossed to my side as soon as he saw me. I didn't want to address the fact I'd been weak and relied on him for a moment, so I went right to business. "Thanks for helping pull that together. The staff did a great job. Jillian was a great choice to send in."

He nodded. "Charlie, Ray wants to see you."

Detective Ray wanted to talk to me. The cops wanted to talk to me, which was not outside the realm of the expected. I shored up my shoulders and crossed the few feet between us and the police.

Detective Ray was a nice enough guy, middle aged, a bit sloppy, perpetually dressed in Hawaiian shirts and shorts. He seemed fair and honest, as much as I knew. Hopefully, this was just routine, and we could immediately get to the part where he found out who had done this. Ray looked me over without a word, then took a moment to glance at a woman in a coroner's jacket, who was busy filling out paperwork near the county van.

He offered his hand, which I shook without thinking. He came to the resort upon occasion, especially with Jimmy Toki. He'd never offered his hand before. I rubbed my hands together, freezing, despite the sweet yet tangy island breeze blowing off the shore just a couple hundred feet away.

"Tell me what happened," Detective Ray said, in his grizzly voice.

Alex moved closer, and I actually appreciated his support, which more than anything told me I was losing my mind today. "I saw Mallory around eleven, when the lights were out on the big palm. Then I left the resort and went into town to check on some details for tonight but mostly for the luau. I called her on the drive back multiple times, but she never answered."

"Then when I got back, I was annoyed I couldn't find her. She wasn't answering her radio either, and her dune buggy was still in its place. I called Alex on the radio and told him I couldn't find Mallory. We were going to look, but we had to open the festivities, so we did that instead. Then we got a call from Ikaika that the waterfall wasn't working. That situation was more emergent than finding Mallory because we needed the waterfall for the events, and we thought she was just slacking or something. We didn't know she was...she..."

I couldn't finish the sentence. We all knew what she'd done. She'd died. I wasn't even entirely sure how. There hadn't been blood, that I could see. Aside from being very clearly dead, there wasn't a lot that looked wrong with her. My stomach turned at the train of thought, and I took a deep, steadying breath. I felt Alex's hand on the small of my back, and some of the tension drained out of me. It was an odd dichotomy. He amped up my stress levels 99 percent of the time, yet in these potentially the worst moments of my life, his solid presence was a comfort.

"Do you know how she died?" Ray spoke and moved slowly. Not like an overweight person or a lazy one, but like a lot of people did when they were living on island time. Too bad island time made me crazy.

I wasn't sure what the deal was with that particular question. Did he know already? "No. I don't...I'm not sure." I could only hope it was painless. She had looked peaceful. Maybe she didn't even know it was coming. I pressed my eyes closed and pulled in a shaky breath. Detective Ray let me alone for a long moment, and by the time he spoke again, I had at least marginally gotten control of myself.

"Do you know who Mallory spent her free time with? We should ask around and see if anyone can tell us where she's been this morning."

I thought hard about Ray's question. The bitter reality was, I worked Mallory pretty hard. The reason Mallory and I existed was to fix resorts with problems. That meant we had a paradigm to follow to leave everything in shipshape in as little time as possible. In most places, we were in and out in weeks. Nearly seven months here at Aloha Lagoon was the longest single place I'd been in three years as a traveling manager.

The longest before that was seven months at a Freemont new acquisition that was beyond a hot mess. I couldn't exactly figure out why I was still in AL. Though I wasn't keen on the way they did things, they got the job done. They could have easily hired another manager by now. However, as long as I was here, I was going to make sure standard operating procedures were implemented. Whether the staff elected to follow those procedures or not once I was gone wasn't my problem. I could about bet that the staff here would nary crack the spine of that SOP manual. However, just changing those things was a full-time job. Mallory wasn't given a ton of time to socialize, though she'd been clearly seeking the time. I just didn't know who she'd been seeking it with.

"She didn't have a lot of free time, Detective. I kept her pretty busy. Although lately, she'd been expressing some interest in surfing. I don't believe she was taking lessons with Brad or anything that concrete, but I once saw her on the beach talking to a number of people, strangers to me, but they looked like locals. And she checked out a couple of books on water patterns and the like from the library. We weren't really friends, so much. She was my employee, and I discourage intimate relationships of any kind between employees and management. I don't know who she knew well."

I was pretty sure she hadn't known anyone that well. Except me. Unless she'd been sneaking out of her room at night to meet people. I supposed that was a possibility, even though we had rooms next to one another on the fifth floor. As long as she maintained radio contact if I tried to call her, I never sought her out after I left the offices at around eight. She always walked with me to my room, and if there was an emergency, she always showed promptly. Beyond that, I couldn't say.

Detective Ray cocked his head. "So you're the only person you're aware she really knew very well on the island?"

The questions felt dangerous, though it was certainly reasonable. "I'm the only person I'm aware of, yes. However, as I said, I don't pay special attention to the social life of my employees. Mallory was my assistant, but she wasn't my friend. She was a very social girl. I'm sure she must have known people—I just don't know who they are. I'm sorry. I wish I knew more."

Regret clawed at me. I really did wish I had listened better, noticed more. Mallory talked a lot. All the time. If I had bothered to listen to her, even some of that time, maybe I would have had something to tell Detective Ray. Maybe I could have even seen this coming and acted on it. Maybe it really was my fault. She'd just talked so much, and she'd never seemed interested in getting any particular response. After a while it became like the hum of the radio, ever present and meaningless.

"How long have you been here exactly?" Ray asked.

That one I could answer without thinking. "Six months, twenty days, and thirteen hours." Not that I was counting or anything.

Next to me I could feel Alex's eyes boring into me. I shifted uncomfortably and diverted my eyes when Mallory's stretcher was wheeled into the coroner's van. I patted my bun, trying to make sure it was all still in place. I needed to go back inside and face the guests, and they could *not* know that someone had just been murdered outside. Just like in the midst of every horrible moment in my life, presentation was everything.

"Oh, one last question. Who is Seth Peterson?"

It took me a second to formulate an answer. Seth Peterson meant nothing to me for a long moment. "He's...he's one of the night watchmen. In his twenties, prior military, I think. Buzz cut, that sort of thing. Why?"

Pulling a baggie from his satchel, Detective Ray held it out but pulled back slightly when I tried to touch it. "Does this mean anything to you?"

It did. I wasn't exactly sure what it had to do with anything though. "Yes, they're the cards that each employee keeps to hand to guests who ask for their names or want to report them for something especially good or, heaven forbid, bad. That one belongs, of course, to Seth Peterson. Where did you find this?"

Detective Ray closed his notebook and slipped it into the pocket of his shorts. "It was in Mallory's hand." With that shocking piece of news, he nodded. "Call me if you think of anything, and I *will* be back to ask you more questions at a later time."

It sounded almost like a threat, though it was likely paranoia on my part. He had no legitimate reason to suspect me. I had no doubt that he would most certainly be back. "Can I call Mallory's parents? They're old friends of my family. I hate for them to find out from a stranger."

Actually, maybe I would see if my parents wanted to call them. I didn't know them well, and my mother especially was the most likely to be a source of comfort in a time like this. Detective Ray cocked his head and evaluated me for a long second. "Yes, you can do that. But please be sure they understand that the department will be reaching out to speak with them soon."

Poor Mallory. Who could have done this to her? I could only hope that Alex's take on the situation wasn't the real one, and Detective Ray had no interest in me outside of a good source of information. Though I couldn't help but be aware that if he was looking for a good suspect just in terms of opportunity, he had an excellent option in me. But an even better one in Seth.

CHAPTER THREE

———

The rest of the night went fairly well, considering the restrictions we were under. The whole outside area needed to be kept under wraps, or someone was going to see the coterie of cops and spotlights on the waterfall. Every guest had to be redirected to the beach, the longer route to any other part of the hotel, like the pools, restaurants, or Ramada Pier for the nightly fire-eater show. I had to be honest. I was super impressed with my staff for coming through in this kind of situation. I had viewed them as so low-key they were nearly falling under the classification of lazy, but it seemed they had merely adapted to the slow pace of the island and were capable of coming through in a pinch. I was proud of them. Like a mom at an elementary school science fair.

When everyone started dispersing to their rooms or huts for the night, I took a chance of glancing at my phone. Someone had been calling all night, and I hadn't noticed my phone was on silent, not vibrate like I'd thought. When I scrolled through the calls, I saw that all fifteen of them were from my mother. That was not a good sign. Normally, I would assume that many calls meant another divorce for her and my father, who had married and divorced one another many times, but this time I suspected something worse. Detective Ray had said he would give me time to call Mallory's family and that he would call them later. I hadn't realized he'd meant later *tonight*. Shoot. I dialed Mom's cell phone, fingers shaking.

I always put work first, especially in an emergency, and I'd had it leveled my way as a personality flaw before. However, it had never felt like one until now. I had worked too long and neglected to see that the information of Mallory's passing was given by a friendly voice and not a detective.

My mother's voice carried from the other end of the line. "Oh, Charlotte, there you are. Thank goodness."

"I didn't want you to hear it from the police," I said, guilt rearing its ugly head.

Mom gasped. "The police? Did she get arrested? She said she was just going to sit there!"

A moment of clarity told me we were clearly not talking about the same thing. "Who said they were just going to sit where?"

"Georgie. She said she would stay at the Coco Moo."

It took me a long moment to decipher the comment. Georgiana was my twin sister, identical, and the last place I wanted her to be, especially on Christmas, was anywhere near me. And I had no clue what the last part meant.

"Georgie is here? On Kauai?" Just asking the question filled me with dread.

"She's there in Aloha Lagoon! She said she was just looking around and that she couldn't get through to you at the resort. I gave her your cell, but she said she'd just wait."

That was wise, as I'd have hung up on her immediately. Georgie here? Good Lord. *Why?*

"Where is she?"

"I don't know where she is now. Downtown Aloha Lagoon, I think she said. She was at some karaoke bar called…Coco Moo?"

I palmed my forehead. There was only one possible place that could be. One of the resort eateries was a café called the Loco Moco Café, where they sometimes had karaoke. Coco moo, well, that was what Georgie used to call chocolate milk.

"Why is she here? You know what—never mind. It doesn't matter. Can you text her and ask her the exact location she's at and text it to me?" I'd figure out what to do with my unwelcome guest when the more pressing business was taken care of. "There's something you need to know. Earlier today…Mallory passed away."

Mom's gasp fully reflected the way I felt about it. "How? I don't understand."

I didn't understand either, and I'd been there. "I'm not entirely sure, Mom. That wasn't clear, but I'm sure the coroner will let me know more when she does her examination. I just...I asked the police to let me call her parents. Or you can if you think it would be better, instead of letting them hear it from the police. Though the police did say they would be calling them eventually."

Mom's voice was remote, stunned. "I will call. This is horrible. She was so young."

When I heard her start to cry, it was very difficult for me to keep hold of myself, but there were employees around me, cleaning up the grand ballroom, which had been effectively thrashed by having every activity there. Nani Johnson, a local ukulele player, was packing it up to go home, and the band, Pacific Rim, was cleaning up their instruments on the stage. Someone would need to cut both of them a check. I made myself a mental note, and concentrating on work instead of my sobbing mother was a relief.

I also couldn't bear to really think about Mallory or the implications of her death right now. There would be time enough for that after the practical was dealt with and when I was completely alone. Mom and I ironed out a few of the details she needed to pass on to Mallory's family, and I hung up after promising I would go and rescue Georgie, who could have managed to get to the resort, had she wanted. It wasn't far, just a couple of blocks. She wanted to make me come for her.

I had no clue why, but it was always some kind of game with Georgie. If Georgie was doing something, the end purpose would be manipulation. Her showing up at Christmastime was nothing more than a dig. But it did bring up one thing that I wasn't sure whether to pass on to police. There'd been another person who knew Mallory in town tonight.

My sister.

* * *

Technically, I wasn't supposed to pick up guests in my private vehicle, whether they were my sister or not, and the available resort vehicle that was dedicated to the upper-management staff was Alex's at the moment, since I couldn't abide by someone conducting resort business on a motorcycle. Unfortunately, I didn't have the keys. I'd given them to Alex. Which meant searching him out and getting them.

Sighing, I headed back into the working throng, searching for Alex. It didn't take long to find him helping Ikaika and some of the younger men on the staff break down the makeshift winter wonderland that we'd been forced to construct. He was sweaty, his shirt hanging open in a way that was very unbecoming of a manager, even if there was no way I could deny it was becoming in general.

I held out my hand. "I need the keys to the Prius."

He cocked his head, putting his hands to his hips. "Why?"

That wasn't a question I'd expected or made a contingency plan to deal with. I didn't want him to know about Georgie, though I had no idea how I would keep her secret until she blew away with the next errant breeze, like she'd been doing all her life. "I need it." I said it like it was a given, and in a manner of speaking, it was. I clearly wouldn't have asked for the keys if I didn't need them.

"Why?" he repeated. Good grief. What was his problem? Why did he care anyway? The good graces he'd managed to get himself in earlier when he'd helped me out were definitely gone. That was a relief anyway. One thing I definitely did not need was Alex trying to sneak out of the box. I didn't have time for that kind of nonsense.

"I have to pick up a stranded guest."

He nodded, pulling the keys from his pocket. "That makes sense. Let's go." He started walking for the door. I had to scramble to catch up.

"What? No. I don't want you to go. I just need the keys."

He kept walking. "My car now, Charlie. Remember, you insisted."

He dangled the keys, and I snatched at them, but I was just too short, and I refused to get any closer to warm, sweaty Alex.

"So if you want to use it, I'm driving. Unless you just want me to pick up this guest."

"Lord no." The words were out before I could prevent them. I flinched. "No, thank you." When we reached the resort vehicle parking area, I spent a moment debating how much it was worth to fight about this. I didn't want him there, but I also didn't want to make this any more of a deal than I had to. My feelings for Georgie weren't something I wanted to share with the rest of the world, and my feelings on anything at all weren't something I wanted to share with Alex.

I gestured to the car. "Let's go."

I decidedly didn't want a fuss at the moment. I just wanted to get Georgie, shove her into an empty room, and pretend she wasn't there until she left. Then I needed to deal with Mallory's death and what exactly that meant, but I couldn't even touch on that now. That was for later.

I strapped myself in because I'd seen Alex drive, and I didn't want to venture that without safety first. The entire cab smelled like him—fresh ocean air, tangy seawater, warm male skin, and the underlying hint of his shampoo or body wash. Something exotic and smoky, slightly Asian. I took a deep breath, then wished I hadn't when the scent wrapped around me, teasing at my nose, trying to tickle my other senses where it was most certainly not allowed. If only tonight hadn't happened. If only we hadn't been forced under the mistletoe. If only he hadn't comforted me. It made everything else so hard.

Alex started the car. "Where to, Boss?"

"Downtown." I glanced at my phone for reference. "Corner of Blossom and Main."

He glanced at me curiously. "That isn't far. Why is a guest stuck out there?"

I shrugged, unwilling to get into the whole thing. Georgie had reasons for making me come and get her, and I didn't even want to guess at her game. She couldn't win if I wouldn't play.

Alex shrugged too and pulled out onto the scenic road that trailed through the acres of resort. To the right was the ocean. To the left, had it been not dark, we would have seen cliffs. Since the sun set around five during December, and it was almost nine at the moment, the road was empty. Everything closed up on the resort fairly early, and it wasn't early.

I felt like I should tell Alex that the person we were picking up was my sister because that was going to be a glaring omission when the time came. He was going to wonder why I didn't tell him, and then what would I say? *Oh, my twin sister slept with my fiancé two days before Christmas, which was also the day before our wedding, and then she gave me a video just to make sure I really understood what she'd done.* That really wasn't the sort of thing you shared with a coworker. Or a friend. Or anyone except a highly paid therapist.

I opened my mouth to speak, but Alex moved first. "How long were you friends with Mallory?"

The question was like a punch in the gut. In reality, I'd never actually been friends with Mallory. She was more than a decade younger than me and my employee to boot. But I had known her the majority of her life, if only on the periphery. She was so much younger than me that we'd never really spent any time together until I'd hired her a year ago. Then after that, the only time we'd spent was business related.

"I've known her a long time. Pretty much her entire life. But not really well. She was younger than me."

He didn't respond, and I wasn't sure if I appreciated that or not. I wasn't happy he'd brought it up at all, and hours later I was still suffering a mixture of embarrassment and gratitude about his behavior after the waterfall incident. I tried looking out the window, but it was dark, and there really wasn't much to see. The reflection of the moon and an ocean of stars off the water and the limited view in the headlights.

"I'm sorry," he said at last, surprising me out of my reverie.

I had no response. I couldn't say it was okay, because it most certainly wasn't. It took a moment for the proper response to work its way into my brain. "Thanks."

"Are you okay?" He shot me a quick look before returning his eyes to the road.

Most certainly not didn't seem like an acceptable response. It took a long time to find one. "I will be."

He nodded, seemingly finding the answer good enough to stop worrying about me, which I didn't entirely understand anyway. Why harass me for six months and then suddenly start acting like my best friend? It was true that I was normally aggressive toward Alex, because he set me off balance, something I disliked. Control was my best friend. It kept me happy and calm. My aggression, however, wasn't the whole cause of his attitude. He just enjoyed giving me crap, and murder shouldn't change that. His behavior had altered, and that made me suspicious.

It was time to change the subject, and we were getting close to downtown anyway. I took a deep breath and let it out slowly, wishing I actually had a happy place to seek out. "The person we're going to pick up is my sister."

His eyebrow cocked, but he didn't ask why I hadn't said anything earlier, which was oddly circumspect for Alex Cho. He was just full of surprises today. I wasn't a fan of surprises. Never had been. Eying him suspiciously, I didn't notice him pulling into the parking lot of the local community center until he pulled to a stop.

Now that we were actually here, it hit me again how much I didn't want to reconnect with Georgie. Honestly, three years was not enough. I could have used another couple of years before burying the hatchet, though I wasn't surprised she was pushing the issue. However, to show up on Christmas, that took some balls. She certainly had those in excess. She was about three seconds from a WWF wrestler in terms of *cajones*. As far as I was aware, there wasn't anything that take-no-prisoners Georgie wouldn't try at least once.

He eyed the crowd wandering up and down the main drag of Aloha Lagoon. "Want me to run over and get her? What does she look like?"

"Well, she looks a lot like me. Pretty much exactly like me. But I'll do it. No worries."

The look he shot me left no question that he was confused by my words. He wouldn't be when he saw her. Actually, the last time I had seen her, her hair, naturally blonde like mine, had been sheared boy short and dyed black. What she looked like now was a mystery. So maybe it really was better that I planned to go after her myself. If by *better* I meant *soul crushing*.

I opened the door and stepped into another beautiful night. Resisting the urge to inhale the inherent perfume of Hawaii, I headed for the entrance. There was something about a sultry Hawaiian night that made me want to linger, which was exactly why I never would.

Gritting my teeth, I braced myself for the hit of seeing my sister for the first time since she'd blithely handed me a tape of herself screwing my fiancé and skipped out of town.

Georgie was sitting on a park bench near the front of an ice cream place, legs crossed, microscopic denim skirt riding up to the point it was barely clothing, as was her way. She'd finally allowed her hair to go blonde again, but it was still super short, and now spiky. She didn't spot me immediately, which wasn't surprising considering the chaos of a festive holiday night on the town. Alex, to my right, noticed her right away though. I could tell by his whistle of wolfish appreciation, because...Alex.

"You didn't say you were twins."

"No, I didn't." There was no point in trying to come up with a good excuse for my lack of information, so I didn't.

Georgie noticed me and perked up immediately, sliding off the bench and pushing her impossibly short skirt even higher. She seemed impervious to all the stares of lust and jealousy following her all along the sidewalk. I'd never been jealous of Georgie. Even when she'd slept with Jared. I'd just been disappointed. In both of them, but most of all in Georgie, who was supposed to have been there for me through thick and thin, because that was what sisters did. Georgie and I might as well have been from different planets, as foreign as our personalities were to each other. And it was impossible to be jealous of an alien.

However, I had depended on her. With our tumultuous upbringing, we'd relied on each other, however different we might have been, to give us a safe port in the storm of chaos. Georgie was outgoing and impetuous. I was a control freak, type A, whatever you wanted to call it. I liked control. Our constantly leaving father and our constantly dramatic mother had been engaged in a soap opera–worthy relationship that consisted of marrying and divorcing with alarming regularity throughout our entire childhood. If times got rough, Dad left, Mom cried, and

Georgie and I just put our heads down, relied on one another, and waited for him to return, which he always did. They'd get married again, and the cycle would start over. I'd never expected Georgie to be reliable, because she wasn't. She had too much of Dad in her. She was a runner. However, I'd also never expected her to turn on me like that.

"Charlotte, it's so good to see you." She threw her arms around me, smelling of coconut oil and rum. I stiffened for a long second, because honestly I really wasn't comfortable with her touching me. She'd never even offered an apology for breaking up a ten-year relationship at the altar. Never even once.

I patted her on the arm in some semblance of a greeting and stepped away as soon as possible. It was very clear that Alex was on to the awkwardness between us, but there was no way I was going to clue him in to the details on this one. Georgie spotted Alex, and her eyebrows cocked into her hairline. "Well, *hello*." She glanced at me approvingly.

I had no idea if she thought we were together—fat chance—or if she thought I'd brought her an early Christmas present. Alex grinned, those interesting creases flashing. I sighed, regretting that I ever had to do this. "Georgiana, this is the Leisure Groups coordinator at the resort, Alex Cho."

I should have said something else, but what was there to say? *Georgie, meet another man I think is insanely sexy. Please have at him, as you do?* I pushed the thought away immediately. Not thinking of Alex and sexy in the same sentence was how I got through every day.

"Hello there, Georgiana." Alex's lethal smile was clearly already working on my twin, not that it took much for Georgie to be swayed out of that microscopic skirt.

Ugh. If only he'd just given me the keys. But he would have eventually found her anyway. Alex had a homing beacon for anything in a bikini, but I wouldn't have had to be present.

"You can call me Georgie," she said, making it clear she was really saying, *You can have my panties as a trophy.*

"Georgiana and Charlotte, huh? Those are big names to give baby girls," Alex pointed out.

I nipped the conversation in the bud. "My mother is obsessed with *Pride and Prejudice*. She had us at the same time as several other people in her P and P club, and all the Lizzys and Janes were claimed early. She didn't want us to have the same names as all our little P and P friends, so she named us after Lizzy's homely friend and Darcy's sister of questionable intelligence." I rubbed a hand across my forehead and begged the universe for patience. "Let's get out of here. Do you have any bags?"

She picked up the pink and green carpetbag at her feet. "Just this. I can't wait to get somewhere quiet and dark. All anyone can talk about in this town is murder. I need a drink."

"You just spent hours at a bar," I pointed out. Then her first comment sunk in. Had she already heard about Mallory? That wasn't the way anyone should find out.

"Murder?" I asked cautiously. "I didn't think it would get around that fast."

These people could talk. It was the perennial curse of a small town, which Aloha Lagoon was, even when it sometimes felt big because of all the tourists coming through. Georgie shrugged, the strap of her bronze tank top slipping off, revealing for anyone who cared to look, which was quite a large number, judging from the stares around us, that she'd elected to spend today without the traditional constraints of a bra of any kind.

"Well, the guy did die three days ago. I guess that's big news around here."

A guy died three days ago? That *was* news to me. She wasn't talking about Mallory, which was a relief, but I paid no attention to news or gossip unless it directly impacted the resort.

"Surfer, out on West Point," Alex filled me in. "Someone shot him point blank, straight in the heart. Left his body on the beach. He was an Olympic hopeful for 2020, but he wasn't a local."

That dismissive "he wasn't a local" said a lot. Most people in AL were as welcoming as they had to be to get money, but surfers from out of town weren't a favorite. Especially when they challenged local surfing gods and took up too much space in the good waves. I couldn't picture someone killing him for something like that though. AL, be it a small town or not, had an inordinate amount of murder. Not that most of it affected the tourists, but still, there was a lot. To have this man and Mallory both be murdered in a three-day period seemed a bit excessive.

Coincidence? I wasn't sure. I couldn't help but remember that recently when I was driving by the beach I had seen Mallory hanging out with surfers. They were the only people I had ever seen her with outside of the resort. Was it possible she'd known that other man?

I would tell Georgie about Mallory once we were safely in the car. If I were polite, I would have let Georgie sit in the front seat, but I had no intention of doing that. The less time she spent near Alex, the better. I didn't need these kinds of additional complications right now. I could only see the way they were eying each other leading to disaster, and we were not allowed any form of disaster at the Aloha Lagoon Resort and Spa.

To my surprise, Alex solved the problem before I had a chance to, opening the back door to allow Georgie inside. She flashed him a smile and some gratuitous skin before shutting the door. Maybe it wasn't about Alex specifically. Maybe she just couldn't help herself. Just like when Alex saw a pretty girl. They were hardwired, like primitive sluts.

When I got into the car, he eyed me, and his expression was laden with meaning. Too bad I had no clue what that meaning was. Probably he wanted to know what was going on between Georgie and me, but there was no way in a thousand burning hells that I ever planned on giving him that information. It was embarrassing enough without anyone knowing. *Especially* Alex. There was something about the idea of him knowing I couldn't keep a fiancé that was beyond mortifying, even more so than the event had actually been.

I took a deep breath and waited until Alex was back on the road before blurting out, "There's something I have to tell you."

It came out sounding almost exactly like the way it sounded when someone was being laid off or when parents were getting divorced just one more time. She eyed me suspiciously. "What is it?"

I licked my lips, my mind cruising through a list of possible ways to phrase the whole tragic situation. In the end, I went with the same thing I'd told my mother. "Mallory Langston passed away this afternoon."

I included her last name because Georgie wasn't the best at remembering details, like that Mallory was now my assistant. If I just said "Mallory," she might not even realize who I was talking about.

"Oh my gosh. Why? I mean, how?"

I glanced back at her, and she really did look shaken. Georgie and I were both very good at hiding our feelings—must have been genetic—but we did it in different ways. Right now, though, being flippant and acting a bit stupid, Georgie's preferred method, wasn't really an option.

"I'm not entirely sure. I just didn't want you to hear it from someone else or in barroom gossip." Since apparently murder was a hot gossip topic.

She fell completely silent, and I was pretty sure she just didn't know what to say. I couldn't fault her. I didn't know what to do. I was completely at a loss, as I'd never dealt with something like this before, and I rather strongly hoped I never had to again. I could only scramble for something practical to think about so I could push away the horror of it all.

"How long have you been waiting?" Alex asked conversationally, when no one spoke for a long time. I thought maybe he was just trying to diffuse the tension, but I really was curious how long she'd been here.

"Oh—" She waved her hand dismissively. "I came ashore this morning. But I didn't spend all that time in Aloha Lagoon. I've been all over the island."

I glanced at her and then sat forward in my seat. Where had Georgie been all this time? What had she been doing? Georgie was the only other person I was aware of who knew Mallory very well on the whole island of Kauai. They'd actually been friendly with one another, as much as one could be with someone a decade younger than you. It seemed impossible to even consider what her motivation for doing something like that could be, but it was also impossible to deny that Georgie most certainly had been in town long enough to have been the one to murder Mallory.

CHAPTER FOUR

————

I pushed the thought away as soon as I had it. Georgie had a lot of faults. She would sleep with anyone for pretty much any reason. Things I wouldn't even have considered sufficient reasons to let someone borrow my phone would good enough reasons for Georgie to let someone borrow her vagina. She ran away constantly, never staying in one place for more than a few weeks at a time. And her departures were always at the worst possible time, leaving others—usually me—to deal with the ruins of the messes she made when she went.

She would be willing to hand me a video of her and Jared in flagrante and vaguely tell me it was for my own good before leaving for Spain. She'd be willing to leave me with an entire wedding to cancel. But nothing would make me believe she'd be willing to take someone's life. Whoever had murdered Mallory, it wasn't Georgie.

It took very little time to get back to the main building, illustrating again how pointless it had been that she hadn't just walked over, and I padded through the empty lobby, Georgie in tow. Alex bid us a hesitant good-bye and headed into the night to the little cottages on the beach that most employees elected to live in if they chose to live on property. They weren't the same as the huts used by the guests, but they were still nice. I wasn't a big fan of sand. Whenever I had things to deal with on the beach, half of it seemed to come back with me, and I spent the next week dumping grains out of everything I'd been wearing.

Georgie took in the elegant lobby, from the granite floors to the perfectly designed lighting scheme, and let out a small whistle. "This place is swank. Very nice. Not too festive though." She would point it out.

"It's festive enough for a five-star retreat. This is not a Motel 6."

I'd denied the staff the right to use the eighty-five million boxes of garish decorations that Phillip had apparently loved. Even if I was still a fan of Christmas, I would have stopped them. "Understated elegance" was one of Freemont's key words, and I was nothing if not a Freemont creation. I had never known Phillip personally, though I had seen him at corporate retreats. He was rather difficult to miss with his deafening voice, overwhelming personality, and considerable girth. However, it was clear he'd done a very good job managing this resort, and his touch was everywhere, usually elegant and understated, the way Freemont wanted it. However, his almost fanatical love of Christmas had left the staff with some very bad ideas of what constituted proper holiday cheer and also some very tacky décor.

"You used to love Christmas. I mean, you know, people here seem to have different taste, but this place would have been a waterfall of white lights on your initiative a couple of years ago."

I shot her a look. "Yeah, weird how I no longer seem to appreciate that holiday spirit." I turned and left her without another word.

I stepped up to the desk and asked Darcy Collins, the night desk clerk, for a list of open rooms. There were no rooms kept for employees. Mallory and I were the only ones who stayed inside the resort in a special set of suites designed for the manager, though Phillip, the only manager this place had ever had before me, and his wife had taken a house in town. The rest lived on the beach, like Alex and those who came from other places to work the summer months, or in town, where there were plenty of small houses staff could rent together to save on funds.

Darcy manned the desk until morning, though we generally accepted no arrivals after nine PM. There was never a bad time for the guests to find they needed something, and someone always had to be there to provide it for them. There was an immaculately well-oiled, though considerably smaller, nighttime crew here at the resort to make certain that from housekeeping up to management there was always someone to solve problems and meet needs at Aloha Lagoon. Darcy pushed her bright red hair from her face and set to serious tapping. She was always perfectly efficient, though I often wondered how she could type with her ridiculously long nails. They were awful too. Sharpened to a point at each tip, which struck me as unbelievably dangerous. I'd take someone's eye out, if not my own. But she kept them perfectly manicured and was clearly able to meet the requirements of her job, so there was no complaint to be filed.

"I'm struggling here. The place is filled up because of Christmas and all." She eyed Georgie. "However, since it's clear this is your sister, I'm going to see what I can do." I had no idea what that meant, but she spent several minutes typing in silence while Georgie took in every inch of the lobby like a dog in a new place. Finally, Darcy threw up her hand in triumph. "Ha. There you are."

She reached under the counter and grabbed two card keys, taking a moment to program them. She slid them into a guest envelope illustrating some of our amenities and handed it across the kidney-shaped desk to Georgie, who had wandered back.

"Room 259. It's on the second floor. I can call Jonah to get your bags?" Darcy flashed me a look as though she wasn't sure I would approve.

My opinion didn't matter, however, since Georgie had no bags. "Oh, no. I'm good. Just this." She held up her one piece of luggage and waved the card keys in the air. "This is going to be so fun," she squealed. "Like being kids again."

I was considerably less interested in a trip down memory lane, and I wasn't even sure why she was here, but she was my sister, and if she was here, clearly looking for something, I would take care of her, just as I always had since we were small. Even though I was just thirteen minutes older, there was no mistaking which of us was the older sister and no mistaking which of us the rest of the family, and seemingly the rest of the world, expected to take care of everything. Maybe because I always had and had made it very clear that I always would.

* * *

Morning came way too early. I hadn't slept well, with the dual stressors of Mallory's death and Georgie's oddly timed arrival. I grieved for Mallory, but there was nothing to be done but tuck my emotions away. The day was very full, and there were a million things to deal with today, and every other one of the five days between now and Christmas. I couldn't let a single thing slide, because this was Aloha Lagoon, and it wore the stamp of Freemont. There was a certain level of perfection to uphold. More importantly, however, this was the place guests had chosen to spend their holidays when they could have been anywhere else. I could never forget that what happened here mattered to them.

When I got down to the lobby, Georgie was already there, working the crowd with a finesse I'd only ever seen in Alex. Too bad they'd be a violent train wreck together.

I spotted the man whose card Detective Ray said Mallory had been holding when her body was found, clocking out of work for the day. Seth was young, maybe his midtwenties, but he'd been part of the night security staff as long as I'd been there. He was a good-looking guy, despite his unfortunately shaved haircut, with vivid green eyes and golden-blond hair, what there was of it anyway. He kept to himself, maybe even more than I did. I wasn't certain I'd ever seen him speaking to another person. So why had he given Mallory his card? If he hadn't given it to her, where had she gotten it? And the most important question of all was, why had she been holding it when she'd died?

I wasn't interested in being a part of finding out what had happened to Mallory. I wanted to pretend it didn't exist at all. Still, the thing with the customer card was really bugging me. I approached him. "Seth, can I speak with you for a minute before you leave?"

He turned and eyed me under aggressive eyebrows, his body language saying that he was considering telling me no. I suspected it was nothing except my name on his paychecks that kept him from doing that. He kept his hands in his pockets and backed up a step when I got too close. He was short for a man, but he was a bruiser, head to toe muscle. If he wanted to be, he'd be dangerous. He didn't speak, but he didn't leave either, which I took as his form of acquiescence.

"You know, I was the one who found Mallory's body last night."

Those eyebrows pulled together. I'd once read that the average person had approximately two percent Neanderthal DNA. I couldn't help but wonder if perhaps Mr. Peterson here had more.

He surprised me though. "I'm sorry. I've seen people die before, but that was on a battlefield. In a place where you feel safe, that must have been very unpleasant."

I nodded. "It was. She…she had your customer card in her hand. Do you know why she had it?"

His only reaction was an almost imperceptible jerk of his right hand inside his pocket. His expression didn't change at all. "I gave it to her. As to why she was holding it at that particular moment, I really couldn't say."

"Why'd you give it to her?"

He didn't answer me for a moment, so long that it became awkward. "I asked her on a date. She couldn't even remember my name. We flirted. I gave her the card. She said she'd remember it next time. Obviously, there was no next time."

He was lying. I didn't know why, but nevertheless, it was clear he was. Maybe he had asked Mallory out. Maybe they'd even flirted. However, that wasn't why he'd given her the card. As a manager, I'd gotten used to hearing some whoppers from employees trying to get out of something—work, trouble, a promotion that would mean more responsibility they weren't ready for. I knew a lie when I saw one. Even when the liar had no facial expressions.

I couldn't really call him on it. There was nothing to say. If anyone was going to ferret out Seth's motivations for lying, it would be Detective Ray, and not me. I nodded. "I'm sorry to hear that you were friends. I mean, I'm sorry for you, I guess, because you were friends. I'm not sorry that you were friends." Could I botch this up any more?

"Same to you." He nodded very slightly, touching his front teeth with the tip of his tongue. I got the feeling he wanted to add something, but he didn't. He just nodded again, then turned and walked away. I watched him go, wondering what to do with the knowledge I now possessed that not only was Mallory holding that man's card when she'd died, he was lying to me about it.

I returned to the lobby, took a deep breath, and crossed to Georgie. "How was your room?" I asked very politely, like I would to a complete stranger. I was probably ridiculous to even be waiting for an apology. It was pointless, as she'd never give one. And even if she did, it certainly wouldn't make up for what she had done, especially when she'd never behaved as though it mattered.

She eyed me almost suspiciously. "It was fine. Afraid Mom was going to ask me if you gave me a nice room?"

Trying to restrain a sigh was unsuccessful. "It's my job to worry about guests," I reminded her.

"I'm not a guest. I'm your sister."

There was nothing I could say to that. Sisters didn't do the things Georgie had done. Right now, I felt like she was a sister only in the sense that we shared the same parents. "There's a breakfast at the Loco Moco. I hear it's very good."

Georgie gave a sigh to match mine. "Okay. I want to know how Mallory died. Can I ask the police?"

I flinched. I wasn't sure I wanted to know, even though I'd have to face the whole thing eventually. "Maybe. I'm not sure they know."

She cocked her head to the side. "How could they not know?"

"Because it just…it wasn't clear. I saw her. I couldn't tell either."

Georgie's face finally softened. "You saw her body? That must have been awful."

My response was something between a shrug and a nod. I had no idea how to respond. It *had* been awful but not as awful as being murdered, and I was a weak person, one who didn't want to know the details.

"The detective handling the case works in town. Maybe he can tell you something." She couldn't help but understand by now that my curiosity didn't extend as far as hers did.

Her expression made it clear she thought I was in the wrong, but there was no changing my mind about this one. I didn't want to know what had caused Mallory's sightless stare and tangled limbs. If I never had to think about what I had seen again, it would be too soon. Nor did I want to have another discussion with Detective Ray. If Georgie wanted to touch on all of that, she was free to do so. I wouldn't be a part of it. If only the specter of Mallory's family wasn't there all the time, telling me I needed to know so that they would know. I pushed it all away.

She gave me a loose wave and gestured outside. "See you."

I said bye and watched her walk through the double glass doors. A couple of men immediately stood from their casual reclined perusals of the paper, or people watching, and followed her outside. She was like the Pied Piper of men. I sighed and scooped up the left-behind papers, depositing them on the front desk.

When I was nearly to my office in the back hallway, Jillian cornered me. "Oh, Miss Conner. I really just wanted to say how sorry I am about Mallory. You must be really bummed."

Bummed. Indeed. "I've known her a long time," was all I said in response.

Jillian nodded. "I know. You guys are always really busy. I'm sorry I didn't have time to get to know her better like some of the night staff did."

I nodded, wondering if this was going somewhere important. "Yes, I kept her busy." It was a stupid throwaway comment. It didn't mean anything.

I felt, more than saw, Alex sidling up next to me in the hallway. He took up all the air around me somehow, making it hard to breathe. I chanced a glance at him, and he looked like he was willing to hesitate for our conversation to finish, waiting his turn to speak with either me or Jillian.

"I saw her a lot at Strangler's Cove."

"Strangler's...Cove?" What a name. Was that a place? A bar? Kauai wasn't that massive of an island, but I made a point of not venturing outside of Aloha Lagoon. There might be something out there that would appeal to me, and I was trying my hardest not to find anything here appealing. Hawaii was a risk. The kind of place I'd fall in love with, if I wasn't ever vigilant. I couldn't afford to get too attached to any place, or anything.

"Yeah, it's a place where some of the local surfers hang out. Pretty obscure. But the waves are bitchin'."

I nodded. Sure they were. Absolutely. The place I'd seen Mallory with surfers definitely didn't sound like the same one that Jillian was talking about. "I did notice that she'd developed a recent interest in surfing."

"Well, I don't know how much actual surfing she was doing. She seemed more interested in the *surfers* than the *surfing*. But she was always out there anyway. I've got an ex who likes to hang with those guys, so I saw her sometimes. Anyway, sorry."

I thanked her and turned. Alex made it clear from his body language that it was me he was waiting on. Not a surprise. We spent most of our time together. More's the pity.

"What's up?" I requested, stepping into the field of electrified air that always seemed to hang around him, waiting to zap me every time I got too close.

"Requisition forms." He handed the papers my way. "I know that place. Strangler's Cove Beach, well, and Strangler's Cove too. I've been there."

"Was it for the bitchin' waves?" I asked.

Laughing, he took the forms back. "No. It was an accident. I parasail. I got caught in a crosswind. Crashed there. It wasn't until I asked around later that I figured out where I was. The water is hard there. It's dangerous. Only an idiot would surf a place like that on purpose. The cove itself is less *bitchin'* and more *tidal wave*. That's a one-way ticket to getting dead the moment you lose control. But there's a beach nearby there. I'd probably have trouble finding the cove again. It isn't even on a map. But I could get you to the beach where I took off that day."

I evaluated him. "For what?"

He cocked his head. "Aren't you even the slightest bit curious?"

"No." There wasn't a lot that he could do to argue with my deadpan voice.

However, unlike Georgie, he didn't leave it be. "I'm sorry, Charlie."

I sniffed, turning slightly away before my expression gave anything away.

"I know you don't want to think about it, because you think you can't afford to."

It really unnerved me how he did that. No matter what I did, he seemed to understand my motivations. "It's a very busy time. I just need to work." I really just couldn't afford to think about Mallory, or I'd lose it completely, and there really was just no time for that.

"If you give yourself the time to grieve, to try to understand what happened and why, you'll be able to work much better."

He really could not have said a more beguiling thing to me. Being able to work better was all I really wanted at this juncture. Mallory's family deserved answers, but all I wanted was to bury my head in the sand. It was a hard fight between my conscience and my fear. Hurt for Mallory's parents won out.

"Can you take me to the beach you took off from between four and dinner? We have to be back for the meal."

We had to be. There was no one else to host. It wasn't the standard habit of the resort to have dinner hosts, but the holidays were different. Phillip had set a precedent. He'd presided over the entire Christmas week like the resort was his home and he was the benevolent host. People loved him for that. It kept them coming back. I was no Phillip, not by any stretch of the imagination, but even I knew what needed to be done.

"Sounds like a plan. That reminds me. You need to wear this."

He reached into the back pocket of his khaki shorts and handed me a folded thing. It wasn't until he shook it out that I realized what it was. Or at least what I thought it might be. "What in the name of all that is holy is that abomination?"

Alex laughed. "It's the mistletoe hat. And Phillip always wore it. I've already had guests from last night asking me why you aren't wearing the hat."

I stared at the bright red trucker hat, adorned on the bill with a strand of utterly ugly fake mistletoe. "I will never wear that hat."

Alex's impatience was sudden and unexpected. Usually he was pretty tolerant of the differing managerial styles between me and the man who had preceded me. The kind and jovial Phillip had size fifteen shoes I could never fill. And a horrid hat that I wasn't even going to try filling.

"Guests love the hat, Charlie."

I shook my head. "I'm sorry. No. It will never happen. You can make me hang decorations. You can make me listen to 'Jingle Bell' remakes until I bleed from the ears. You can make me do fake yuletide smiles while everyone gets all...jolly. You *cannot* make me wear that hat."

His lip twitched. "What is the deal with your dead hatred of Christmas?"

I flinched. The last thing I wanted to talk about was Christmas. Even though I used to live for Christmas, it now seemed easier to ignore all of it. Jared had been a huge fan as well, running the line of Christmas cards for a huge corporation of card makers. It had seemed like fate to have our holiday nuptials. Now I just loathed every Mele Kaliki moment.

"Listen, you can handle the being jolly, and I'll handle the being efficient. Perfect solution."

His lips twisted. "We'll return to this later." He tucked the horrid hat back into his pocket.

"No, we won't," I promised sweetly.

He might be inclined to bring it up again, but I had no interest in discussing it. As far as I was concerned, the mistletoe hat was a thing of the past. I could see that gleam in his eye, the one that said this would come up again, but I would just continue to ignore it.

We had a short discussion about the work that needed to be done today, and we agreed to meet in the employee parking lot at four, given that something didn't come up to stand in our way. I was torn. I hadn't lied to Georgie. I didn't want to know what had happened to Mallory, and I didn't want to know why. I wanted to close my eyes and ears to all of it until I could block out the parts that might cause me to stumble, the emotional side of what had happened. I also knew that there was no one here who would fight for Mallory's family. They were a faraway element, a foreign concept. They deserved to know. I couldn't agonize over it at that moment. There was work to be done.

The first order of business was to handle the shipment of conifers from the mainland that some of the guests wanted for their rooms or huts. Pine trees were certainly not native to any island in Hawaii and had to be shipped across the Pacific to end up in homes, or in this case, rooms. The cost was ridiculous, but Aloha Lagoon got people what they wanted. Even if that meant shipping trees in from somewhere colder. I smiled brightly at every guest I passed, because smiling was as instinctive as breathing when in the presence of guests. I didn't have Phillip's effusiveness, but I truly did care about the guests and their happiness.

A couple of children ran through the lobby, nearly knocking me over, having a loud argument about whether Santa, or *Kanakaloka*, as the natives called him, would arrive on a surfboard or on a Skidoo. Neither was correct actually. In the way I always absorbed local knowledge, I knew that most people credited Santa with arriving on an outrigger canoe pulled by dolphins. Barefoot and wearing a pair of shorts and a flowered shirt, of course. Because…Hawaii.

The kids' mom followed behind, struggling with a massive bag of the kinds of accoutrements that seemed to be inherent to children. They were on their way out to the beach, like almost everyone would be today.

Including me, apparently.

The day passed quickly. Even though it was another five days to Christmas, the giant Christmas Eve luau wasn't something that happened overnight. There were dozens of different people involved in the process of prepping for such an enormous meal. Over the years, even the population of AL the town had started joining AL the resort for our feast. It had eventually replaced whatever the town had done alone. I wasn't knowledgeable in preparing luaus, and the list seemed endless. Luckily, Alex was experienced with luaus, and he was ever efficient.

I saw Georgie on occasion, small peeks near the pool or in the lobby. I still had no idea why she was here, but as least she was staying out of my way. There wasn't much more I could ask. My occasional meetings with Alex were at least civil, and he kept his shirt mostly buttoned, so I considered that a win.

At four, one of Hawaii's ever-present ukulele players, Nani again, took the stage in the main ballroom to play some traditional Christmas music. Outside, in the area that had been cleaned of any sign of Mallory's death, another band was channeling the Beach Boys. There was something for everyone and two hours to kill before dinner. I finished the last of my paperwork and locked my office, headed for the parking lot. I braced myself for as much as two hours spent in a small space with Alex, the stuff my nightmares and inappropriate dreams were made of. What I hadn't anticipated was the sudden presence of Georgie.

As though she'd been watching for me, she appeared out of nowhere, like from behind a palm or something, and materialized at my side near the front door. I said hello vaguely and kept walking through the power doors, hoping she'd get the idea and find something else to do. It didn't work. She kept following me.

"Where are you going?"

The question made sense, I supposed, but since I was predisposed to be irritated at her presence, it just made my teeth grind. "I need to go somewhere."

It wasn't really an answer, but it was as good as I planned to give.

"Where?"

Ugh. This was like we were teenagers again, when she'd grill me until I ended up giving her information I hadn't wanted her to have. Information she'd then use against me. "I just have an errand to run with…" I didn't want to finish that sentence. It was stupidity to have started.

"Alex?" Georgie flashed me one of her signature lascivious grins. "He's seriously hot. Good choice, there."

"Good choice," I repeated vaguely. I wasn't getting into this with her. Nothing I'd ever done with Alex was my choice. He'd already been here when I'd arrived, and neither Juls nor

Rachel was here now to give me the help I needed. He was really the only option. That didn't imply a ton of choice.

I restrained the urge to warn her away from Alex, but I didn't even know who the warning would be for. Georgie? Alex? My own misplaced, much unappreciated lust for the man? Who knew? So I didn't say anything at all.

"I have to go," I blurted out, snapping out of my momentary fugue.

She followed me out to my car where Alex was already waiting, and I didn't know how to tell her to just get lost. Regardless of my feelings on the subject, she was my sister. Before Jared, we'd been everything to each other. She was the only person I felt safe to trust and safe to love. Then she'd ruined it all. For some reason I couldn't begin to imagine, she'd chosen to visit me, without warning, at the absolute worst time of the year.

"You don't have to go," I finally offered, desperately grasping for, at the very least, polite, if not kind of sisterly.

Alex cocked his head, taking in the both of us. "We're going out to the beach to see if we can meet up with some of Mallory's friends."

I closed my eyes for a second, restraining a sigh. He *would* tell her immediately what we were up to, when I had gone to great lengths to avoid her knowing.

To Alex, she actually addressed a request to go with us. "Can I go too?" She turned imploring eyes on him, acting as though I didn't exist. Even though it was my car and she'd followed me outside. Georgie always spoke to men first, if it was an option. It was just her way. Maybe they were easier for her to manipulate, or maybe she just liked them better.

My respect for Alex rocketed up another notch when he turned immediately to me, eyebrows cocked questioningly. I had no doubt that if I said I didn't want Georgie along, he would tell her no. That was something I wasn't sure I'd ever experienced before. Obviously, Jared hadn't spent a very great deal of time saying no to Georgie. I shrugged, faking indifference.

He opened the back door for her again, even though this time we were riding in my car. Then he jogged around and claimed the passenger seat. This time the smell of Alex in such close confines didn't come as a shock, but it wasn't pleasant either. Well, it *was* pleasant. It was freaking hot. Which is why it wasn't pleasant. Alex was a complication that I couldn't afford to disregard as an enemy to my peace of mind, my sanity, and my continued work performance.

It took not quite thirty minutes to get to the beach that Alex had been talking about. It was outside of Aloha Lagoon but not so far it wouldn't attract some of the locals. Like almost every beach in Hawaii, it was occupied. Even the remote beaches usually had two or three random surfers or one intrepid family picking across the shoreline.

For a moment I was struck breathless by the sheer beauty of the jagged rock line above us, the vivid hues of the setting sun, the intense green of the vegetation around us against the intense blue green of the waves slapping on the shore. Then I forced the awe away. There was nothing in Hawaii that I was willing to fall in love with. Not even a single beach.

"Wow," Georgie breathed, taking in the riotous explosion of oranges, yellows, and pinks of the sun setting over the Pacific. "This is amazing."

Alex nodded, taking it all in with pride, as though he'd given birth to Hawaii and raised it, working two jobs to put it through college. "The most amazing place on earth. Come on. Let's catch these guys before they decide to leave."

This wasn't the beach where I'd seen Mallory and the surfers. That beach had been plainly visible from the highway. But if someone else had seen her here, it couldn't hurt to check it out. Even if the pickings of surfers was slim. We crossed the beach, where I ended up taking off my shoes again because…sand. Always with the sand. I ignored the somewhat pleasant feeling of warm grains between my toes and concentrated on catching the three men in swim trunks who were clearly showing signs their party was breaking up and they were headed out.

"Hey," Alex called, and they all turned to face us. Alex jogged on ahead, striking up a conversation with the men, who seemed like they were at least paying attention, even if they didn't have any answers.

It took longer for Georgie and me to reach them. By the time we got there, all four men were joking and chatting like the oldest of friends. Actually, for all I knew, Alex did know them. He was a parasailer, a surfer, and heaven knew what else. We reached them just in time to hear one guy with a brutally shaved head say, "Oh, yeah. We know that chick, but not really well. She hangs with Squid. Ask him. He'll know more."

I was going to give the benefit of the doubt and assume Squid was a person and that Mallory hadn't spent her off time in the water trolling for cephalopods to hang with. Although, there was no reason I could think of to trust any man who wanted people to call him Squid, but that was another story.

For a second the guys noticed Georgie, or more specifically her fantastic lack of clothing, in her short-shorts and pink bikini top, and fantastic bounty of cleavage. All the conversation stopped while they were struck dumb. There was a long awkward moment where they simply stared at her. She stared at the sea, totally absorbed in the slapping waves and oblivious to the admiration.

Alex ran a hand through his hair and also glanced out to the ocean longingly, as though it physically hurt him to be out here and not get in. "Where can we find Squid?" he asked instead.

The shaved-headed man shrugged. He was gaunt and hard looking, probably the result of being an athlete, but there was something Spartan about his appearance that suggested he was used to pushing himself hard and depriving himself of anything not necessary to live. The smallest of the group, a man that I could see was really more of a boy, raised his hand. Apparently he was young enough that he still needed to be called on to make a comment in a crowd. He was probably eighteen, give or take, and his orange swim trunks hung on his skeletal frame.

Alex pointed at him. "I think Squid likes your beach, Alex." He still struggled with acne, and his voice broke when he talked. "I see him there a lot."

I had no clue which beach was considered to be the sole property of Alex, but I was sure that he knew at least.

Alex nodded. "Thanks, Big Steve."

The third man was a portly, middle-aged guy with a grizzled white beard and very small swim trunks. It was possible he was nearly as white as I was, though his color could clearly only be attributed to genetics and not a very concerted effort to avoid being in the sun, like my lack of tan. He nodded gravely. "Also, if all else fails, Squid likes to eat at Sir Spamalot's. He's there for lunch almost every day."

Alex brightened at that information. Lunch every day made Squid an exceedingly easy mollusk to track. That was good, considering how narrow our time was currently. *Wait a minute.* What was I thinking?

Going to the beach one time was something. Planning a trip to the local hangouts to find Squid was another matter entirely. I still wasn't sure I wanted to know the why or how Mallory was dead. Half of me just wanted to work. Half just wanted to offer comfort to the people who had given me an endless supply of lollypops at every barbeque when I was little. Mallory's family. For a moment, I had forgotten that at the end of that merry chase was a cold reality I still wasn't ready to face. Maybe it was time though. Maybe I needed to face it.

It took several minutes for Alex to say good-bye to the men, and it involved all sorts of fist bumps and slapping. Once their ridiculously involved secret handshake was finished, we all piled back into the car. It was too late to do anything but immediately return to the hotel and prep for the dinner crowd. It had taken us an hour to get there and back, and the conversation had only lasted maybe ten minutes. I was no detective, but that seemed like an exceptionally bad cost-benefit ratio to me.

CHAPTER FIVE

———

Once we were back, I went to my room to change for dinner, because people loved to dress for dinner during Christmas. I'd learned that the hard way the night before when I'd gone to dinner desperate and frazzled after discovering Mallory and found the majority of the women dressed as though we were on a cruise ship. Out of politeness I informed Georgie about the unspoken dress code and went to change my wrinkled suit for a much-nicer pencil skirt and a silk blouse.

My suite had been designed to be lived in, and it was definitely more of an apartment than a hotel room. I was equipped with multiple walk-in closets, a kitchenette, and a whirlpool tub and steam shower. I didn't really need that kind of a setup. I moved often as a consequence of my job, and my typical stay was under two months. I could have spent my days in the same room the guests used and been fine. But the suite was here and meant for the manager, and so here I was.

I sorted through the closet, looking for something nicer than I was wearing and less ridiculous than the red carpet fashion show I'd seen the night before. I packed light. Because I needed to be able to leave at a moment's notice. Not just because the company might ask me to. I just…needed to be ready. I did have a single evening gown in case of hotel events, but there was no way I was breaking it out for this. Alex had already cautioned me that this period of ridiculous dress-up would end on Christmas Eve during the luau when everyone would shimmy out of those slinky dresses and back into flowered shirts and khaki shorts.

Georgie was standing outside my room in the quiet fifth-floor hallway when I emerged, which was an unpleasant shock. I'd made a point of not telling her which room I was in, and this area of the hotel was not occupied. It contained only the manager's suite and several unused offices. Of course someone had told her. Why wouldn't they? She was my identical twin. It wasn't as though anyone would assume I wouldn't want her to have that information.

"Can I talk to you, Charlie?"

I flinched. "Not if you call me 'Charlie.'"

Her head cocked. "Alex does. I just assumed you were cool with it now."

I sighed. There was really no way to explain why I let Alex do it, but the reason wasn't that I was "cool with it." "Alex is the one and only person who is remotely permitted to call me Charlie."

And he was permitted only because I couldn't stop him.

"Hey, you guys make a great couple. Seriously. You can practically see the electricity between you two. Sitting in the same car is like being caught in a thunderstorm." She grinned. "See, that's what you never had with Jared. That's why it didn't work."

There were so many things wrong with her statement that I didn't know where to begin. "Alex and I are not a couple. Not by any definition of the word. Unless you mean a couple of managers forced to work as a unit, and then, yes, I suppose you could use the word couple. And Jared and I didn't work because you had sex with him and filmed it. Oh, and then gave me the tape."

I hadn't really meant to bring it up. It didn't help anyone. But there it was, just floating in the air in a cartoon bubble. Impossible to make it disappear.

She sighed. "So you're still pissed about that."

She said it as though I was still pissed about the time in second grade when she'd borrowed my Garfield shirt without my permission and then gotten paint on it during art camp. Any person, reasonable or otherwise, would still be unhappy about what she'd done.

"You never even apologized," I pointed out, keeping my voice completely even. There was no point in letting her know how much I was still wounded. And no matter what, she probably wouldn't understand that it wasn't about Jared, a man I really hadn't been particularly good with. It was about her. About what *she'd* done, not what he'd done. Because she was my sister, and she'd really let me down.

Mouth pressed tight, she sighed. "Look, I didn't apologize because…maybe the way I did it was wrong, but Jared was a jerk. And he was a boring jerk, at that. You never would have walked away from him, and it was almost a done deal. I was running out of time, and I had to do something."

She really had justified it in her head. As though it was all perfectly rational to do what she'd done. Like the ends justifying the means didn't make her an emotional terrorist. This was pointless. It would always be. I wasn't even sure she was telling the truth in attributing her actions all to wanting to save me from myself with a little prewedding coitus.

"What do you want, Georgie?"

"I need a job." She blurted out the words without any kind of cushion for the transition from her screwing me over to her begging me for a job.

"Seriously?" She made my head spin. "What happened to Gentry?"

Like me, Georgie had a degree in hospitality, though she hadn't gone on after her bachelor's. For the last three years, since the day she'd walked out after giving me the tape, she'd been working for a cruise company called Gentry Ocean Liners. Doing her own little Julie impersonation, running games aboard the activity deck. Owned by deeply southern American royalty, Gentry was a huge travel empire, owning yachts, hotels, resorts, and even private islands. It was a good job for anyone.

Her tongue stabbed into her cheek, and I could see it pushing out. Georgie only did that when she was literally biting her tongue. Whatever she told me wouldn't be the truth. At least not all of it.

"I had a...problem with Marty. I need a new job. I disembarked in Hawaii, so I just hopped over to Aloha Lagoon. I mean, not to be rude, but you clearly need someone to replace Mallory, and I'm as qualified as she was. More, if you count real-world experience."

That was technically true. But while I hadn't been friends with Mallory, I'd liked her. Georgie wasn't my favorite person at the moment. "That's nepotism," I pointed out.

"It would only be nepotism if you hired me above other applicants because I was your sister, and you and I both know that would never happen." She was right about that. We were silent for a long moment while I debated how to put her off long enough to come up with an excuse to not hire her. Beyond that I didn't want to, of course.

Her sigh was small, nearly silent, mostly manifested through the rise and fall of her bony shoulders. "I have nowhere else to go, Charlotte. At least let me do Mallory's job for a few weeks to save up some money, and then I'll be out of your hair."

What could I say to that? I didn't know Marty, but I knew from a casual conversation with Mom that he was her boss and had been for three years. I had no idea what had happened with him, but after all the years she'd been working for him, if he was going to do something terrible, I would have thought he'd have done it before now.

"Okay, but I work my assistants hard. Are you ready for that?" I would actually be taking it easy on her, because she wasn't really trained, and I just didn't want to fight with her about her lack of work ethic. It wasn't worth it. I was really just giving her a few weeks of pay for doing nothing, instead of just a straight-out donation.

"Absolutely. Marty is a work machine. I've never worked so hard in my life as the last three years."

Her face pinched again, and there was a moment where her shuddering sigh seemed like the biggest thing in the room. What had this Marty guy done to her? Surprisingly, I had a momentary flash of sisterly indignation on her behalf. Maybe I wasn't still that angry after all.

* * *

The rest of the night and the next morning went off as smooth as a new jar of peanut butter. I wasn't sure how the repeat guests were going to accept me as their new "host," but wherever I might have fallen short, Alex took up the slack.

If Alex didn't do the job, surprisingly, Georgie did. Looking shiny and rather modest in her Aloha Lagoon khakis and burgundy polo, Georgie was certainly likeable. I was lucky enough to be surrounded by people able to do the one thing I couldn't—be charming.

She was also up first thing in the morning, waiting for me when I got to the lobby. I was suspicious but grateful. Alex was still bugging me about heading over to Sir Spamalot's for lunch, looking for Squid. I was torn about whether or not I wanted to go, but if we had any chance of breaking up a workday, it would be because we'd already done hours of work in the time before lunch.

I really had no desire to meet with Squid, but the trip to the beach hadn't made me feel any better, and I believed that Alex was right. Maybe I should just ask the police how she died, go to my room and have a good cry, and just be done with the whole thing. But I couldn't embrace weakness to that extent. It was better to act than weep, if those were my only two options.

At noon I left and met with Alex outside. I was worried Georgie would try to come again, but she was nowhere to be found. That was both a blessing and a curse. I didn't want her along, but I wasn't keen on spending any more time alone with Alex than I had to. Especially when he refused to stay inside the box I'd shoved him in. Alex outside of my "nemesis" box was not something that would behoove either one of us.

Alex was standing near the big palm, hands in the pockets of ridiculous pants, which were either really long shorts or really short pants. Or maybe they were capris for men. Manpris? When he saw me, the left side of his gorgeous mouth cocked, flashing that signature fascinating crease in his cheek and that one raised eyebrow. I looked away, concentrating instead on the sidewalk, a pile of sand, the big palm. Anything that didn't make my pulse kick like an angry rabbit.

Once we were safely in the car—mine again, since it smelled less like him, not that I would tell him that was the reason—he changed radio stations for a few minutes without even asking, settling on the station he'd started with. We could have walked. It wasn't that far, but cutting out time waste, and sand, was always my goal.

"So what's the deal with you and Georgie?"

I glanced at him quickly before darting my eyes back to the road. "There's no deal."

He laughed, which annoyed me. "Well, we both know that's not true. So tell me the story. She steal your boyfriend in sixth grade? Puppy liked her better? Parents compared you two? People accidentally got you confused at really awkward times?"

I sighed. There was really no good answer to this question. A dark part of me that rarely reared her ugly head suddenly wanted to make life awkward for him since he was pressuring for answers. That squirming darkness superseded my desire to keep my business from being his.

"All of the above. Then she had really kinky sex with my fiancé the day before our wedding and taped it. She gave me the data stick right afterwards and then left town. I haven't seen her since."

Alex ran a hand through his hair. "I'm sorry. That sucks. Jeez."

Then I felt bad for making Alex feel bad for me. I had issues. For years I'd refused to tell anyone what had happened between Georgie, Jared, and me. I hadn't even told my parents, who'd happened to be married at the time. I'd just handed the data stick to Jared after I'd watched it, and kicked him out of the apartment. I didn't even make excuses, nor was I remotely interested in hearing his. I sent an email to everyone invited to the wedding stating very matter of factly that the wedding had been canceled. Then I called corporate and asked for the first available position at any resort not in Chicago.

My mother was still trying to get answers about why I'd canceled the wedding, but she wouldn't be getting any, because I wasn't going to tell her that, and oddly, Georgie never had either. There were a couple of reasons for that on my part. She wouldn't have wanted me to walk away. In her mind, life wasn't life unless you were invested in a Tammy Wynette–level of standing by your man. She would have, and in fact had, seen undeniable proof of cheating and simply dismissed it as an older form of "boys will be boys," which was code for "men are bastards, but I'm codependent." The other reason was simply that I didn't want her in my business. She'd be burdening me with her terrible relationship advice from now until forever.

I wouldn't tell anyone. Except, apparently, Alex. Because...who knew why.

I couldn't look at him, so I just kept driving, though we were nearly to Sir Spamalot's. Hawaiian people's obsession with Spam was something I would never understand, and I'd never eaten at Sir Spamalot's, but I still knew where it was. I knew where everything was on every one of the numerous acres of Aloha Lagoon.

"You want me to kick her out of the hotel?"

I did glance at him then. Was he serious? It was clear he liked Georgie. Did that mean...he liked me better? That was both shocking and excruciatingly uncomfortable. I couldn't ferret out the answer in my head. "Are you serious?"

He scowled at me. "Of course I'm serious. How long ago was that?"

"Three years. It's okay. I shouldn't have been planning to marry him anyway. He..."

How could I explain Jared? How could I explain that his anal-retentive perfectionism wasn't a good foil for my serious personality or my need for order and control? You'd think two people like that would have done well together, but we hadn't. All Jared had done was congratulate me on my perfectionism as long as it didn't interfere with his. How could I explain that we were two people who'd fallen into a relationship as college freshmen and then spent the next ten years being too self-satisfied or busy to bother seeking out a relationship that actually would have mattered?

"We weren't a good match. Georgie was right about that much. Maybe she just wasn't right about how she broke us up."

In just less than twenty-four hours, I'd somehow come to accept her explanation. It made sense anyway. Georgie probably didn't like me much, but she liked Jared even less, and she'd always been very vocal about that, right from the moment they'd met. In her convoluted way of thinking, where sex was a solution for anything, it probably did make sense to use it to break up a bothersome relationship when neither party would listen to your advice.

That didn't make it okay though.

"Why is she here now?" Alex asked.

I shrugged, keeping my eyes focused outside the window, even though we'd pulled into a spot. I was not interested in seeing whatever look he might have on his face. I didn't want his sympathy, his umbrage on my behalf, or anything else. I just wanted to pretend I'd never said it.

"She needs a job."

He didn't say anything else, thankfully. I didn't want to talk about Jared anymore, nor did I want to be questioned about why I would elect to hire my sister, who'd done something like that to me.

Sir Spamalot's was just off the main resort road, and as always it was busy. Centered around Spam-inspired food and that boisterous Hawaiian hospitality, Sir Spamalot's was every local's favorite. Personally, I was not a fan of canned meat, but even I had to acknowledge that the place was creative and popular. I realized belatedly that I had no clue what Squid looked like.

"Do you know Squid?" I asked, feeling like an idiot for just saying that name out loud.

Alex shook his head, looking very cheerful for someone who had no idea who we were looking for.

"Then how will we find him?"

Shrugging, Alex opened the door and hopped out. "Look for someone who looks like a squid?"

I scrambled to catch up, doubting the chances of success with his plan. As it turned out, I shouldn't have been. Like everything else Alex touched, the seemingly ridiculous idea was a good one. We approached the tiki-hut-looking outdoor café and immediately set eyes on a man who even I couldn't deny actually looked like a squid. With his very white skin, long face, bulbous eyes, and eight thick dreads—two longer than the rest—if anyone looked like a squid, it was this guy. I was still debating how offensive it would be to ask him if he was Squid—since if he wasn't, he might be slightly peeved by the question—when Alex approached him.

"Squid? Mo and Big Steve said we could find you here."

He nodded. "Ah, hey, bra. 'Sup?" He didn't appear remotely curious as to why we'd approached him or how we'd identified him. However, it was also clear from his glassy eyes, slack mouth, and the overwhelming scent of eau de weed clinging to his clothing that he was so very, very stoned. So it might simply be that those questions never even registered as valid ones.

"They said you're friends with Mallory. From the resort?"

His vague expression spent a slow moment rearranging into raised eyebrows. "Oh, yeah. Sure. Mal. Why?"

If he didn't know she was dead, I certainly didn't want to be the one to tell him. I'd had that privilege too many times already. "Do you know who else she hangs out with a lot? Maybe who she spends the most time with?"

The question seemed to confuse him for a long moment. He reminded me of a sloth as much as a Squid. His reaction times were just so slow. I could only hope that he didn't surf that high, or he'd be living a shortened life too. "She has this boyfriend. Don't remember the dude's name. Bill? Hill? Oh, maybe Phil!"

The fact Mallory had a boyfriend was shocking, and it was news to me. I wasn't even aware she'd spent so much time out. When did she even sleep? However, if we were relying on just Squid for information, it seemed very likely we might never know what the man's name was. But we did certainly seem to know what it rhymed with anyway.

"Do you know where she liked to hang out?" Alex asked.

I let him do the talking since Squid seemed to like him, and if he wanted to talk about anything related to the beach, Alex was the only one who'd be capable of having that conversation. I liked beaches. When I wasn't wearing heels. Alex was the resident expert on all things water sports, and it seemed best to just hang out and let him work. Of course, the subject might never come up, but nevertheless, I liked to err on the side of caution.

Squid suddenly looked suspicious, which surprised me because it suggested he was more with it than I'd thought. What did he have to be suspicious about though? We were the ones with the questions. Actually, maybe that was why he was suspicious.

"She likes Strangler's Cove Beach."

Alex nodded. "That's where we saw Mo, Big Steve, and that other guy. Anywhere else?"

Squid scratched his head very slowly in the blank scalp space between two dreads. "She likes that club Spikers on the other side of the island. Why are you asking? Don't you know where Mal is? I can tell from your clothes that you're from the resort. Aren't you, like, her bosses?"

"We were," Alex said. "She died recently."

The shock on Squid's face was not feigned. He really hadn't known that she'd been killed at all, let alone that she'd been murdered. He clearly wasn't the reason she'd died anyway. That was one person we could take off the suspect list I definitely didn't have brewing in my mind.

"Aww, man. That sucks."

Profound truths from our friend Squid. Alex thanked him, and we headed out toward the car together, blinded by the sunshine when we left the straw covering of the café that shielded us in shade. He blinked for a moment against the sudden light and then turned to me. "Did you know Mallory had a boyfriend?"

I shook my head. "Not a clue."

"Do you know anyone at all named Bill, Hill, Phil?" he asked me, instead of giving his opinion on our varying managerial styles.

I shrugged. "There's Phil from the kitchen staff, but he's married. And there's also a Bill who works in valet parking, but he's barely five feet tall, only about seventeen, and has some serious skin condition of some kind. Mallory was gorgeous, and I would imagine she'd be more selective than that."

The truth was I had no idea what kind of men Mallory liked. She'd probably told me at some point during her endless ramblings, but I hadn't been listening. I rarely ever listened to anything she had to say that wasn't about a resort. It was a slap in the face to realize what I could have learned about her, had I only been willing to pay attention. Though I would never be Alex, it was certainly in order that I pay more attention to the reality of my employees and not just their working conditions and efficacy.

I was a good manager, but I was *not* a good leader.

It was a shocking and humbling realization. Give me a resort any day, and I could have it running in tip-top shape in no time. Give me a staff of employees, and I could leave that resort in two months knowing only who was in charge of what and their names so I could be sure to be able to reach them. Connecting with people wasn't really my forte. It was one of the reasons I liked to keep moving. If I stayed at a resort too long, it would begin to be awkwardly obvious how hard I worked to keep this strictly professional at all times. I could never be Alex, nor did I want to be, but I could be more than I was.

"Seth from the night staff told me that they'd been flirting lately. He gave her his card so she'd remember his name. He didn't mention anything about her saying she was already dating someone, nor did he say they'd gone out. That seems like a pretty glaring omission, if they had."

Alex cocked his head. "Seth doesn't rhyme with Bill, but it couldn't hurt to ask him if she mentioned having a boyfriend."

I noticed Detective Ray and a woman I didn't know getting out of a car in the lot. When he saw me, his gaze honed directly in. He left the woman, who may have been his wife—I didn't even know if he was married—on the sidewalk and crossed over to us.

"Miss Conner. Alex." He nodded at us. It struck me suddenly that it was such an odd way to greet people to just say their names. I'd done it before, but it was so weird to identify someone and have that be a greeting. Like nodding at our toast and saying "toast" before eating it.

"Any new info?" Alex asked, running a hand through his flyaway hair. If it was possible, the sun actually intensified that smell, the scent of Alex, the reason we weren't driving his car today, and for a moment I was shamefully distracted from the conversation.

When I reentered the world of the not-pointlessly-lusting, I realized Detective Ray was already in the middle of an answer. "...broken neck, we think."

The words made my stomach clench and then flip violently. I thought about throwing up for just a moment, but luckily the feeling passed.

"Mallory died from a broken neck?" I repeated, my voice wavering shamefully. Alex's hand darted out and rested lightly on the small of my back. It wasn't a violating touch. Not even a significant one, but it stopped my urge to hyperventilate almost immediately.

Ray shot me an evaluating look. "Yes, she did."

"Did you know that Mallory had a boyfriend?" Alex asked.

Ray shook his head. "Can't really say what we know and don't know in an active investigation. Her body was released to her family yesterday to be returned to Chicago."

That didn't help much. Which was probably the intention. I had to ask because I had to know the answer. Was it something I'd done that made her die? Had she noticed something wrong, crawled inside to fix it, and died in a freak accident? I couldn't imagine her doing it, but I had to ask anyway. "Did it...did she die from the fall?"

For a moment, Detective Ray's look was pure sympathy, but it only lasted for that small second. "No. She was already dead."

I closed my eyes and swallowed hard, struggling for control. Well, at least there was that much. Alex stepped a little closer to me, and I let him because, once again, when it got hard, he was an odd source of comfort I wouldn't have expected.

Next to me I heard Alex's voice as if far away. "Then why or how did she end up in the waterfall?"

For a long moment Detective Ray didn't speak. Long enough that I finally felt okay opening my eyes.

"I'm not sure. I suspect it was some kind of message. We just have to figure out who it was to and what it was about."

The idea that a person would murder an innocent human being just to send a message to someone else was horrifying. I could barely speak. When I did force words past my thick throat, I wasn't even sure Detective Ray could hear them.

"She didn't...she didn't suffer...right?"

I didn't want to hear the answer, but now that I knew how she'd died, I was sick with the possibilities. I would never sleep again unless I knew the cold facts. If she did suffer, it would be better to know and think hard on it than to suppose while I lay in bed awake. I could feel Alex's fingers curve against my back, and against my will, I folded into his strength. I shivered.

Slowly, Detective Ray shook his head. "I don't think so. You still can't think of a reason someone would want her dead?"

I shook my head silently. She didn't suffer. At least there was that.

"And you can't think of anyone who knew her better than you?"

I couldn't bring myself to point a finger at my own sister. Again, I just shook my head. Alex shot me a brief look but said nothing.

Detective Ray nodded. "I'll be seeing you, Miss Conner."

He returned to the woman, and they headed up towards the counter, while Alex and I stood in total stillness for a long moment. "Hey," Alex called after Detective Ray. He turned. "Did you ever find out why she had Seth Peterson's card in her hand?"

Ray cocked his head. "We talked to Seth."

It wasn't an answer, but I figured it was the best we were going to get out of the tight-lipped detective. He nodded again and turned back to the counter. Alex pushed a hand through his hair and used the hand on my back to direct me toward the car. I should have done something to end him touching me, but for the moment, I didn't want him to stop. He made me feel safe. Protected. Which was exactly the reason I should have stopped him.

At the car he paused. "Want me to drive? I don't mind."

I shook my head. I couldn't give up that much control just for the sake of comfort. I would drive.

We drove in silence until we were nearly across the length of the resort.

"I think we should go to the club. What did he call it?"

"Spikers," I responded absently, keeping my eyes on the road and my mind on anything but Mallory. That was a weird name for a club. It sounded like a warning to the ladies about the quality of people present at the club, to be cautious not to put down your drink.

"Right. We should go tonight. I have no idea where it is, but I'll find it."

I shook my head. "We can't do that tonight. We're busy." I realized how shrill I sounded and dialed it down a notch. It wasn't his fault that Mallory had died. At least I was pretty sure it wasn't. No, definitely not. In a million years, no matter how many faults I wanted to lay at his feet, Alex would never be a killer. "We already took way too long a lunch, and we don't have time for something like that."

Alex leveled a hard look my way, and for once it actually worked. "We need to make time. The resort isn't the only thing in the world, Charlie."

Ouch. It wasn't the only thing in the world, but it was the only thing that made me feel better. "I really don't think this is a good idea."

We pulled into the employee parking lot. "Well, I do. And I'd like you to go as well. You can get the men to talk to you easier than I can, and I'll target the ladies. Someone has to know something."

I laughed. I didn't mean to—it just came out. "I'm not exactly man nip, Alex. I'm…vanilla. And uptight. And…" I stopped myself before it got depressing. "If you want someone men will pay attention to, bring Georgie."

His expression burned, his dark eyes searing into me. "Believe me, Charlie—you're hot, and you could distract someone into saying things they don't mean to say." Without another word, he hopped from the car, leaving me alone and confused and a teensy bit inappropriately turned on.

CHAPTER SIX

———

Several of the staff, including Georgie and me, spent the afternoon placing wreaths made from the traditional Hawaiian choice of poinsettias on every door in the resort, as well as the doors of the huts on the beaches. It was another tradition started by Phillip. The man had truly loved him some Christmas. All Hawaiian people seemed to, with a kind of spectacle that fit their everyday fascination with the colorful and extreme, but Phillip really had taken it to a special kind of level.

However, I wasn't about to stop his traditions now. Except for toning down the decorations just a tad and the stupid mistletoe hat, which I'd rather start myself on fire than wear. I wasn't even Aloha Lagoon's permanent manager, and it wasn't my place to interfere with traditions that had begun before me and would continue after I was gone.

There was a random concert going on out on the beach, and honestly, I wasn't even surprised anymore when I saw something like that. It could have been just a group with a sudden urge to jam. However, it was more than likely a party. Some of the locals were in the midst of *Mahahiki*, a traditional Hawaiian celebration to respect mother earth, which had come before the Christianity thing. It wasn't so big anymore, mostly faded away to make room for Santa and Christmas trees, but there were still a few who saw it as another excuse to party.

The calendar had once been divided into only two seasons, *Kau*, which was summer and considered to be the dry season, though so far I hadn't seen even a moment I would have considered dry. There was also winter, or *Makahiki*, which was considered the wet months and several months of taking it easy, which was a good reason to party. Not that these guys needed much of a reason to have another shindig. It seemed to be inborn around here.

If there was any kind of war going on between people, fighting was banned during *Makahiki* so that people could get down. Luckily, we were way past warring people looking to prove superiority over their neighbors. Now it was mostly random festivals and concerts, trying to give a vague reminiscence of the old culture.

Eventually, I left the others to finish the task and returned to my office to check on the preparations for the luau. Because the town had agreed to combine their massive local luau with ours, there were multiple sources of money involved in the cost of planning. There were also multiple people working the planning. But with only a few days left before Christmas Eve, we were way past planning and on to panicking.

People were already readying the pigs for slaughter in just a couple of days, the chocolate pies, the fruit cakes, something called almond floats—whatever that meant—and the inauspicious-sounding green tea ice cream. Maybe it was good, but more than likely it was only good if you'd grown up with it, and it sounded suspicious to me. I was a little homesick for the idea of a nice dead bird, instead of pig, and a couple of dinner rolls, but when in Rome.

Once dinner hit and Alex and I had done our hosting duties, we met in the corner of the main dining room, where happy guests were laughing along with the strains of Benny Hoku and his Ukulele "Wahines" playing live music. Outside, there were games for the kids and an ice cream bar with so many toppings the parents were probably going to hate us come bedtime, when their kids were too sugar high to sleep.

"I found Spikers. It's on the other side of the island. About as far from Aloha Lagoon as you can get. Which may be why Mallory chose it," Alex told me, just as Georgie decided to join us.

"What's Spikers?" she asked.

Of course. Why did she always pop up right when I needed her to not be there? Actually, this time I might have needed her to be here.

The look Alex gave her was a shock to me. There was no open friendship in it. What had happened while I wasn't paying attention to cause that one? I probably shouldn't have even been curious, but I was. I was sure we needed her, regardless of how much Alex might think I was capable of being a femme fatale. Just the memory of the look he'd given me was way too hot to dwell on when things needed to be done. Or ever, if I was smart.

"I need your help. There's some club on the other side of the island that Mallory frequented. I need you to go there with us and be hot. See what information you can get."

Georgie's mouth pursed. I would have thought she'd by dying to get to a club. "Why don't you just go and be hot?"

I glanced down at my tan linen suit and red blouse, added in an attempt to be even vaguely festive. "I don't do hot."

She rolled her eyes. "We look exactly the same."

I really hadn't expected this argument. "No, I assure you. We do not."

She waved me off. "Wardrobe. Come on. I'll fix you up. I'm sure I've got something perfect. What kind of club is it?"

Eyebrow cocked, I glanced at Alex for help. He was still standing there, looking more pensive than disapproving now. I shrugged. "A club kind of club. People probably drink there?"

Sighing, she turned to Alex too. "What kind of club is Spikers?"

"Europop dance."

At least he knew the answer. I didn't even know what that meant.

"I definitely have something. Let's hit my room. You don't want to be too early. You'll stick out, and no one Mallory liked will be there anyway."

Alex grabbed Georgie's arm, not hard but definitely enough to get her attention. "I want to talk to you."

Some kind of message was communicated between them with a glance, and my stomach twisted. They'd definitely been spending time together that I wasn't aware of. Not that it was any of my business. My only business was getting this resort through Christmas, and now, apparently, figuring out who Mallory knew besides me.

"I'll be right behind you," she told me. "You know where my room is, right?"

I nodded. Of course I knew. I knew which guest was in every room. I wasn't going to say a single word to her, or to Alex. If they wanted to have a relationship, one of any kind, it was none of my business.

None at all.

I forced myself to not even look their way until I reached the hallway to go upstairs. They were standing close together, and Georgie was speaking quickly and urgently. Alex stood with his arms crossed over his chest, legs braced, everything about him conveying the message he did not approve.

Not my business.

I went upstairs and waited in front of Georgie's door. I had a master card key, but I wasn't going to invade her privacy. I didn't feel we were close enough for that. It took her maybe five minutes to join me upstairs. She didn't mention anything Alex had said, not that I was surprised by that.

She opened the door and ushered me inside, heading right over to pull open her closet, dramatically revealing about twenty outfits. I honestly couldn't figure out how she fit that much stuff into a single bag. That was a marketable skill.

She pulled out a tube with several slits cut through it, the holes covered in a black mesh.

"Good lord." I stepped away. "What the hell is that thing?"

She rolled her eyes. "It's a dress. Okay, maybe that's a little much for you. Let's keep looking."

I stared at the offending garment as she tossed it on the bed. No one should ever, ever, ever have had any reason to where that, anywhere. Ever.

"How about this?" I snapped my head back her way, watching as she displayed another tiny black dress with one strap and an uneven hemline that wouldn't even cover my butt—which was likely the point—but that dress was a short train to Nopeville for me.

I shook my head. "Unless you're Pebbles, there's no reason you should be wearing that dress."

To my surprise, she laughed. "Okay, this is going to be harder than I thought. What about...no." She tossed another tube dress, this one teal blue lamé. She pulled a couple more dresses—both covered in sequins, one silver and one gold—and threw them on top of the others. No wonder she could fit so many outfits in one bag. They were all made of spandex and tailored to fit a twelve-year-old.

She waved her hand. "This isn't going to work. Here, let's do this instead." She reached inside and produced a pair of pants, which I appreciated, though I was less appreciative of their skintight cut and the fact they were made of leather. Then she added a black shift top with a larger swingy kind of bottom, like a bell shape, that I had to admit, reluctantly, that I actually liked.

"Go put this on. Then we'll work on shoes and jewelry."

I headed for the bathroom, eyeing the pants suspiciously. At least I could wear a bra with this outfit, which didn't seem like a possibility with the rest she'd shown me. My bra and I had a relationship that I appreciated. She kept the ladies in check, and I kept looking like a professional—and not part of the world's oldest profession.

"You're going with us, right?" I called through the door, nearly falling over trying to get the pants on.

"I don't know. I think you can handle it."

I shook my head, even though she couldn't see me. "I don't think I can. So you should come. Besides, we can cover more ground that way."

It took Georgie several seconds to respond. "Well, okay, I guess."

She fell silent, and I finished struggling into clothes that were probably a size too small for me and intended to be tight anyway. But finally I was dressed. When I got back out of the bathroom, Georgie was already dressed in the teal blue tube dress, which of course she made look good even though it was inherently hideous. Her clothes were an abandoned heap on the bed. I'd folded mine and was holding them awkwardly.

She snapped them out of my hand and threw the pile next to hers. The next hour was a mad rush of strappy stilettos, hair spray, makeup, and general agony. Also, I couldn't comfortably sit, so all of that was done standing up, in four-inch stilettos. When we were finally both ready to go out and meet Alex, it was already after ten. No worries for us about arriving unfashionably early.

Alex had also changed. His dark blue jeans weren't tight at all, but they were cut well, for maximum fit. Combined with a plain white V-necked shirt and a fitted black sport coat hanging open, it was clear he knew how to dress for a club, unlike me. His black hair was mussed—kind of spiky, kind of just messy, completely adorable. I concentrated on everything else I saw in the lobby.

He whistled in appreciation. "Nicely done, ladies." Whatever he'd been angry with Georgie about had apparently been resolved. He was all appreciation now.

We loaded into my car again without discussion, possibly because it didn't say *Aloha Lagoon Spa and Resort* on the side, like Alex's did. Possibly just because I was the last one to drive. It certainly wasn't my choice, as I was crippled by my shoes and the creaking of leather as I hobbled across the parking lot, yards behind them.

The drive to Kapa'a wasn't short, but it was no longer than two hours. A bigger town away from the people who knew Mallory would have been a perfect escape for a young girl searching for the kind of fun she didn't want to get back to her boss. I didn't know just what sort of fun she'd been seeking, but this was a long way to drive for a good time. Alex's phone directed us to Spikers, and the name turned out to make a lot more sense once we pulled into the parking lot. Though it was clear from the thumping music and blinding lights that Spikers was definitely a hopping nightclub, the area right next to the building was also busy, with a late-night volleyball game, a full team on each side of the massive net.

"Mallory liked volleyball," I said, the words suddenly seeming like the saddest statement I'd ever made. It reminded me why I was here. My head was filled with a giggling teenage Mallory, arms around her mother, crowing over her latest high school team victory. Those days were gone for the family. When she was alive, it was poignant memories of childhood. Now, for a long time all the family would have was pain.

The other two seemed to feel the strange gravity of it as well and flashed me somber looks. We sat in the car, observing an unexpected moment of silence. Finally, I pulled myself together and straightened my shoulders. We were already here, and we were going to get this thing done.

"When we get inside, split up. Alex targets the women. Georgie targets the men. I'll go outside and talk to the volleyball players."

That seemed like the best option for me anyway. I just didn't have what it took to seduce information out of people, despite Alex's and Georgie's proclamations to the contrary. Talking to a bunch of sweaty, aggressive people was much more my speed. No one argued, and we split up at the door. It was warm outside, as it always was, but a few of the people around the net were making a nod to the season with tacky Santa hats along with their bikinis and Speedos. I didn't want to break up the game, so I headed for the sidelines.

It was cheap of me, but I didn't want to talk about Mallory's death. If they didn't know she'd passed away, let them hear it from one of their friends. Instead, I watched the game in silence and then eventually spoke to the woman next to me. She was short, brunette, and very perky looking.

"Do you come here a lot?" I asked, speaking loudly to be heard above the chaos.

She nodded. "All the time. There's always a great game going, and if I'm lucky, I can hop in on the next round. Best playing in town, and great drinks and hot men inside if I get bored." She winked at me.

"I never even knew this place was here until today, but I heard one of my friends comes here a lot. Mallory Langston?"

The girl nodded, her curls bobbing. "Oh sure, I know Mal. She's got a mean serve. Half aces."

I had no clue what that meant, but I nodded encouragingly. "I never knew she had all these friends I'd never met. Who else does she hang out with?"

"I've seen her with people from Aloha Lagoon mostly. You know, she works up there."

I nodded. "Yeah, so do I. I just didn't even know people came out here."

"She hangs with a bunch of surfers. I think she might be dating some English dude, and I saw her once with this crazy OCD guy who works at a restaurant near the resort where she works. There are a couple of guys who live here in town who seem to like her. One's Eurotrash, but the other's another surfer. She sure likes surfers."

"So I've discovered." She either didn't notice my wry tone or didn't make anything of it. Mallory's obsession with surfers wasn't something I knew about before the last few days, that was for certain.

None of what this woman was saying was really of any help to me, except for the mention of Poncho, the OCD cook at the Loco Moco. Even for someone who didn't get out much, Poncho was recognizable from the short description. The rest were completely useless without names. From the way she was talking, she didn't even know their names.

"Are any of them here tonight? Just so I can say hi?"

I was trying for casual, but it probably didn't come across that way. Oh well. An actress I was not. She shot me a questioning look. "Well, Eurotrash is here. I saw him go in. None of the others are, that I know of."

There wasn't much use in asking her what Eurotrash looked like. That would be a step over what would be appropriate in casual conversation. If she called him that, I could probably figure it out. Someone who looked like what the girl's nickname suggested was probably a bit recognizable compared to the rest of a small island town. Even at a nightclub.

"Thanks."

She nodded, returning her attention to the game. "Tell Mal hi for me."

I wished I could.

I went across the other side of the net and repeated the conversation with two others who didn't even know Mallory. At this point, it seemed like the only appropriate thing to do would be to go inside and look for Eurotrash or maybe Mallory's mysterious English boyfriend. The inside of the club was insanely packed. Which made sense, as it was, as far as I was aware, the only real nightclub on the entire island. I spotted Georgie in the mad crush, only from her spiky white hair. I couldn't find Alex in the sea of dark-haired men, especially when it was pitch black inside, unless one of the spotlights managed to wander my way.

Because I didn't know who Georgie had already questioned, I decided to talk to her first. It seemed to me that if there was anything to be found out about Mallory at a place like this, there were so many people here; I couldn't imagine how we would find it. We couldn't question everyone, so the only thing to do was to strike up conversations with as many people as we could and hope they panned out.

I had to scream Georgie's name, even when I was standing right behind her. She was at the bar, chatting up a blond man in his late thirties clad in a non-Hawaiian-like three-button suit with pinstripes. He looked as uncomfortable as I felt, and I had a pang of sympathy for him and whatever, or more likely whoever, had dragged him there. I'd been in those shoes. Usually with Georgie but also with Jared, who'd just loved having business meetings at public places like clubs and restaurants.

She turned and smiled at me. "Charlotte, this is Niall. He's from Ireland."

I waved at Niall and considered that he might be the person that volleyball girl had been referring to, but I simply couldn't imagine that anyone would refer to him as trash of any kind, whether he was European or not. He flashed me a relieved smile, as though he recognized me as one of the awkward ones, a member of his party.

"Hello," he shouted, his accent heavily Irish and completely adorable.

"I need to talk to you for a minute," I told Georgie, indicating the dance floor with my shoulder. Somewhere on the other side of the room was a bathroom. In there we might even be able to hear each other.

She shook her head. "You need to dance with Niall. He hasn't danced all night." She laughed as though anything about this was funny, and I wondered if she'd also been drinking during the thirty minutes I'd been outside talking to the volleyball people. She shoved my awkward self with one hand and awkward Niall with the other until we were on the fringes of the dance floor.

I eyed him. "I don't really dance," I said, mentally murdering Georgie.

He shrugged. "Me either. I'm here with my brother, who does dance. See—he's over there." He indicated to a man who was groin grinding with some woman in a dress exactly like the first one Georgie had offered me. "Shall we be terrible together?"

I agreed, and we headed a little farther in so we couldn't be seen being awful. "Do you come here often?" he requested, flailing his arms around. He really was a terrible dancer. No question about that. I did my part by occasionally doing an awkward shimmy that might count for dancing if one was either very generous or very drunk. Best both, probably.

"I don't. I'd never heard of it before today. Mallory does though. Do you know her?" It was as suave as I knew how to be.

He frowned, his nose wrinkling like a shar-pei. "I've only just flown in today."

I shook my head. "No worries."

Another strikeout. Niall seemed like he was in a pretty good mood for a man dragged to a nightclub on the same day as a transatlantic flight. I would have been spitting nails if placed in the same situation. Clearly he was a good-natured man who did not know who Mallory was or whom she'd spent her time with. Which meant I was out here looking like an idiot for no reason.

We talked about how long I'd been in Hawaii, and I suggested he visit Aloha Lagoon before leaving the island. When the music ended, I was eagerly anticipating getting back on the fringes, but it was not to be. An arm snaked around my back, and I reacted by elbowing the person, who turned out to be Alex, in the stomach. He didn't seem irritated. He just laughed and grabbed my fist so I couldn't hit him again.

"Relax, Bruce Lee. It's just me."

I glared at him, which seemed to have little effect on his glee. "What do you want?" I realized I was being a little ungracious, considering I'd just gut-punched him. Niall was staring at me like I'd appeared in front of him out of nowhere, so maybe I'd come across as nicer before. "Sorry about that. You startled me."

Alex's grin was lethal. I hated seeing it. "All good. What I want is for you to dance with me." He turned to Niall. "That's not a problem, is it, mate?"

Niall shook his head. "Of course not, Alex. I didn't realize you knew each other."

I glared at Alex, even though he didn't really deserve it. Was there anyone he didn't know? Niall had been in town one day, and we'd been in this club for less than an hour. Alex was a social machine.

"We work together," Alex told him. "She's my *boss*." He winked as though there was some hidden dirty meaning behind what was essentially a true statement.

This time I had a good reason to glare, so I took full advantage.

He ignored me, grabbing my hand. "Let's dance."

I had a chance to tell Niall good-bye before Alex dragged me into a dark corner where the people "dancing" next to us were actually breaking some laws about public indecency. "I don't dance," I shouted, trying to be heard over the blaring of a speaker situated just to our right.

"It's a slow dance. Listen. Everyone can slow dance."

Some man was moaning along with a bluesy R&B riff, and Alex was right. The music wasn't exactly slow, but it was slower. With about as much gentleness as he'd displayed dragging me over to that spot, he slid and arm around me and spun me around so that I was the one with my back facing the wall and his back was to the crowd. His body pressed hard against mine, and I was spending every single moment trying to control my heart rate and pulse. All the individual cells in my body weren't particularly interested in the sensible opinion that having feelings, even just dirty ones, for Alex was a very bad idea.

"Can you hear me?" he asked, mouth pressed to the lobe of my ear.

I nodded, not trusting myself to speak. I was afraid what would come out would sound a lot like *I think you're scorching hot.*

"Good. I met Niall earlier. His brother Henry is a permanent resident of Kaumakani. I think he knows Mallory. He seemed hesitant to admit it, and I think he suspected I'm really Mallory's jealous boyfriend. He doesn't want to piss me off."

I nodded. That made sense and was really unfortunate. "I thought you were going to be talking to the women?"

He shrugged. "I talked to everyone who got close enough to strike up a conversation. Niall is very friendly. He brought Henry over to meet me. Henry is *not* very friendly. Unless you're a girl."

I shrugged, realizing that I was keeping the flow of the music, forgetting momentarily how awkward all of this was. "I'm a girl. Maybe he'll talk to me."

He shook his head. "Have Georgie do it."

His hands were on my hips, and I could feel the outline of every individual finger through the butter-soft leather. He was so distracting. It was awful. "I can take care of myself," I reminded him indignantly.

He grinned. "Of course you can. You can take care of yourself better than anyone I've ever met, which is part of why you are so hot. But in this case, Henry likes himself some trashy girls. Look at everyone he's dancing with. Even in that outfit, you could never pass for his kind of girl."

There were so many parts of this conversation I had no idea what to do with. I could take care of myself better than anyone Alex had ever met? I was so hot? Alex thought Georgie was trashy? Or at the very least that she pulled off trashy better than I did? It was all mystifying. And unfortunately, it was the last hint of me being able to pay attention to what I was supposed to be doing instead of the fact I was in Alex's arms.

"Now let's get out where he can see us, and convince Henry that I'm not Mallory's possessive man so that he'll be ready for Georgie when she comes."

He spun me around until we were back in the middle of the crowd, and Henry was conveniently bumping and grinding with a girl wearing a dress that looked like it was composed fifty-fifty of Lycra and duct tape. Alex pulled me in close just as the slow song came to a stop. I tried to pull away, but he didn't release me.

"I don't dance."

He shrugged. "You don't have to dance. Just act like you think I'm hot, and rub yourself up against me. If you can make it match the rhythm, so much the better."

The problem was I didn't have to act. Alex was molten hot. I spent all of my time trying not to think about it. I didn't want to embrace it now, just for the sake of proving something to Henry. I was already weaker than I should be after the stupid mistletoe kiss and the way he'd been continually making it impossible to ignore that he was capable of being as nice as he was sexy. I seriously didn't need this kind of complication in my life. Which was why I'd put such a concerted effort into disliking Alex. Now he was trying to ruin it all.

I turned off the part of myself that was eagerly reminding me over and over, *Hey, did you know you're rubbing up against that guy? You know, the one you spend all your time purposely* not *fantasizing about?* I hated that part. It needed to be put to death, just like any wayward part of me—and there were a few select ones—that were enjoying this charade.

The thumping, monotonous song didn't even have words in English. They sounded like maybe Swedish or German. It got on my nerves for its sheer repetitiveness, but even I had to admit it had a good beat. "Brace yourself," Alex said into my ear.

I had no idea what he could be talking about until I felt his hands move up my thighs, nearly cupping my butt. Like we did that sort of thing every day, he used the grip to guide me along with the music. I nearly elbowed him again. "You're too stiff, and Henry is watching."

I realized indeed he was. He was right next to us and eyeing us curiously. It was now or never, which was really just a lame justification to let Alex feel me up and rub myself against his hard body. But it was totally not justification to enjoy it. I just couldn't help that part. I was almost sorry when the song and the good excuse for touching Alex was over.

All it took to end that, though, was to remind myself that Alex and Hawaii were synonymous, and I wasn't doing either of those things.

My brain was back, but that didn't mean my body was back under my control. My heartbeat was frenetic, and my skin was brushed with a thin sheen of sweat over the goose bumps Alex's touch had left. I needed a minute to get control again.

Alex leaned over to speak with Georgie, and I headed straight for the bathrooms, probably my only option for escape for a few minutes. I hoped he was telling Georgie to move in for the Henry kill, because we were so not dancing again. No matter what we might learn at the end.

I spent a good thirty minutes hidden in a stall, breathing deep and scrambling to get back my much-loved control. When I felt like my old buttoned-up self again, I decided it was safe enough for me to return to the bar and see what was going on with the others. I emerged to an energetic techno version of "Wannabe," because what could make a club visit better than a little circa nineties Spice Girls action?

I took a deep breath and headed for Alex and Georgie, now deep in conversation. They probably thought I had issues with constipation, as long as I'd been gone. Neither one asked me anything though. When I got to their side, Alex pulled out his phone and stared at the screen. "It's really late. We better get back to the resort."

That was a remarkably adult thing to say, and I was a bit shocked that I hadn't been the one to say it, since I'd anticipated being the mean one who made everyone go home. I could tell by Georgie's face that she wanted to object, but I was her boss now, and she was probably still trying to make a marginally good impression. She needed the money to get back to Chicago.

We headed for the car, none of us speaking until we were safely inside and no one could hear us. I worked off the stupid shoes, wishing there was a way to get out of those pants before I died of suffocation.

"Hey, thanks for dancing with Niall," Georgie said, shooting me a grateful look. "The poor guy was desperate for company, and he wouldn't leave me alone. It was impossible to ask anyone anything with him right there."

That made her behavior more acceptable, but I was still slightly embarrassed about my foray onto the dance floor with Niall, who was clearly Ireland's worst dancer. I didn't need any more help looking stupid on the dance floor, thanks.

"What did you learn?" I asked, pulling back out onto the road headed for Aloha Lagoon.

"A girl told me Mallory was here sometimes with 'some dimpled super hottie' from Aloha Lagoon. She said his name is Keanu. How could I possibly forget that name? Do you know a Keanu? And the most important question is, does he look like Keanu Reeves? Because I'd be happy to question him if he does."

Alex laughed. I didn't know who Keanu was, so I couldn't say.

"No," he said. "He's a white guy. Light hair. He does have some high-powered dimples though, which give him major mileage with the ladies, for which I am dead jealous. Don't get too excited though. He's an accountant."

Georgie grinned. "You know how to ruin a good fantasy. That's it. I didn't learn anything else useful. Though I did get groped by some dude with a man bun, but he was incredibly attractive, so we'll decide later if that's a success or a failure."

Alex had Georgie pegged. For her "he's an accountant" would be like saying "he's a leper," whether he was a dimpled super hottie or not.

"What did Henry tell you?" I asked Georgie. I was dying to know if rubbing up on Alex had given us anything at all, except for me some fantasy fodder that I didn't need.

She shrugged. "He didn't say much. He did admit he knew Mallory after he saw you and Alex dancing. He just said she 'liked to have a good time' and she had 'lots of friends,' which both pretty much sounded like he was calling her a slut, if you could hear his tone of voice. I'm really not sure where he has room to talk. He's clearly a grade A manwhore."

"Did he give you any names?"

Georgie shook her head. "Nope, but he did say she had someone teaching her to surf, because she talked about it all the time. So we should probably figure out who that person is."

Alex cocked his head. "Weird that Big Steve, Mo, that one guy, and Squid didn't know." It *was* weird. Either she'd been hiding it from them too, or they were hiding it from us. I couldn't figure out a reason for either. "Then, while we were waiting on you, I think I also got felt up by the same guy as Georgie. He swore it was an accident. Charlie, what'd you learn?"

Somehow I'd gotten the most solid information. Checking out the volleyball net had been a good thing. "I talked to a girl out by the net who said Mallory came with a bunch of people from AL. Most surfers, also Poncho, which I really can't figure out yet. And she said that Mallory had an English boyfriend, but she didn't know his name, nor did she say he was there, though she was very into her game. So we should probably figure out who that guy is as soon as possible."

"Hmm. Did you know she had a boyfriend?"

I shot Georgie a look. "I didn't know anything about her at all. Oh, and I think that Niall's brother is Eurotrash."

Alex shot me a look that was half amused, half horrified. "He's a little skeezy, but that's a bit harsh."

"No, that's a name. Eurotrash. That's what the girl at the net said. That Mallory spent a lot of time with a guy, and the volleyball girl called him Eurotrash, as though that was his name. She said he was there, but she couldn't give me more information than that. Judging from the fact he looks like he stepped out of an *International Male* catalog, I'm guess she means him. So he probably knew more about Mal than he was willing to tell you."

We spent another couple minutes discussing the experience, but there really wasn't anything else to be gleaned. I drove in silence for a long time, while Georgie snored in the backseat, even though she was the one claiming it was still early. Alex was awake, but he let me drive in silence, which I appreciated. It let me think.

Mallory's boyfriend was English, not Irish, and the girl at the net had distinguished him from Eurotrash, who I was pretty sure was Henry. So he was pretty much eliminated as a potential boyfriend. Finding him might be an issue. Hawaii was a melting pot of cultures and nationalities since there were so many tourists, many of whom came from other countries. He could be almost anyone and anywhere on the island.

It was almost one when we pulled up in front of the resort, jolting Georgie from sleep with an unglamorous snort that

I had to admit I found a little amusing. She wiped her mouth and stretched. "I'm going for a walk on the beach. You in?"

I wasn't sure if the invitation was directed at Alex or me. I glanced at him.

"Not me. Five comes early," he said.

When I looked, Georgie was staring at me. I shook my head. "No thanks. I need to get some sleep. This really is a huge time of year for us. We shouldn't have even taken the time to go."

We shouldn't have, but Alex was right. I felt better now that I was doing something, getting some kind of answers that I could pass on to her parents. I couldn't bring Mallory back to her family, but I could maybe tell them why she was gone. If only it didn't make me feel so much less sick and powerless to keep trying to work and pretend it didn't matter.

Alex and I trekked across the parking lot, and I stopped to greet several people returning from some kind of Christmas party, judging from the fact they were wearing Santa hats and bathing suits and reeked of vodka. I asked if they needed anything, which was greeted with hysterical laughter, like I was the Jay Leno of Aloha Lagoon. They shook their heads no, which elicited more laughter. I stopped at the door and asked Marcus, one of the night watchmen, to follow them discreetly and make sure they got safely to their rooms.

Left with only Seth, who was writing in a log on the counter, I approached him. "Today we learned Mallory had a boyfriend. Did she tell you that?"

He glanced from me to Alex and Georgie. "She mentioned she was dating someone." He didn't offer anything else. Talking to him was excruciating.

"I guess their relationship wasn't that great, if she was into you," Alex offered.

"She had concerns about the future of their relationship." It was all he said. Then he proceeded to stare at us without blinking once. He was so creepy. Maybe that was criminal in and of itself, but we had no evidence he was up to something, and if Detective Ray had questioned him and let him go, there was probably a good reason for that.

We said good-bye to the night watchman and crossed to the desk. At that point we split up—Georgie heading for the back entrance to the sand, me heading for the elevator, and Alex heading back outside for the beach huts.

He paused at the door. "Let's go over to the Loco Moco tomorrow afternoon and see if Poncho and Keanu can tell us anything useful."

Out of routine, I wanted to say no. The closer we got to Christmas, the busier our days got, and I was exhausted and overwhelmed by everything that still needed to be done before the end of the week. However, I couldn't help but feel that I owed it to Mallory's parents, to Freemont, to the guests who called this resort a second home, to solve this mystery.

"Okay." I nodded.

He looked at the ground for a long moment, like he was debating something or his mind was far away. Then he raised his eyes and met mine. Like an idiot, my pulse immediately jumped into hyperdrive. I needed to get my shield back up, and fast. If just meeting the man's eyes kicked my libido into action, I was in trouble.

He licked his lips slowly, which really didn't help. "Good night, Charlie."

I could barely breathe. Striving with all of my might for casual, I probably failed miserably. "Good night."

For a moment, he looked like he might say something else, but then he just slid his hands into his pockets, turned around, and walked out into the night without another word. Deeply shaken by an exchange that had barely even been an exchange, I headed for my room on trembling legs. I needed to make a list of all the reasons I didn't find Alex attractive. I would do it in the morning. Then I'd read it every day until I was out of this place.

CHAPTER SEVEN

———

It took a whole lot of coffee to get my brain engaged in the morning, and I drank so much by lunch I was considering just investing in some kind of IV drip. It made me feel a bit better to see that Alex looked like crap as well, and I was pretty sure Georgie was hung over, though I'd never seen her drink anything the night before. The rooms did have minibars, after all. But to her credit, she did just as I asked her to do,

It was an insanely busy day, and I was approached to help decide which pigs we'd use for the Christmas Eve luau. I was perfectly fine eating meat. I wasn't perfectly fine picking a porker to be murdered in two days' time. I asked the committee, which consisted of several AL community members and business owners—including Gabby LeClair, who ran Gabby's Island Adventures; Rick Dawson, owner of Rick's Air Paradise helicopter touring service; and Reverend Blake and Pastor Presley—to use their discretion. I told them I trusted them to make that choice, which I hoped would gain their trust in return. The truth was, the food at the Luau was something I wanted to enjoy eating, and I would have no part of perusing it while it still had a face.

I spoke with several restaurants and locals who were providing the rest of the food for the luau, like the *poi, lomi salmon*, which was a delicious tomato and salmon salad that even I could get behind, *poke*, which was a raw fish salad that I could not, *haupia*, a traditional Hawaiian dessert made from coconut milk, and *opihi*, freshwater snails I wasn't exotic enough to remotely brave. In one more day, the committee and the cooks would begin working on the *imu*, an underground oven used to cook the Christmas pigs, *Kalua*-style.

I gritted my teeth and made smiles for all the Christmas wishes and endless holiday tunes on repeat. I took lots of pictures for ecstatic families who were living out their dream holidays.

At four, Alex and I packed it up and headed out to the beach. At some point, he must have relayed the information about today's events to Georgie, since she was already there waiting, dressed in microscopic shorts and a bohemian top with lots of fringy things. I wasn't sure when she'd become an official part of our not-official investigation, but it was clear she had. I'd been irritated at first, just because I was irritated with her in general, but she was coming in handy, and I was starting to enjoy having her there, despite circumstances when last we'd met.

Some small part of me delighted in seeing her again. I still had less than positive feelings about her actions with regard to Jared, but she was right—I hadn't loved Jared so much as I'd been content with him. My feelings were hurt that she'd betrayed me, but they weren't hurt that she'd betrayed me with Jared, which didn't make a lot of sense empirically, but it did to me.

The Loco Moco was fairly quiet, one of the reasons we'd chosen this time of day. It was too late for lunch and too early for dinner. Poncho was in the kitchen meticulously arranging all the ingredients for the dinner rush. Volleyball Girl hadn't been kidding when she'd referred to Poncho as OCD. The guy was more particular than I was, and that was saying something.

Alex leaned over the counter. "Hey, Poncho, can we talk to you for a minute?"

He shrugged, putting down his carefully folded hand towel and heading for the door to the main dining area. "What can I help you with?"

Poncho was an older man, maybe in his early sixties, and of all the places I could picture him, a nightclub was the dead last. "We're looking for friends of Mallory's. From the resort? Someone said they saw you guys hanging out at the club in Kapa'a."

He nodded. "Yeah, sure. I saw her there." He didn't follow that up with any information.

"Were you friends?" Alex asked.

He shook his head. "One night there was a salsa party up there. All salsa music and tons of my pineapple salsa. It was a pain in my butt, but I made a lot of money. I saw a couple of people from the resort up there. I heard about Mallory. That's sure too bad, and what with the holidays and all."

We nodded and agreed.

Poncho's story made a lot of sense. Unfortunately, it didn't help us much. He'd been there to work and not to hang out. It couldn't hurt to ask though. "We're really trying to find her boyfriend. Do you know who she was dating?"

He shook his head. "I barely saw her at all. She came and talked to me about my salsa. She was a big fan. She came back and talked to me about a dozen times during the night, but it was all conversation that didn't really mean anything. I saw her dancing with lots of men. I didn't notice she had one particular special friend."

I was amused by the use of the words "special friend," but it was clear he'd paid enough attention that night to have an idea of what she'd been doing anyway.

"When was that?" Alex asked.

"About two or three months ago, I guess."

We nodded and said thanks, and Poncho returned to the kitchen. Georgie hadn't spoken the entire time, and I was largely silent as well. I knew who Poncho was. Alex clearly actually knew him. It was best to let him take the wheel. I didn't know Keanu at all, even by reputation, so that was definitely going to be Alex's domain.

When we were alone again, Alex directed us toward the Loco Moco's offices upstairs. I remembered Alex saying that Keanu was an accountant, but according to the sign on his office door, he was also the assistant manager. Sitting behind the desk, Keanu was, as Georgie had heard, a super hottie. He wasn't my type, as I preferred darker men, but with his sun-streaked brown hair and intelligent blue eyes, Keanu was definitely easy to look at. He smiled when he saw Alex, and they exchanged one of those weird man handshakes that looked like some kind of secret meeting sign.

Alex was also right about the dimples. They were lethal. Probably the only thing stopping Georgie from draping herself over the desk like a mink were the piles of accounting ledgers all around his desk. It was too vivid a reminder for even her to overlook.

"Hey, we're looking for people who might have hung around with Mallory Langston over at Spikers. We heard you like it there. Did you ever see her with anyone particular?"

He frowned, taking us all in. "I heard that you guys lost an employee. It was Mallory?" We nodded. He didn't look deeply shaken, which led me to believe he didn't know her well. "That's awful. She was so young."

There was a moment of agreeing it was an awful thing, and then Keanu moved on to the question. "I go to Spikers sometimes. It's really far and kind of a pain. I actually drove up with Mallory once, and Big Steve."

Big Steve had not mentioned that tidbit when we'd spoken to him. Also, I very much doubted that Big Steve was old enough to drink, but he must have had a fake ID or something.

"We heard she had a boyfriend. Do you know him?" Alex asked. "We'd just like to have a chance to talk to him, since we were closest to Mallory."

I glanced at Alex. Maybe we were closest in proximity, but I was starting to doubt that we had known Mallory at all. However, I wasn't going to contradict him.

Keanu shrugged. "I didn't know of one. She hung out with a lot of surfers. And I saw her around with Autumn sometimes. You know, Autumn the photographer?"

I did know her. Like everyone else on the staff, I wasn't friendly with her, but she photographed a lot of weddings done at the resort. She was good too. As a person, I didn't know her very well, but I was getting so I could spot an Autumn Season photograph seconds after seeing it. I could spot her red hair in a crowd too.

"Can you tell us anyone else she hung around with? Even if they weren't really close?"

He shook his head. "A guy named Joe. Another surfer named Stan. I'd hit the beach and ask some of the surfers."

"We already did that. They didn't have much to say."

Especially, they'd failed to mention that Big Steve was hitting the town with her or that she'd been taking lessons from someone, though I had no idea who. Alex thanked Keanu, and he walked us out of the restaurant and into the sunny December afternoon. It seemed too bright, somehow, for the matter at hand. Like if a person was going to die, there should be a suitably Dickensian atmosphere even in Hawaii. We headed back to the resort, walking in a row, all of us silent.

"I'll talk to Autumn," I said at last.

Alex nodded. "You should."

The afternoon went well, and I had only a small break before dinner. I planned to take care of paperwork that was getting ignored in favor of investigating and Christmas preparations. On my way out of the office, I was stopped and serenaded by a group of slightly tipsy and very tanned guests. Alex and a couple of other employees also joined our crowd. I clapped politely for them and wished them happy holidays, while everyone else cheered and hooted like they were a Broadway show on tour, but my sincerity must have been lacking.

As I was walking away, I heard one of them say, "I don't think she's very festive."

Another said, "Well, we can't expect everyone to be Phillip."

A woman giggled. "No, some of them are Scrooge instead."

Sighing, I decided going back and apologizing for my lack of festive cheer would just make things worse. Making a mental note to amp up my fake holiday shine, I almost made it to my office before Alex stopped me with a hand on my arm.

"Hey, we need to talk. Right away."

I flinched immediately. "We need to talk" was such a heavy-sounding thing to say. Like he was planning to break up with me, which he couldn't do, as we were decidedly not together and never would be, no matter how delectable he looked today or any day. Because I wasn't doing Hawaii. Or Alex.

"Fine."

We were closest to my office, so he opened the door and gestured inside. Once both of us were on the other side of the door, Alex locked it, which seemed inappropriate, or possibly only seemed that way because it gave me an inappropriate thrill of anticipation. If only he'd kept his mouth to himself on opening night and his hands to himself at Spikers.

Now I was weak.

"Is something wrong with the resort?"

My panic was settled immediately when he shook his head. "Not as such. However, Charlie, we've got a problem."

I rolled my eyes, like the child I'd worked long and hard not to be. "As ever we do."

He glanced down at the floor and then back to me, rubbing the back of his neck. The muscles in his jaw worked, the corded strength of his neck emphasized by the casual gesture. Why did he have to be so hot? It was a special brand of hell reserved just for me.

"You need to lighten up. The guests are starting to notice your distinct hatred of Christmas. What's the sitch? We're going to have to do an intervention soon, because if you piss off the guests, you're not doing your job. And heaven knows that Charlotte Conner always does her job."

The way he said it was like an insult. So I always did my job. Was that a crime? Possibly. But my lack of Christmas cheer clearly was. I took a steadying breath.

"I heard the comments from the guests as well. I am not a fan of Christmas. I am trying very hard not to let that show. I typically work at resorts where Christmas is low-key. Hawaii is a different sort of party. I appreciate you bringing the matter to my attention." The last words were said between gritted teeth. From his expression, I could see he heard it but didn't comment, which was just as well.

He cocked his head and licked his lips. "Wear the mistletoe hat."

My mouth twisted. "I'm not wearing the mistletoe hat."

Did we have to do this again? I would die before I would wear the mistletoe hat. No sane person would ever wear the mistletoe hat. He pulled it from his back pocket, as though he'd been carrying it with him every day since our first conversation.

"Phillip always wore the mistletoe hat. Everyone is talking about the distinct lack of hat," Alex pointed out.

I glanced at the offending hat and hissed, "I'm not wearing the hat."

Alex slapped it down on my head, probably ruining my bun. "It doesn't hurt. It will make the guests happy. Happy guests are our real job, Charlotte, and I know that you know that."

Charlotte. It gave me a pause as I reached to tear off the offending headgear. It was too big, being made for Phillip, and hung down over my eyes. "Charlotte" meant that Alex was serious. The guests wanted that stupid-ass hat.

I pulled it off, praying my hair was still in place. "I can't wear the hat." I glanced at him. "Here. You wear it. You're as good as I am as the face of Aloha Lagoon. Wear it with as much pride as anyone can muster with this ridiculous thing on their head."

His mouth twisted, but he complied with my request, snatching the offending thing from my hands and slamming it down on his own head. "Christmas means a lot to this resort, Boss. Don't screw it up for these people. They're counting on you to continue the traditions that could be lost with Phillip. And traditions are what keep bringing them back year after year. Think back. You've got to have a couple of happy holiday memories. Something you can pull out and enjoy. If you can't do that, put on a happy face and fake it, because these people need that."

His voice was low and serious, and it was clear he meant it. He knew what made this resort a place that people kept returning to year after year. That people chose when they could have been home with family in some snowy wonderland like Boston. Instead, they were here with us. Because the traditions and memories they held of Aloha Lagoon were also a part of their family. A part of their history.

I nodded. "You're right. I'm sorry. I have…negative feelings about Christmas. I need to keep them in check. I would appreciate it if there were some traditions of Phillip's that you would take the mantle for, including the mistletoe hat. I'm sorry, but I can't wear it. It's too big for me anyway, and I can't be the serious face of this resort while wearing it. I appreciate your compliance on this issue."

His lips tilted, the hat hanging over his right eye, the mistletoe half cocked, leaning to the right as well. "You appreciate my compliance in the wearing of this stupid hat.

Thank you, Charlie, *I* appreciate *that*. You should have worn the hat."

I sighed. "And why is that, Alex?"

The grin kicked up a notch, sneaking into weaponized territory. My gut clenched. "Because now I'm dangerous."

He was always dangerous. Way too dangerous for my own good. I licked my lips. Did I even want to know? "We don't do dangerous at Aloha Lagoon. We do friendly, happy, and efficient."

"If I'm taking Phillip's mantle, and Phillip's ridiculous hat, I'm also taking the rules."

Why *did* it sound so dangerous when Alex said it? What could the rules possibly be? I shrugged. "You go right ahead with that. I recommend you start immediately. Somewhere other than my office."

"Oh, but I'm not done telling about the hat."

He was grating on my patience, and something about his expression told me I wasn't going to like his answer. "I'm not sure I understand what you're getting at. What are the rules exactly?"

"I get to choose the new rules."

I rubbed my eyebrow, praying to get through this conversation. "You get to choose what?"

"Phillip had only one rule. Whoever wears the hat gets to choose the rules. All the Aloha Lagoon employees are subject. For Phillip, his rule was that whoever he stood near, they get the mistletoe, because he got the hat."

The words were starting to sink in. "Are you kidding me? He made every employee subject themselves to kissing? That's sexual harassment!"

Good lord. Phillip hadn't seemed like that kind of man at all. I was sorely disappointed and a little bit sick. I would need to call every employee into my office so we could discuss their experiences and what kind of repair would need to be done.

Alex laughed. "Not if you had seen it. A peck on the cheek. That was all. But now I have the hat."

My mouth dropped. All I could picture was him tonguing every single female employee in the place. Well, I could also picture them enjoying it.

"Alexander Cho, I will not have you laying one on every employee in this place. I don't care what Phillip did. It's highly inappropriate, and the fact it was just cheeks barely makes it outside of the realm of completely unforgivable. Don't make me report you to corporate, because I don't want to."

I didn't want to. And I didn't want to address the sick feeling in the pit of my stomach that Alex was so twisted he would actually do that. Whatever I said about him, I had expected better.

His smile shifted slightly. "I would never do that, Charlie. I would hope you know me better than that."

His expression made me want to apologize. "You're the one who said it," I nearly shouted.

"I said Phillip made the rule, and it was cheeks. Phillip made the rule whoever had the hat gets to choose. I only said those weren't my rules. It's my hat now. And I make the new rules."

This was ridiculous. A confusing conversation that was starting to really upset me, though it shouldn't have been. Phillip's behavior wasn't acceptable, but it wasn't exactly completely condemnable either. No doubt the staff had been compliant because it was meant in fun, and if anyone had cared, Phillip would have stopped. At least, I hoped he would have. I had never actually met him while in life.

"Phillip shouldn't have made people kiss him, Alex. It's inappropriate. They're your employees, not your personal harem."

"I know that. I don't appreciate your suggestion that I can't tell what's completely inappropriate and what's not." The smile was completely gone now. "I only meant I'd switch it around. That anyone can kiss me if they want. I'm game. Honestly, I…I'm not sure what to do with the knowledge that you think I'd take the hat as a free ticket to feeling up our employee base."

I licked my lips again. My mouth was unbearably dry. "I didn't mean that. I was talking about Phillip."

He pinned me with a hard glare. "I would never press myself on someone who didn't want me. And I would never take advantage of an employee, even one who did want me. I had no idea you'd take my teasing seriously, but I can't help but appreciate this insight I have now into the type of person you think I am."

I shook my head. This was out of control, and I freaked when things slipped out of my control. "Stop. That isn't what I said."

Because even when I'd pictured him kissing the employees, I hadn't pictured it as harassment. Most of them had made it clear that they would be very into getting some mouth-to-mouth resuscitation from Alex Cho. He always humored them, but he never made a move. Not on any of them. Not in all the time I'd been there. The realization was a bit shocking. Girls were always hanging on him, but he was never hanging back. I'd never followed the behavior of the others through to processing the behavior of Alex, a person who always behaved as a boss among our staff, not as a man.

"Some things you don't have to say, because they're just very clear on your face and in the words you *do* say. After six months, I thought...I had hoped you at least respected me as a fellow member of your management staff. I'm troubled, and frankly I'm...I just... Excuse me. I have work to do."

He turned to leave, the disgust rolling off him in palpable waves, completely at odds with that stupid, damnable hat, still perched on his head. I blinked, my heart pounding into my throat. I'd lost control of this conversation completely. I had no idea what to do next. That was a prospect with which I had absolutely no familiarity. I always knew what to do next. Except when I accused an honorable person of planning to sexually harass our entire staff, and I did it completely by accident.

"Alex, please stop." I was afraid the words wouldn't come out of my rapidly constricting throat.

For a moment, I was sure he wouldn't listen. The voice I'd used wasn't as his boss—it was as a person, same as he was. It was begging for a brief reprieve from the censure I most certainly deserved for the message I hadn't even meant to convey.

But he did stop, his hand on the doorknob, the line of his body rigid with whatever emotion I'd invoked by accident. I swallowed hard, torn between begging him to look at me and appreciating the fact he wasn't.

"You have never been anything but completely appropriate to our employees. I'm sorry. I didn't mean you wouldn't be. Not even for a moment. I was just surprised that Phillip would have started a tradition like that. I don't...I don't believe you'd ever take advantage of someone under your command that way. It just...it was just confusion. I..."

This was hard. Probably much harder than it needed to be. Alex left me twisted in knots, no matter what the subject was. But the fact he believed I would see him like that, that he believed I would accuse him of molesting people who relied on him for his livelihood. That was hard to come back from.

He finally turned, his nostrils flaring. It was his only show of emotion, next to the rigid posture he displayed. "You..."

My breath came out in a shaky rush. "You're an excellent manager, Alex. You could have taken control of this resort six months ago without a single hitch. Corporate sending me here caused more problems than it ever could have solved. And I'm sorry. I'm sorry I'm here, and I'm sorry you believed I would accuse you of something like that. I never would. You are the perfect person to run this place. I don't know why I'm still here, but corporate made a mistake. This office should be yours."

I was trembling once the words were out, almost heady with the relief of admitting the truth of our situation. Alex was a better manager than I was. At least of Aloha Lagoon. There. I'd said it.

Alex looked at the ground for a long second, the bill of the hat completely concealing his face. When he slid it off and threw it on the chair, I could see some of the anger in his gaze had gone, replaced with some repressed emotion I couldn't identify. "I never wanted this office."

I threw up my hands. "Who cares about the office? I'm saying you deserve nothing but respect for the way you handle this resort. I respect you, Alex. You're a truly talented leader who understands how to get people do what needs done without using force or coercion. That's a gift. Not many people have it."

He blinked at me wordlessly, and I blinked back at him, deer caught in a headlight. Why wasn't he saying anything? Or at the very least doing something? The urge to force him to respond itched under my skin. I had never forced anyone to do anything. At least not physically. There was no way I was going to start now.

But didn't he understand what I was saying? He was more than my equal. He'd exceeded me at my own game. If I'd considered it ever happening, I would have expected I'd be bitter. Or grudging. Or something. All I felt was the electric power of his presence that always pressed around me when we were stuck together in a small space. I was unbearably aroused by knowing he'd spanked me at my very best skill, running resorts.

I stepped in his direction anyway, the smell of his skin teasing my nose. "I just...I...why aren't you saying anything?" I blurted the words out when I got close enough that I could have touched him. His dark eyes burned into mine, never wavering. He was so dangerous. This was why I fought with him. To avoid this very thing.

"Charlie," he didn't continue. I had no clue what he was going to say. I couldn't even think straight. The heat of him was weaving around me, stealing my ability to breathe. Why didn't he speak so we could leave this room? It was much too small. He closed his eyes. "Stop looking at me like that."

The words were hoarse. Not at all what I'd expected him to say. I had no clue what he meant by that. Words barely made sense at all. The urge to touch that Adam's apple bobbing in his throat with each hard swallow was almost unbearable. I bit my bottom lip to stop myself from leaning forward and pressing my mouth to that spot, running my tongue over the rough hairs of his afternoon shadow. What had happened to my brain? I'd had one once, and I really wanted it back. But I couldn't remember where to find it.

I managed to control myself enough to keep my mouth to myself, but my fingers had other ideas, running softly over his Adam's apple, the pads tickled by the growth on his skin. His labored breaths, short and harsh, burned my skin.

"*Charlie.*" The word was another pant, hot against my face. Was I really that close to him? Why had I disliked the name Charlie so much? There was something so sexy about that word, the way he growled it between clenched teeth, like it was torn from his body, as unwilling to say it as I'd been to hear it.

I didn't even remember moving, but I was incredibly aware of the moment when I felt his mouth brush mine. His skin was molten hot, his lips giving under mine, letting me slide an exploratory tongue against the smooth inner skin of his bottom lip. I had no idea if the raspy breathing and the trembling between us was him or me, but it was definitely me that tangled my fingers into his thick, dark hair and pulled his mouth down hard over mine.

I lost myself for a second, drowning in sensation of giving in to what I'd actually wanted from him from the second we'd been thrown together. That was the harsh truth I didn't want to face. Alex got under my skin. I wanted him. I respected him. I needed to stay away from him so very badly. But right now, I couldn't remember why. Oh, yes of course. Because I was leaving Hawaii. Because this was transitory. Because I didn't do complications, and I didn't do permanency, and Aloha Lagoon would be nothing but a memory, first chance I got. I was supposed to be a professional. That last part was the thing that finally got me.

I tore my mouth away from his and ran my hand over my heated lips. "I'm sorry, Alex. I'm sorry. I didn't…I'm in charge here."

Slowly, his eyes opened. The dark heat of his gaze burned me. For a moment, everything between us was still. Then he grabbed me by the waist, turned me around, and slammed me so hard against the door that it momentarily knocked the breath from my frame. It was his turn to do the aggressing, and he wasn't shy about it. Nothing like me.

He sipped at my lips, teased with his tongue, delved deep, aggressive and hot, before tearing his mouth away only the slightest hint of an inch. "I'm not."

I'm not. He was not in charge. He wasn't required to maintain professionalism at all times. And he was the one doing the aggressing. That. Changed. Everything.

I bit at his mouth, nipped his tongue, fought him with the same forceful press of burning flesh that he gave me. He hiked me up against the door, his hands touching every inch of exposed skin, with small teasing glances, leaving goose bumps in his wake. This was so dangerous. But I could do nothing to stop myself from tearing at his clothes, pulling his shirt until I could get my hands inside, running them over the tight muscles of his stomach.

I pushed at him, kissing deep, hot, on the verge of outright violence. He let me control him, pushing him across the small space of my office. We stopped suddenly, slamming hard into something. *My desk*, a tiny hint of sanity told me. He turned me again, pressing my butt against the hard ridge of the wooden top. We scrambled at the stuff on top, pushing away anything that prevented him from hoisting me onto the ridge, never tearing our mouths away from each other.

The clattering crash of whatever I'd been keeping there hitting the floor should have returned me to sanity, but it didn't. I didn't care about any of it. I just wanted to rip into Alex, to bite every inch of him, to scrape my nails hard against his skin until every atom was somehow marked by me. Those thoughts should have alarmed me, but I couldn't find that much sanity. All I could do was melt deeper into whatever this was.

His hands pushed at my skirt, wrapped around my legs. I had just simply not known that anyone kissed the way he did, with such intent, with the burn of promises that I didn't doubt for even a second he could keep.

"What's broken, eh?" It took a second for the words to even sink through the haze of burning red lust that had covered my brain and left me without any of the faculties I prized so much. Ikaika's voice. Through the door. He rattled the handle. "You okay in there, miss? You lose a bookcase or something?"

Alex stilled, slowly pulling his mouth from mine, a sigh moving through his entire body, the heat of his breath teasing across the bare skin of my shoulder where he'd managed to work my shirt partially open. He was a mess, mouth swollen like he'd been punched. His shirt was completely undone. I didn't even remember doing it. The sheen of sweat against his tan skin sent another burning thrill through my body, my legs almost giving out beneath me.

When he caught my gaze, his eyes fell shut. I could feel his struggle to control himself riding hard through his frame. I didn't want to control myself, for the first time in my life. I wanted to get at him. Crawl into him, touch every single inch of all that he was, inside and out.

I couldn't find my voice. Ikaika had a master key. It worked even on my office. If I didn't answer soon, he would come in. That was something I definitely didn't want. I opened my mouth, but no sound emerged.

Alex pulled in a hard, slow breath. "All good, Ikaika." His voice sounded almost normal, the trembling of his words mostly concealed. "Some stuff got knocked off the desk. Please help Silas do a sweep of the beach."

Ikaika didn't respond, and for a second I feared he would push it, but he didn't. My frame slumped against the desk when he said, "Okay, Alex."

I could hear his footsteps walking away from the door. Reason was slowly creeping back in, and with it, regret and humiliation. What the hell? What the hell, what the hell, what the hell? Was I out of my mind? I had to work with this man! He was my closest workmate. The person with whom I spent the bulk of every day.

I clutched at my rumpled shirt, gaping half open, the top button uselessly hanging on the slightest hint of a thread. Alex turned back to me, something black in his gaze. I opened my mouth, brain grasping for any words that would make all of this go away. What had I been thinking? Was I completely out of my mind?

"Don't..." Alex held up a hand and then dropped it. "Don't look at me like that." The words were low, aching with emptiness. He flinched at the same time as I realized those were the same words that had started all this. The look, however, couldn't have been the same. "Don't tell me you're sorry, Charlie."

My mouth worked silently, because the only thing that wanted to come out was that very thing. "I don't...I'm..."

I let the words trail off. I couldn't say anything else. I was the worst kind of fool. Where was the self-control on which I prided myself? Where was the order and reason? In my entire life, even during my ten-year relationship with Jared, I most certainly wouldn't have come remotely close to getting naked on company time and banging on company property. Seriously. What. The. Hell?

"I have wanted that from the moment you walked off that plane after Phillip died." Alex's voice was rough, scratchy.

The words sent another hot wash of lust ripping through my body. Alex was so dangerous. I should have listened to the warnings my brain gave me. Right from that same first moment, when my body had stood up and said hello when he showed up at the airport to greet me.

"I won't be sorry. I won't."

I spent another useless moment struggling to find words that meant anything. I *was* sorry, and I couldn't help but be. This would go nowhere. We still had to work together. I still planned to leave Hawaii the instant that my transfer came through. He would have been wise to be sorry. I was so very sorry.

He shook his head, disdain clear in every inch of his tight face. Whether it was for me, himself, or merely for the situation, I really couldn't say. I swallowed against the lump lodged hard in my throat. If only I'd controlled myself. Why did it have to be so disastrous, the one time that I couldn't?

He turned and walked away without looking back, leaving the door hanging open behind him. I pressed my hand against my useless mouth, surveying the damage that was my office. Papers were everywhere. My keyboard was on the floor. A coffee cup was spilled—thank goodness it had been mostly empty. A stapler, my phone, several ledgers, all of it spread on the carpet. I hadn't even cared. I leaned over and rescued a potted plant. Since I knew it was a mistake, and I truly believed it, why did every atom of my being long to run after him now?

CHAPTER EIGHT

———

Somehow, I made it through dinner with Alex by my side and didn't do or say anything that made it more awkward. Not that it mattered. It was insanely awkward without any additional contribution on my part.

I was beyond ashamed of myself, and looking Alex in the eye was impossible, and not just because he was wearing that stupid hat again. I should have controlled myself. I knew better. I knew. And I'd slipped anyway. In such a major way.

After dinner was over and we were taking care of details, Alex grabbed my arm to still me, sending goose bumps skittering across my skin. "We need to talk," he said, his voice low and husky.

Another shudder tore through me. "I think that's the worst possible idea," I whispered back. The last time we'd needed to talk we'd ended up making out on a desk. Talking alone to Alex was the first step to slipping up again. I knew that one now from firsthand experience. I'd wanted Alex before we'd met in my office. Now it was burning under my skin and still just as inappropriate.

He cocked his head to the side, trying to get a good look in my eyes, when I was trying very hard to not meet his. "We can't keep sidestepping this, Charlie. You and I have been ignoring this for six months."

I made the mistake of meeting his eyes, and there was no question that my inhale was a gasp and my exhale sounded very much like a moan. "Yes, we can. I'm sorry. I just…I lost it for a second. We're not *ever* talking about this."

He sighed. "You want me, Charlie, and I want you. How long can you pretend it doesn't exist?"

The words were like a shocking caress, and they tore right through me. If I had defenses at all against Alex, they sucked. I wasn't sure I had any real ones though. "Forever," I hissed. "We need to work." The only thing to do was get attention back to the right place. I needed it to be about work to keep my sanity.

"Life can't be nothing but work," he argued quietly.

"Yes," I said, much louder and firmer. "It can."

I turned and left the room and was incredibly thankful that he didn't try to follow me. I presented a strong front, but the truth was, he was right. I wanted him. The only thing keeping me in check at all was the flimsy knowledge that relationships at work were a terrible idea and that I was gone the second an opportunity came. He was an almost irresistible temptation, and I just needed to stay away from him. I had Christmas to get through and Mallory to think about. I didn't need another complication. Alex was an ocean of trouble, and if I opened up to him at all, he would flood in and drown me.

I waited until all the work was done and went looking for Autumn. During the Christmas festivities, she was here every night, taking commemorative photos for the guests to remember their holiday season. It was good money for her, and for us, because people loved memories and wanted to come back when they saw the photos again down the line. I pulled her aside.

The first thing she did was lay a hand on my arm. "I'm so sorry about Mallory. I haven't had a chance to speak with you yet, but I know you'd known her a long time."

"Thanks." I cocked my head. "How'd you know that I'd known her a long time?"

She looked surprised by the question. "Well, she told me. She said your parents are friends."

"That's true." Autumn was a better resource than I might have expected. I wasn't aware they'd known each other so well. "We're looking for other people who might have known Mallory. Especially people she might have gone surfing with. Or a man she might have dated."

Autumn unzipped a large portfolio, red hair sliding into her face as she reached down to sort through it. "I went through my pictures yesterday and found the ones that had Mallory in them. Just in case you wanted them or maybe her family, since I guess they probably came and got her body."

"Yes, my mother told me her funeral was in Chicago this morning." Under different circumstances, I would have flown there to attend, but days before Christmas, it was simply an impossibility.

She nodded, handing a pile of glossy 8-x-10 photographs my way. The pictures of Mallory left a dull ache in my chest. I pulled in a hard breath and sorted through them resolutely. Most of them were just Mallory, doing what she did best, talking, laughing, being young and alive. The unfairness of it all caught my air and trapped it for a long second until I forced it out on a shuddering sigh. Autumn flashed me a sympathetic glance, and I ignored her. I couldn't afford to be overcome by emotion. Now was not the time.

The seventh photograph was finally something I was interested in. Mallory standing on the beach, talking to two men. Both had their backs to the camera, but one was instantly recognizable as the overweight man from the beach. The one that Alex had called Mo. The other man seemed to be a stranger. He was fit though, his heavily muscled back a canvas for three largish tattoos. One was just a Celtic cross, which was easy to recognize. I couldn't make out the other two in a picture taken from such a distance. But there had to be a magnifying glass somewhere in this resort, and I was going to find it. Maybe Alex would be able to identify the man by his tattoos. Or maybe Autumn could.

"Do you know this man?" I tapped the back in question.

She shook her head. "I have three different pictures of her with him though. His back was always away from the road, but I'd stop to take coast pictures, and there she'd be with that guy every time. The other people tended to change."

So it seemed very likely to me that this was Mallory's elusive boyfriend, still very elusive. Although if I ever saw his back after this, I would know for certain it was him. She took the pile back and sorted through it, handing me the photo I'd been looking at and two others, both similar beach shots with several people caught in the lens. Each time two of those people were Mallory and her tattooed friend.

"Can I keep these?" I asked.

She nodded, handing me the whole pile, including the photos I couldn't stand to look at. I tucked them at the bottom of the pile, then thanked her and headed back to my office. It took some digging, but I found a large square magnifier buried at the bottom of one of my desk drawers and took a closer look at Mallory's friend and his back. Every picture was from a different angle, so I could take multiple looks at his tattoos.

One was the predicted Celtic cross. One was some kind of flower, which I thought was odd. It didn't look like a hibiscus, which was the state flower of Hawaii, and that would make a little sense, I supposed. This looked like something else, though I had no clue what. The last was some kind of symbol, maybe Chinese, maybe Japanese or Korean. I wasn't sure. I knew who would know, but there was no chance I was calling him into my office. I was going to do everything in my power to avoid being alone with Alex Cho ever again.

I scooped up the pictures and the magnifier and headed back to the lobby. Alex was talking to some guests, filling Phillip's massive Christmas shoes quite nicely. It really was better to just let him do the schmoozing. Especially when the matter was the holidays. Not that I would ever have another Aloha Lagoon Christmas. I waited until their conversation was finished and the family headed outside, presumably to watch the fire-eaters, before approaching.

He looked up from the papers in his hand, and his gaze burned as I crossed the room. It was almost unbearable just having him watch me walk. Cocking one eyebrow, he waited for me to speak. "I got these photos from Autumn. These were taken of Mallory in the last few weeks. Three of the photos have this man in them. I don't suppose you'd recognize another man's back?"

He glanced at the pictures, brow pulling together. "No, but those tattoos are interesting. Do you have a bigger picture?"

I handed him the magnifier, cautious to make sure we didn't accidentally touch each other in any way. I knew my strengths, no question. I knew what I was good at. But I also knew where I was weak, where I would cave if given the slightest chance. And Alex was weakness number one in my book. I'd done fine resisting my feelings when we were adversaries. Now…now I wasn't doing fine.

He cocked his head and studied the photos for a long time, while the staff cleaned up around us. "Well, the cross is easy to recognize. One in every five guys in college had one like it or similar. The rest…I'm not sure."

"Do you recognize the character?" I pointed to the Asian tattoo.

"Well, it's not Korean."

"Do you read Korean?" I was insatiably curious, now that I'd let him in a little. Everything about him would be catnip to me if I wasn't very, very careful.

He shrugged. "Some. But I just know it isn't because of the way it looks. Here." He moved a foot or so to the bar and flipped over a napkin, pulling a pen from his pocket. "If we take symbols everyone wants on their wall or whatever, like peace or love, you'll see what I mean."

He drew something quickly, in small, careful strokes, then pushed the napkin across the counter in my direction. "Here are the Korean symbols for love and happiness. Do you see the circles at the bottom of each?"

I nodded. Both characters were resting on a circle shape, and happiness had two circles. He grabbed the napkin back and sketched again. "I just know these from Asian class. My parents made me take it every year. There were a ton of Chinese and Japanese kids in there, because there's a lot in Hawaii, so we all got to learn a bit of each language. Here's love in Chinese and Japanese. They're practically identical."

I noticed he was right. The only difference between them was a few small marks in the middle of the character. "They do look different from Korean. You're right."

He nodded. "Whenever you see circles or ovals, you are looking at some other language than Chinese, for sure. I'm thinking this character is in traditional Chinese, though I'm not sure what it says. Give me a minute to try to figure it out."

He spent long, silent minutes flipping through an app on his phone. My phone rang, and I saw it was my mother on the other end. Now that my parents were back together again after their last divorce two weeks after my would-be wedding, Mom was always happy and usually a delight to talk to, but now wasn't a good time. It was possible it was about Mallory's funeral or something though, so I answered.

"Why didn't you tell me you have a boyfriend?"

She didn't even say hello. Who led with an introduction like that?

"I don't."

Alex glanced up at me, looking mildly curious. There was no way I was letting him be privy to this conversation. Because I knew exactly who my mom was talking about and exactly who had delivered this information her way. I covered the mouthpiece. "Will you excuse me?"

He nodded slightly, watching me as I ducked into the nearest available empty room, a filing room behind the concierge desk. "Mom, I don't know what Georgie told you in your nightly call, but I definitely do not have a boyfriend."

She sounded skeptical. "What about this Alex man Georgie told me about?"

Restraining a sigh, I propped the phone between my ear and shoulder, peeping out of the room to make sure no one was getting close. "Alex is my coworker. That's all. Regardless of what Georgie says."

She was silent for a long, disapproving, second. "Georgie says he's very handsome."

I shut my eyes, praying for patience. "He is. But that doesn't change the fact he's my coworker, making it highly inappropriate to even consider a relationship. He's not my boyfriend."

She sighed, finally electing, thank all of heaven above, to abandon questions about Alex. "Georgie says you gave her a job."

She sounded almost critical, which I certainly wouldn't have expected. If I'd given it thought, I would have anticipated that she would be unhappy if I *didn't* give Georgie a job.

"Yes, I did. Is that wrong?" I wanted to cut to the chase and get back to the pictures and any clues they might provide.

"No, I suppose not. Why isn't she working for the cruise lines anymore?"

I paused. "She didn't tell you?" I'd assumed that whatever her problem with Marty was, she'd shared it with our mother, the person she dumped all her personal information on.

"No. I just don't understand it. She's been working there for years."

I didn't understand it either, and I was mildly curious, which was another sign that I was starting to forgive Georgie, despite myself. "All she told me is that she was having problems with some guy named Marty."

"Marty?" she repeated incredulously. "Martin Gentry Marty? That Marty?"

"I have no idea."

My brain worked. *Martin Gentry.* I kept abreast of everything that happened in the hospitality industry. I knew about the Gentrys. Gentry Cruise and Leisure was merely one branch of the massive Gentry hospitality empire. The Gentrys: older parents, Martin and Cecelia; a single living matriarch, Martin's mother, Felicia; two sons, Martin and Davis; and a daughter, Eugenia. All were part of that small contingency of America's ultra elite. Their worth was something akin to the people they'd built their empire with, the Rothschilds, the Carnegies, the Hearsts, and the Rockefellers. If someone broke their worth down into the amount each of their small family was worth, I guessed it was somewhere around tens of millions a person.

Whether the Martin Gentry that Georgie worked for was the senior or junior, there was little doubt that they would have ruled over the ship Georgie had worked on. That probably meant he got away with some pretty questionable stuff if he wanted, and there was no one to call him on it. No wonder she'd felt like she had no choice but to run.

"All she said was that she was having issues with Marty and she had to leave her job."

"Now, I just don't get that at all." Mom sounded truly distraught, and I was confused about her allegiance to a job that Georgie had probably left for a very good reason.

"Maybe he was sexually harassing her, Mom. Or trying to make her do something illegal or morally reprehensible."

"No way," Mom immediately shot back, like I was talking about her favorite person in the world. "Marty would never do something like that. And what's more, I suspect you don't know this, because you've been ignoring Georgie for years, but Martin Gentry and Georgie are best friends. And I mean true best friends. Thick as thieves."

Thick as thieves? Who said that outside of a regency-period drama? "Mom, have you been into the *Pride and Prejudice* stash again?"

"I'm serious," she huffed. "They are very close. Like 'spend every waking moment together for years' close. They must have fought about something, but he definitely didn't do anything to hurt her. I would stake my life on it."

"Do you know this man?" If I sounded skeptical, I couldn't help it. Mom always sided with the man in a relationship, as though the possession of testosterone and testicles automatically made him right.

"Actually, yes, I do. I've met him several times."

Okay, that was a surprise. If Georgie had been bringing him around for years, that meant two things: they weren't having raunchy sex or she wouldn't have brought him home, and they probably really were best friends. Georgie wouldn't travel with someone she didn't like. She was perfectly content hopping on a plane by herself and seeking out the wilds of the world without anyone to keep her company. If she elected to invite company, it was because she enjoyed being with Marty Gentry. So if that was true, what had happened to drive her away?

It didn't matter. I didn't have time for one more mystery. I had enough on my plate already. Georgie and her BFF would just have to sort out their own problems. "Ask her, Mom. She hasn't told me anything."

"Well, it's no wonder. You've made no attempt to keep up with her life."

I took a deep calming breath and reminded myself that my mother didn't know what Georgie had done or why Jared and I had broken off our engagement the day before the wedding. She knew the reason was good, because I never did anything without a good, solid, practical reason, but she didn't know anything beyond that.

"I have to go. We're really busy around here. Talk to you soon."

There wasn't much she could say to that. She said good-bye. We made mutual kissing noises, as was our habit, and I hung up, desperately glad to be done getting grilled. Taking a deep breath to fortify myself, I rejoined Alex in the lobby.

"Discover anything?"

He glanced up from his phone. "I'm still trying to find the character. I'm installing an app that will let me take a picture of the character, and it should let me know." He held up his phone triumphantly. "There it is. Okay, let's do this thing."

He took a photograph of the photograph, while I held the magnifier over the tattoo. The program worked, and I didn't want to get close enough to him to be able to watch the process with him. I could tell when it finished though, because he seemed confused by the results.

"What is it?"

He shook his head and then held the phone out to me. There on the screen was an identical black inked symbol, and the translation underneath read *opium*.

While I digested what that might mean, Alex's eyes moved to the flower, and he stared at it for a long time, angling the photograph in several directions. "Do you know what this is? I can't even see it as a super-stylized hibiscus."

I shook my head. "It does seem a little familiar."

"To me too. I've seen it somewhere lately. Somewhere I was." He was silent for a long second, staring intently at the photograph. Finally, he dropped it triumphantly. "I know where I've seen it. It was growing all over the place after I dragged myself out of the whirlpool in Strangler's Cove."

I took in the pale purplish, loose-looking petals. The middle was also carefully inked in, a weird pod-ish sort of thing, pale green and protruding from the petals, which looked like it was wearing a hat made of microscopic green bananas. Around the middle pod, dozens of smaller little pod-ish things jetted out.

"That is a really weird flower. Are you sure you saw it here on the island? I don't think I've ever seen anything like that. Although my mother had poppies that looked a bit like that growing in her garden."

Alex stilled. "Poppies? A man who has the word *opium* tattooed on his back also has a flower tattooed on his back, and it didn't immediately occur to us that it might be an opium poppy? If we ever had an edge, we're losing it."

He picked up his phone, typed in *opium poppy*, and we watched together as pictures of endless poppy fields generated on his screen. Grim faced, he turned my way. "That's definitely the same flower I saw. Whoever Mallory was dating, it's possible he knows something about opium growing right outside of Aloha Lagoon."

CHAPTER NINE

It was a long day trying to get to the afternoon so we could go check out Strangler's Cove. We agreed that this was no place to make assumptions. If we were going to take this information to Detective Ray, we needed to be very sure. Alex was open about the fact the waters had been rough, and he'd been a little disoriented and panicked after being caught in a whirlpool. Maybe the flowers he'd seen were not the same as the tattoo after all. There was a very marked difference between garden-variety poppies and opium poppies. If they were the same, we'd know.

Getting to Strangler's Cove was not something that Alex knew exactly how to do. He'd gotten there accidentally, by literally having one. The only thing he really knew was what he'd already told me. That it was near to the beach where we'd met Mo, the man whose name no one really seemed to know, and Big Steve, and that there was a massive whirlpool nearby. Approaching it by boat wouldn't be possible for that reason. If we tried it, we'd be down before we even got close enough to see the shore.

After the daily rush and plans for Christmas Eve were over, we grabbed up Georgie, who was working in the lobby bar for the day, and headed out to the beach Alex did know, in Alex's car. We parked on the road and didn't go toward the beach, instead following a path into the mountainous terrain near the beach. The theory was that maybe we could climb to the place Alex had landed by crossing over the terrain, rather than approaching by water.

It was an insanely unpleasant hike even though I'd made a nod to the exercise by wearing suit pants instead of a skirt, and flats instead of heels. Though the view was extraordinary, this wasn't really the kind of place that someone would go for a leisure hike. The path was slight, the terrain rocky, and the vegetation thick and unforgiving. I could see prints in the soil, so there were people making this trek, but it had to be very purposeful. No tourists were wondering up a trail to take some pictures.

When we reached the top, we could see the barren beach where we'd met Mo and Big Steve. There was only a single man standing in the sand, and it was clear he was on his way out. There was no apparent reason the beach was empty, except it was a small beach with hard waves nearby, and it wasn't the kind of place surfers preferred. Directly in front of the peak, I could see only the edges of the cove and the brutality of the whirlpool that Alex had talked about. My stomach twisted, envisioning Alex trapped in that maelstrom. As we watched, the water suddenly relaxed, the massive whirlpool becoming a relaxed circle of softly rotating water, instead of the violent churning of moments before.

"What happened?" Georgie voiced my very question.

Alex shook his head. "I'm not sure. It seems to be on some kind of nature-driven schedule. I caught the end of it that day, which is why I'm standing here right now. I promise you that much. That's some powerful water. I was still trying to get out of the cove when it started again. It's a pretty short break. Maybe ten minutes tops. I clung to the side of the mountain down there and tiptoed around to the beach. It took me like an hour to get on solid ground again. Obviously, we need to find a better way to get in and out, which is why I brought these."

He held up his backpack, then set to unpacking climbing ropes, carabineers, and a number of other items whose use was a mystery to me. Climbing was not something I did. Nor was it something I wanted to start doing now. But this could be the difference between understanding what had happened to Mallory and leaving the solving of her murder to fickle chance. It was worth the climb. Plus, Alex clearly knew what he was about.

He set to drilling the climbing anchor into the rocks. "We can climb down. It isn't completely impossible. This isn't really a dangerous mountain on the way down. I might even free climb it. But I don't want you guys to take any chances. The way up is a little bit tougher. But there are still ledges. I couldn't do it when I was here because I had an injury from the whirlpool. That obviously won't be the case here."

He took one look at my face and flashed me a reassuring smile. "It isn't bad, Charlie. I just want to make sure you guys are safe since you don't do a lot of climbing, so I brought everyone a harness and ropes. We'll be top roping with a belayer. It's usually safer to rappel alone, but since we aren't actually rappelling, just hiking down while playing it safe, I think top roping will be fine."

He might as well have been speaking another language, for all it meant to me. I nodded stupidly, and he flashed me another smile. He was trying really hard to be comforting, anyway. He was right. I could see a very thin path winding down the not-quite-entirely-sheer rock face. There was technically a way to hike down this cliff. But I wasn't going to be sad to have a safety system set up. I was surprised that he hadn't tried to talk us into having him go alone. Then I remembered his comments about how capable I was. Maybe he really did believe I could do hard things, even with little practice.

He helped us both into harnesses, and I ignored that the process basically involved him feeling me up. I just concentrated on the shoreline below and the whirlpool that was picking up speed, starting on its violent cycle again. It still wasn't distracting enough, but he made no commentary on my erratic breathing before moving on to Georgie. Once we were all prepped, suited up, and roped together and connected to the climbing anchor, we climbed over the side and started down the mountain.

The path existed for sure, but it was so thin someone's foot seemed to slip off every minute or two. Rarely was it Georgie, who clearly knew more about climbing than I would have assumed. Mostly it was me. Alex might as well have been born a mountain goat. I made myself feel better by remembering that he did this kind of crap for fun. He had an advantage. And some really weird ideas of what was fun.

It took probably nearly forty-five minutes to reach the bottom, even with the aid of the ropes to keep us from plummeting to our deaths. Alex immediately stripped out of the harness as soon as we hit dirt, and we followed more slowly, mostly because I couldn't figure out how to free myself, and Georgie ended up having to help me.

The cove was gorgeous, overgrown with greenery, embraced by walls of volcanic rock. It was big, much larger than I'd pictured in my head. Maybe half the size of a football field. Some of the plants looked local, and I'd seen them before on the island. However, Alex was right. The entire cove was covered in opium poppies, cheerfully skipping in the light breeze coming off the ocean. They looked a lot like their more innocuous sister plants, save for the weird pod inside. I knew from last-night's research that the pod was where the opium came from, and also an instantly recognizable way to identify these plants.

It was so bizarre to know this was here, and had been here for some indeterminable amount of time, and no one knew. Except for the people who had planted and were cultivating it, of course. What a lucky day they must have thought it was when they'd discovered the makeup of Stranger's Cove. It was the perfect place for an operation like this because no one could get to it by accident, unless it was truly one heck of a crazy accident like the one Alex had suffered.

Alex moved through the crop, taking dozens of pictures with his cell phone. Opium poppies became heroine, and heroine hit the street. I had no idea how many poppies it took to make a dose of heroine, but there was a good chance the street value of this field was no joke. I took several minutes to make a long scan of the entire cove from my space just under the cliff side. I was interrupted suddenly when my heart jumped to my throat after the ropes behind me slammed to the ground at my heels. I stared up but could see nothing. What I could see, without any trouble at all, were all three of the harnesses crumpling to the soft dirt beneath my feet. Either Alex hadn't done that great a job of connecting our rope, which I did not believe since I'd seen him screwing those anchors into the hard rock, or someone had purposely found a way to disconnect our rope.

Considering we were standing here in the middle of someone's illegal gold mine, my money was on the latter. And we were sitting ducks. From their vantage point above us, whoever was there would have no trouble picking us off one by one, as long as he had a long-range rifle or something else that could make the distance. I searched the cove for Alex and my sister, but visibility wasn't great through the lush jungle-like growth. I could make out a bit of Alex's head but little else. They needed a warning, and we needed to get out of here with whatever evidence we already had. It would have to be enough.

I picked my way through the loam that sunk under my feet, desperately trying to get to the others. The urgency was burning under my skin, and no matter how fast I moved, it didn't feel like it would be fast enough. I didn't want to yell too loud and get anyone else's attention. By the time I could see them both, I could see the shore too. It was only a few feet in front of me. They were having some in-depth conversation, staring at Alex's phone. I opened my mouth to call out a warning, but all it turned out to be was a scream as brutal hands pushed me hard from behind.

The force was enough that I bypassed them both and ended up face first in the ocean. In theory, this wouldn't have been a problem. I wasn't Olympic material, but I was a passable swimmer. What I was not, however, was a person capable of extricating myself from a violent circle of churning water. I barely touched the surface before the tide grabbed me and yanked me hard into the maelstrom. I tried not to panic. With everything that was in me. Calm and rational was the very air I breathed, but without air to breath, that was hard to hold on to.

I didn't want to fight, because I wasn't sure what would make it worse and what wouldn't. If only my would-be killer had pushed a few minutes earlier. The water would have been calm. Of course, that was intentional. It was clear the people above us, and with us, had been here all along, waiting to make a move on us. Calm waters wouldn't kill us. So they'd merely waited until a better option that *would* came along.

I couldn't hold my breath anymore, and not fighting wasn't helping. I was still getting tossed like a ragdoll, my lungs screaming for the release of fresh, sweet, air. Of course, it was an illusion. If I took the breath I desperately wanted, I'd just end up at the bottom of the Pacific, never to be seen again. I pushed against the swirl, but it was impossible. I simply wasn't strong enough. Especially since I'd let it go so long trying to figure out how to best extricate myself. Maybe it would have been better to just react instead of thinking in a situation like this one.

Abruptly, I realized that the dark forms in the churning water beside me weren't wood pieces or even fish. They were other people. I knew that no person, no matter how villainous, or even likely how stupid, was going to chase me into a situation like this to try to make sure I was finished. It was probably Alex and Georgie, because whoever was running this operation needed to get rid of us before we could give away their position or offer any evidence to back it up. What better way than the killing field that nature had conveniently offered up?

They disappeared. I didn't know where to. Maybe down. This wasn't the way I wanted to die. This wasn't the way I wanted to lose the people I loved. I clawed for calm, desperate not to use up my dwindling air on panic. I had to spend it swimming, even if it was against an endless tide. Suddenly, I was jerked in the opposite direction, against the rotation, my limbs screaming out in pain, my lungs just screaming. The sudden movement was so violent and unexpected that I couldn't control my response. I gasped, pulling in a hard mouthful of salty water, leaving the door open for the entire ocean to take me.

Belatedly, I realized the counterforce was another person, likely Alex, judging how much bigger he was than me. Unless the person who'd tried to kill me was now oddly trying to save me. Unfortunately, I'd already inhaled water, and now I was choking, unable to hold my breath, and I was seconds from losing consciousness. Unfortunately, there wasn't a lot I could do about that.

It was over for me, and I knew nothing else.

When I finally regained any semblance of awareness, I was lying between poppies and volcanic rocks, spewing water from my lungs into the lap of unsuspecting Alex—and a bit on Georgie. While I was still choking and Alex was pushing my stomach, brutally forcing water from my furious lungs, Georgie held my limp hand, her eyes darting all over the cove. I blinked away tears, a combination of belated terror, exhaustion, and physical abuse. My sister was here. I squeezed her hand as well as I could manage, laying limply in front of Alex, violent coughs wracking my frame every few seconds.

I blinked at Alex, trying to find the words to thank him. I didn't know if he'd been pushed too, or if he'd simply come in after me, but I was very aware that without him I would be dead. There was no question at all. I was nearly dead, even with him. When I tried to speak, my throat was ravaged, irritated beyond where I could make sound come out. Maybe he understood the emotion in my eyes. Maybe he was simply touched by the process of saving the life of another human. Whatever it was, he pulled me into his arms and held me tight, his face buried in my neck. All three of us were wet, wrung out, exhausted, and possibly we were still in very real danger. For now all I could do was cling to Alex, hold my sister's hand, and struggle hard to regain the breath I'd nearly lost forever.

There wasn't enough time for me to recover the way I needed to. Georgie was the first to speak. "We have to get out of here. We don't know if they're still around. I wish we could have seen them well."

Them. That meant there were more than two, because the one above us couldn't have gotten down so quickly, and if Georgie had seen two, there were at least three. We were still in danger. I tried hard to sit up, but I couldn't. I had to rely on Alex to even get into an upright position. All of us were much worse for the wear, hair in faces, clothes ripped or simply missing, like the jacket I'd been wearing. We were a hot mess, and I wasn't sure I was strong enough for either of the two ways out of this cove—up or around.

I waved them away. "Go. I'll stay here. Just bring the cops back. I'll be fine."

"No."

There was no room for argument in Alex's single-word response. I wanted to argue, but I couldn't find the energy or the words. I didn't want to be left here. I also didn't think I could make it out. It took a long moment of just breathing to find the power to speak. "I can't do it. I'm sorry. It will be fine. I'll be here. They must have left by now."

Alex glanced hurriedly around the cove. "I'm sorry, but I don't believe that. I bet the only reason they didn't outright shoot us is because we surprised them unarmed. There's no way they're going to leave us here to spread the word of what we found. I won't leave you here, especially when it'll be dark any minute."

I shook my head. What could I say? Was there any chance at all I could change their minds? "We can't all stay here. They're going to come back eventually."

"No, you're right. We can't stay here. We're going to leave the way I left last time. Around the side of the cliff, over there." He pointed right, where water was slapping hard against the rocky outcropping that he apparently expected me to climb when I was still having trouble controlling my limbs.

I shook my head. "I can't."

He grabbed my face in both hands, cradling my cheeks like I was fragile, and maybe I was. I felt fragile right now. But his words didn't reflect that. He spoke very clearly, eyes pinned to mine. "You can, and you will. I will help you."

He had to be tired. He'd not only pulled himself out of water stronger than I could ever hope to be, but he'd also pulled another limp, unconscious human being to safety. Maybe Georgie too. He had to be exhausted, but he was 100 percent focused. I could see it in his eyes. Thank goodness he enjoyed pushing his body to the limits as a hobby, or all of us would be so screwed right now. If he could do this, I could do this. I nodded, letting him and Georgie help me to my feet.

On wildly shaking limbs, I struggled to walk across the cove. I no longer had shoes. Neither did Alex. In fact, he was mostly naked, wearing only torn shorts. That was the risk he ran when he didn't button his ever-loving shirt. Georgie had one shoe, a white racing tank she'd been wearing under her Aloha Lagoon uniform, and part of her shorts. I was blessed to still be wearing suit pants and a pale pink shell that had once been covered with a white suit jacket. I'd had no idea water could be enough to simply tear clothes from a body.

The safety of the beach might as well have been a million miles away with the combination of injuries, bare feet, and jagged volcanic rocks. Alex knelt, grabbed a sharp rock, my pants leg, and a couple of leaves wrapped around the rock. I stood still while he cut strips from my pant legs, Georgie keeping watch.

When he was finished, he fashioned makeshift feet coverings for all of us, tossing Georgie's one shoe aside. We walked to the corner of the cove, none of us speaking. I could feel every stab of the rocks under the light linen of my pants material, not intended as footwear. I was certain the others were no more comfortable. Alex was trying hard to conceal a limp. He was hurt and didn't want us to know it, but when I caught a glimpse of his ankle, I saw a deep gash in the skin, probably from rocks under the water. I bit my tongue and looked at the expanse we would be expected to cross. There was a ledge, as thin as the path above us, leading around the cliff. It was maybe two hundred feet from the cove to a place where we could safely enter the water and not be sucked down. It might as well have been miles.

I drew a deep breath and focused on those feet. I could do this. *We* could do this. There was a new symbiosis between the three of us. We were a unit we hadn't been on the way down. I no longer cared what Georgie had done. It was ancient history. She was my sister before she was anything else. Together, we'd do this thing. And Alex. I couldn't think about how bonded I felt to Alex at the moment. It was dangerous. He pulled a length of thin rope from the pocket of his cargo shorts, hardly more than a shoelace in width, tying all three of us together.

He grabbed my arms again, focusing our gazes, not allowing me to look away. "We are going to do this. You *can* do this. One step at a time. I know that you're hurt, and you're exhausted, and you're weak. But if we can get to the place where the water is calmer, we can get to the shore on the other side. Just keep looking forward."

I nodded, drawing power from his intensity when I didn't have my own to spare at the moment. He took the front, I was hanging in the middle, and Georgie pulled up the rear, all of us tied at the waist. It was painfully slow going, both literally and figuratively. My twisted ankle screamed in frustration. By the time we were halfway across, my feet were mangled beyond being able to feel them. It was a blessing. I could see how much pain Alex was in. The cut had to be deep, and with the salt water and sand that had to be inside of it right now, I had no doubt the agony was acute. Georgie was breathing hard, her struggle silent behind me.

I slipped. The rope slowed my fall, and Alex and Georgie pulled me back to the ledge.

Alex slipped. He caught himself, using his bare hands to grip the volcanic rocks. He left bloody handprints behind us as we went. I didn't know how long it took to get to the place where we could safely enter the water. Two hours? Six years? I had no clue. It was long past dark when Alex finally stopped, slipping slowly into the water and helping us each enter behind him. The ocean was blessedly calm. We couldn't reach the bottom, and we were in no condition to swim.

We clung to the cliff, working our way along until we crawled onto the beach. For several minutes, we lay there in the dark. It was true that the people who had pushed us could be around, but I assumed they were gone by now. And frankly, I just couldn't move. If we couldn't see them, hopefully they couldn't see us either.

Eventually, we got to our feet and trudged the remaining feet to the car, crawling in and sitting there for another few minutes, headlights off, trying to pull ourselves together. Then Alex started the car, and we drove to the Aloha Lagoon Police Station, a single-story stucco structure in the middle of town. It was wonderfully brightly lit, and just looking at it made me feel safer.

The officer who met us inside the door took one look at us and said he had to call Detective Ray. We probably looked almost as torn up as we felt. We sat, bleeding feet stretched out in front of us. Alex's leg was no longer seeping blood but was now swollen beyond recognition. Mine was merely slightly swollen. Bedraggled hair, dirty faces, and pale skin. The officer asked Alex if he'd like to clean and treat his bleeding hands, but he merely stared at them for a moment and then shook his head. None of us had spoken since we'd left the cove.

Finally Detective Ray showed up wearing sweatpants and a T-shirt, clearly having just come from home and not expecting us or any other matter of grave importance. He looked us over silently for a long minute. Then he shook his head and asked, "What happened to you three?"

* * *

The story took a long time to tell, though not nearly as long as it had taken to play out. I couldn't tell from his expression if he believed us or not. He was as unreadable as his office was messy. I couldn't make heads or tails of anything on his face or on his desk. He didn't speak much. Merely asked us questions, if he had them, and let us carry on with the narrative. His only real tell was when his eyebrows pulled together suspiciously when we talked about the poppies.

Alex patted down his pockets and sighed. "I lost my phone."

Georgie shrugged. "I lost my pockets, let alone what was in them."

I still had both legs of my pants, and I could still feel the phone in my pocket. Of course, I wasn't surprised to discover I couldn't get it to turn on. It lay unresponsive on Detective Ray's desk until I just gave up. It was dead for now. Maybe forever.

Detective Ray pinned us all with hard glances. "You shouldn't go into dangerous situations investigating things. These matters are best left to the professionals."

I was aghast. It was only his attitude that had driven us to that cove in the first place. I couldn't help but wonder if these opium poppies, and whatever force was behind them, were the things that led to Mallory's murder. Had someone done to her what they'd tried to do to us? Had she discovered too much? Or maybe she'd been involved with the process of growing them? How would we even know?

Alex held up a hand. "We had no idea it would be dangerous. It was completely abandoned last time I was there. All we wanted to do was take a few pictures."

Detective Ray glanced down at his disgusting desk. "We'll call Rick and take a copter down tomorrow to take a look. Don't go near the cove again."

He was safe with that one. I never planned to go to the beach again, if I had my way. Let alone Strangler's Cove. We drove back to the resort, barely awake, all of us struggling to keep our eyes open even though it wasn't too late. We'd missed dinner. I wasn't sure I'd ever eat again anyway. When we hobbled into the hotel through the service door, as to avoid scaring the guests, Darcy, the night clerk, came out of the break room, gasping in horror.

"What happened?" She dug those hideous nails into her palms.

"We had an accident at the beach," I explained, without any elaboration. I didn't really want this getting around. At least not until Detective Ray had time to get the proof.

She fussed over us for a few minutes until we were able to shake her. We walked Georgie to her room, and I stopped Alex before he tried to walk the half mile to his cabin on the beach. "This is stupid. Get a room in the resort for the night. You don't even have shoes!"

He flashed me a small smile. "I won't have shoes tomorrow either."

"But at least you'll be better healed. Come on. Don't do this."

Shaking his head, he slid his fingers between mine. "Charlie, you did really well out there. Thanks for not drowning." His lopsided smile punched me straight in the heart.

"Thanks for not letting me drown," I whispered.

He shook his head. "I would never let you be hurt, if I could stop it. *Never.* I'm going home to get some sleep. I'll talk to you tomorrow."

"Let me help you," I said, reaching out my hand to take his again but then dropping it. "At least let me clean and bandage your feet and find you a pair of shoes."

He shook his head one more time. "It's okay." He nodded one time. "Tomorrow, Charlie."

It was just a form of good-bye. Telling me he'd see me tomorrow. But there seemed to be some kind of promise in it. Something that sent chills skittering across my skin. I nodded, not able to find my voice, and watched him hobble away. Then I went to my hotel phone and called Georgie, telling her to come upstairs and use my much-nicer suite to address her cuts and bruises.

She sounded a bit uncertain, which she probably couldn't be blamed for, considering the context. It was just that I'd merely realized that Jared's loss hadn't been nearly as traumatic as the thought of the real loss of my sister. I'd somehow reasoned I had time to be angry, but it was clear that might not always be true. I'd learned my lesson the hard way today.

When Georgie showed up, I ushered her into the shower first, taking some time to lay out on my luxurious bed and enjoy not being dead. My feet were no longer numb, and they were seriously pissed. I couldn't imagine how Alex's must be feeling, with the additional injury he'd gotten. My ankle was twinging, but in retrospect, without weight on it, I could tell the sprain wasn't bad. I'd recover. When Georgie came out, I directed her to my first-aid kit to address her feet, since I was positive her bag she'd come with contained nothing but spandex and maybe condoms. Then it was my turn in the bathroom.

Once I was finished and my feet were sufficiently cleaned and bandaged, I sat on the bed and regarded Georgie, sitting in a chair near the door, as though she was waiting for the first opportunity to leave. Maybe she just thought I'd take the first opportunity to kick her out.

I sighed. We would have to address this, though I wasn't particularly keen on it. "What you did to me was wrong." I decided not to bother sugarcoating it. Georgie wouldn't.

She sighed too. "I know. But marrying Jared would have been wrong too. You realize that, don't you?"

"Yes. But it was still wrong. I'm not mad anymore. Truly. But you could have at least said you were sorry."

Her second sigh was long and slow. "I am sorry. I'm still sorry. But I felt like if I told you that, you might decide Mom has the right of it, always believing or accepting any excuses a man might give. I was afraid once you started forgiving people, you might start forgiving Jared as well as me. And that wouldn't have been okay. I figured I'd just take one for the team."

"You're nuts," I said. "But I recognize you were trying to help in a very odd kind of way."

I also recognized that she was right to fear something like that when we'd been trained about love at the feet of our parents. Love meant forgiving people for anything, no matter how horrible it was. I lived in terror of becoming that person—

the one who gave up everything because I couldn't bear to be alone.

She shrugged. "Hey, it worked, didn't it?"

Her logic was so mystifying, but I loved her anyway. "Yeah, it worked."

"Listen, Charlotte. I know your relationships aren't my business, even less now than they ever were before, but I hope you understand that he really cares about you."

I stared at her. "Jared?" It was such an absurd thing to say that I had no idea what to make of it.

Her upper lip curled. "No, not Jared. *Lord, no*. Alex. He really cares about you. I mean sincerely as a human being cares about you." The words caught me off guard and sent my stomach into a tailspin. "We saw you fly past us, and the backpack was off and he dived in after you, without a second of hesitation. Then some douche pushed me in too, and Alex pushed me out onto the shore and dived back down. Honestly, I'm not sure he would have helped me at all if he could have found you first. And if you had seen his face when we realized you weren't breathing. It was agony and terror. Pure and unadulterated." She shivered. "I've never seen anyone look like that before. If you really haven't considered it before, I think you should now."

It? I could barely wrap my mind around her words. I had no idea what "it" was. The thought of Alex's overwrought emotions crippled me. It was beyond painful to imagine him hurting over anything, let alone me. That told me above anything that I had some runaway emotions to get back under control.

"Considered what?"

"Just exactly what your relationship with Alex is."

I took a deep, shuddering breath. "Strictly business." The words came out much more calm and sure than I'd expected, much to my appreciation.

She eyed me suspiciously. "Really?" Her disbelief was tinted with outright disgust. "If there's one thing I know, it's men and the signs they give when they want a relationship with someone. Alex is giving every one of them. Are you sure, really sure, you're not into it?"

"Really." It was so easy to say. Maybe not as easy to believe in my head. Or even in Georgie's, judging from her skepticism. I needed to change the subject immediately. "Mom asked me why you quit your job."

Georgie's face shuttered immediately. "What did you tell her?"

"What you told me. That you were having some trouble with some guy named Marty."

She flinched, maybe because I'd told Mom. Maybe it was just the mention of the name. She took a shaky breath and stared at some point to my left, gaze unfocused.

"Mom said that wasn't possible. She swears you and good old Marty are best friends forever."

Georgie's mouth twisted bitterly. I had no clue what to make of her reaction. So far nothing in her behavior backed up Mom's claims that she and Marty were "thick as thieves" after all. But then she contradicted her expressions.

"That's us. BFFs, straight to the end."

She was saying something positive, but her depression and vulnerability were showing through her normal Georgie bravado.

"Did you fight?" Now I was turning into my mother, but I wanted to know what was going on with this Marty guy.

She shook her head, wordless for a long moment. Pure alarm shot through me when I saw moisture gather on her lashes. She blinked hard and sat up straighter. "There was no fight. I just walked away. I don't want to talk about Marty. Not now or any other time."

There was a brutal finality to her words. If I brought up Marty the BFF one more time, I had little doubt she'd be up like a shot and out of my room. Actually, I wouldn't have been shocked if she'd be out of the hotel and gone when I woke up. Clearly, Marty Gentry, he of the millions of dollars and mysteriously negative friendship, was a sore spot that had not yet even begun to heal over.

I lay down on the bed, my eyes ridiculously heavy, and gestured to the wide expanse next to me. "The slumber party option is open, but I can't stay up for another minute."

She seemed amused but declined, leaving for her own room. Ironically, once she was gone and I was free to sleep, I couldn't even begin to. The events of the afternoon played over and over again. All the places it could have gone wrong. All the things that could have meant the end of any of the three of us. The thought of it, playing on repeat, was enough to keep me tossing well into the night. Finally, at two AM, I grabbed the room phone and dialed Alex's bungalow number, telling myself that there was nothing overly personal about calling an employee to enquire after his welfare. If it was the middle of the night, well, sometimes I needed to take certain actions before my workday was truly done.

He answered on the first ring. Just a single low, smoky word. "Charlie."

I shivered. "I just…are your feet and ankle okay?"

I couldn't figure out how to vocalize what I was feeling or thinking at the moment. I picked the most concrete concern: the condition of his hands, leg, and feet when he'd left me.

"They're fine." I could hear the quiet amusement in his voice. "All cleaned and patched up."

We were both silent, and I felt like an idiot for giving in to the urge to call when I had no good reason. I was about to offer a lame good-bye and hang up, when he spoke again. "Thank you for calling." His words were quiet, but it wasn't hard to hear the sincerity. "It's late, Charlie. As much as I'd like to take this moment to have some much-needed conversations, we ought to get some sleep."

"Were you sleeping?" I asked, guilt creeping in.

"No." There was amusement underlying his words. "I was laying here wondering if it was too late to call you and if you were sleeping."

I closed my eyes, struggling to breathe calmly. I had no idea what I was doing. This was just stupid. I had absolutely no future with Alex, but I also couldn't deny that my feelings for him went far beyond gratitude for saving my life or even lust after our random make-out session in my office. He was dangerous.

"Good night, Alex."

"Good night, Charlie," he murmured, his low voice so incredibly seductive. I could listen to those two words every night for the rest of my life and never get tired of hearing their throaty growl.

I hung up immediately.

CHAPTER TEN

———

Morning came far too soon, considering how late I'd continued to toss and turn—until I'd passed out from sheer exhaustion. No matter what I tried to do, I still looked like crap. There would be little professionalism in my appearance today. I also had to wear ugly soft-bottomed flats to baby my battered soles and angry ankle. I trudged down to the lobby, where I was dismayed to discover both Alex and Georgie had beat me to work. How was that even possible?

Wordlessly, Georgie handed me a cup of coffee and continued staring into the distance. She looked hung over even though I knew she wasn't, and I began to suspect that was her default look for lack of sleep. How many times had I thought she was hung over when really she was just exhausted? The question made me uncomfortable only because I'd made a lot of assumptions about Georgie over the years, and if that one was wrong, how many others were?

Alex nodded to me but also didn't speak. All three of us stood in silence watching happy guests gear up for another holiday happy day, all of us surly, and Alex with that idiot hat perched on his head and his mouth twisted in the dismay of being out of bed. I felt exactly the same, sans stupid hat.

That was how Detective Ray found us. His mouth was pinched and his eyes hard, and that more than anything made it clear to me that something not good had happened. He crossed to us and immediately handed a couple of photos our way. Alex took them first, and we leaned in to look. It was Strangler's Cove, I supposed, but not the way we'd seen it last night. All the opium poppies were gone. The entire thing had been brutally cut, leaving nothing but a few smashed flowers and hundreds of sliced stalks. Of all the things I'd expected Detective Ray to find, this was certainly not even on the list.

Georgie and I were silent in horror, and Alex's only response was a single curse.

"I take it you're going to say it didn't look like this last night," Detective Ray said.

We nodded, voices overlapping as we told our story again, pointing out how many poppies there had been, how we'd been nearly murdered, how someone clearly knew we were onto them. Obviously, they'd come back during the night and cut down their crop, clearly feeling they were left without choice. Now we would be on their hit list because we'd just ruined what was no doubt many thousands of dollars of a big cash crop.

Detective Ray testily flipped his notebook closed. "They probably cut down the crop so they could harvest whatever was to be had before they lost it all to us. I'm sure not all of it was ready, but some to them is better than all to us. Stay close to the phones. And for heaven's sake, stop sticking your nose in this."

We worked through the morning, finally getting back into the swing of things. With only a few days until the big Christmas Eve luau, there was plenty to do, and my concentration was spotty at best. A member of the luau committee came by to show me a picture of the happy porkers who were about to bite it for the festivities, so there was that. I broke for lunch and headed for the lobby, hoping to find Georgie and Alex and see if they wanted to have lunch and talk about the bomb Ray had dropped on us. If the drugs were gone, was the chance also gone to find the person who had murdered Mallory?

Both were in the lobby—Georgie working the crowd and talking to some delighted teenage boys, and Alex talking to some of the members of the waitstaff, likely about tonight's dinner. After she finished talking to the boys, Georgie moved through the room, laughter and smiles following in her wake. Georgie had a skill I'd never been able to learn. She knew how to make people feel good. I only knew how to keep people in line. How to get things done. It really was no wonder that Jared had caved in to her and jumped into bed at the first available opportunity.

I rubbed the grit of exhaustion from my eyes and watched her cross the room, khaki uniform shorts swishing around her long, tan legs. I lived in Hawaii, and somehow she still managed to look tanner than I. That had to be some kind of a marketable skill.

When she stopped in front of Alex, he flashed her one of those charming grins, cocking his head to the side.

He liked the way I looked. I knew that was true. But we didn't mesh. We were like oil and water, touching but never merging. Georgie, well, Georgie was just his type. Funny, clever, gorgeous, charming, easy. Everything I was not. My throat caught, closing up like I was struggling with the byproduct of anaphylaxis. Not unless a person could be allergic to bitterness and jealousy. I had done this by repeatedly telling Georgie that I wasn't interested in Alex, that our relationship was strictly business. No one could be blamed for her flirtation but me, myself, and I. Didn't she know when someone was lying like my father after a weekend "working"?

Their conversation was low, casual, clearly flirting. When she gestured up, my gut clenched. She was pointing at the hat. The stupid mistletoe hat. He'd made it clear that even when it wasn't someone extra desirable like Georgie, he would kiss anyone who asked. That was his new rule.

The emotions that tore through me were far more intense than anything that had come at the loss of Jared. Nothing had overwhelmed me then but humiliation and wounded pride for my ignorance and stupidity. This was a burning wash of hot jealousy. I had to bite down on my tongue to stop myself from crossing the room and announcing to both of them that Alex was mine. That every inch of that clever brain, every inch of that tanned skin, every curve of that mouth, it all belonged to me. And the urge to protect that, an idea that wasn't even true, welled up in me, struggling to break free with violence.

After watching Alex bend and press a kiss to the edge of her mouth, I longed to kick my own sister's ass, despite our recent understanding. I hadn't even wanted to do that when she'd actually slept with my fiancé. Mostly I'd just been disappointed. A little bit let down. Disillusioned that family would always do what was best for you. Rage, well, apparently violent jealousy was something I saved for men I couldn't even consider.

Alex stood straight. My pulse slammed hard. I could hear the staccato beat of my heart in my ears, the rest of the room just a rushing of water. I didn't know what he was saying to her. I couldn't read lips. He stopped in what was clearly the middle of a word, suddenly noticing me.

I didn't know what my face said. I did my best to shutter the burning resentment I felt, but his raised eyebrow told me I wasn't entirely successful. The right side of his mouth cocked. Just the slightest hint. There was something smug in it. He turned back to Georgie, said something else to her, and then flashed her the thousand-watt smile before turning away.

He grabbed the radio from the belt. "Charlie," he said, the word sending goose bumps skittering across my skin as I heard it come through my radio. "Can you please meet me in my office for a moment?"

I could only hope everyone else in the building who could pick up this radio frequency couldn't hear the way he said my name. That teasing stroke of intimacy when he rolled the word across his tongue.

I swallowed hard. I didn't want to. I hadn't forgotten the last time we'd been in an office together. It wasn't him who was the problem. It was myself I couldn't trust.

"I can't do that at the moment," I said, my throat constricting, my body traitorously screaming how much I definitely *could* meet him alone.

He licked his lips, very slowly. I nearly moaned into the radio. Out of the corner of my eye, I registered that Georgie was still there, watching our exchange. That she could probably even hear our words. But I couldn't focus on that.

"This is a very important conversation, Charlie. About a subject that is still sensitive here at the resort." He was trying to sound professional, but he didn't. Not to me. I was about to start hyperventilating. "I *really* don't think you want me saying what I have to say on this open line."

Oh, good Lord. No, I didn't. I didn't know what he had to say right now, but I definitely didn't want to hear it at the same time as everyone else. I took a deep breath and pressed the button. "Of course. I'll meet you there in five minutes."

His gaze burned, even across the room. My entire body was nothing but the molten lava that flowed, hot and thick, all over Hawaii. This was so dangerous. My pulse thumped hard, kicking at my throat. I couldn't even swallow. The sane part of my brain had turned off. The part that was left wanted to scream "I want you." Right into the radio. It was a very good thing that I couldn't speak.

I glanced at Georgie, realizing she was still there. Still staring at me across the room. Her look told me that if she'd ever believed my claims of strictly business, she certainly didn't now. She'd be an idiot, which she wasn't, if she couldn't tell there was something a little bit more than coworkers and a lot more like people who'd been trying to strip each other naked days before. Her eyebrows shot up into her hair. I refused to acknowledge her expression.

Back straight, I averted my eyes from Alex and crossed the room, headed silently for his office. At least it was a different locale than before. That could only help me stay focused on whatever it was he felt we needed to talk about and not on the man himself. That was good. The way it should be.

I stepped into his office and shut the door behind me. I hadn't watched his progress, so I was surprised to discover I was alone. Somehow I'd managed to beat him, even though he'd been closer. Waiting impatiently, I paced from one end of his office to the other before he finally turned the knob and stepped inside, locking it behind us. I watched his deft fingers turn that lock and felt the breath knock from my body like a punch in the stomach. I was one hundred different kinds of stupid to be here right now.

Trying to ignore the sheer power of his presence after yesterday's events, I kept my face impassive. "What's the problem?"

The corners of his mouth turned up in a grin so contagious I wanted to join in, even though I knew I wasn't going to be half as delighted by what he was going to say as he clearly was.

"You're jealous."

Those were neither the words I'd expected nor wanted to hear. I actually flinched, even though I was begging my face to give nothing away. "Really, Alex? *That* is why you called me away from work?"

He was still grinning. I didn't want him knowing I was jealous. It helped nothing in our lives, our work environment, or our hotel situation, and it was embarrassing besides.

"I called you away from work because that's what I'm going to do every time you stare at me across the room as though you'd like to consume me alive, because I can't stand it. I see you looking like that, and I swear to you that every time—every single time—I will find an office, an empty room, even a freaking closet. And then I will do this."

There really wasn't any warning, although I should have figured it out from his words. His hand snaked around the base of my skull and pulled me forward, tilting up my head until my mouth was directly under his, and then he was kissing me. He kissed like it was going somewhere. And it wasn't. When his hands were buried deep in my hair, my bun was a thing of the past, and I couldn't quite catch a breath, I pulled away from him, pushing at his chest.

"Alex, stop. You can't just kiss me whenever you want."

His smile was proprietary, wolfish. "I'm not. I'm kissing you whenever *you* want. You are not nearly as good at hiding it as you think you are."

There wasn't even anything I could say. He was about the hottest thing I'd ever seen, and there was no denying it. But that didn't make workplace relationships okay. "Workplace relationships are not okay," I reminded.

He laughed like nothing could be funnier than me mentioning regulations. "You don't need to be jealous of Georgie. She's not attractive to me, even a little."

"She looks just like me," I pointed out, bizarrely indignant that he would say that, even though I was the one saying it was against the rules. And why was he standing so close to me still? Every time I exhaled, our bodies touched, and every inch of me that even remotely touched any part of him was screaming for attention. He needed to back away.

His grin was irresistible. I wanted to kiss him just because of the way he smiled, which told me I definitely needed to get out of this room.

"In Korea, one of our favorite dishes is called *Tangsuyuk*. It's like sweet and sour chicken. Do you know why it's a favorite?"

I shook my head, unable to speak when his fingers were trailing a path down the curve of my neck. It took all the power in all the atoms in my body not to drop my head to the side, giving him freer access.

"The key to really good *Tangsuyuk*, the thing that makes it so delicious, is a perfect balance between the sweetness…" His mouth hovered near my neck, replacing his roaming fingers. His breath sent goose bumps chasing along my skin. My legs were actually shaking. "…and the tartness."

Some inarticulate noise worked its way from my throat. I needed my brain back so I could figure out how to get out of here. Or maybe even just what he was talking about. "We make the sauce from tart apples, so it's sweet," he whispered, his tongue dipping into my ear. I gasped, my entire body trembling. "Then we add vinegar, because too much sweet isn't good. Then we add crushed red pepper flakes, called *gochugaru*, so that every single bite is…irresistibly…" His teeth nipped softly at the skin of my neck. "…deliciously spicy."

The throaty moan was definitely coming from me, but I would never make a sound like that. At least, I never had before. His mouth worked at my neck, pulling, biting—if he gave me a hickey, I would kill him. But I couldn't stop him. I couldn't even breathe.

"Georgie is all sweet," he whispered, returning his attention to my ear, his finger tracing the tender skin at the collar of my shirt, leaving shivers in his wake. "All sweet is for children. Grownups know that nothing is more delicious…" He kissed me very softly, and I let him, because apparently I'd lost all modicum of self-control I'd ever possessed. "…than something…" His tongue flicked inside my lips for only a hint of a second. I was panting now, clutching his shirt uselessly. "…that burns against your tongue."

Then I was against the door again, and I was all for it, my nails digging into the hollows of his cheeks as he invaded my mouth. I was so insanely hot for him. There was no point in denying it. I wanted to do things with Alex that were probably illegal in all forty-eight contiguous states, *and* Hawaii. Then I wanted to do it a second time, because I was very, very sure that once wouldn't be enough.

From another man I wouldn't have believed his words. Not with the constant casual flirting between he and Georgie. But I believed Alex. I couldn't make complete sense of that, but somehow I knew he was sincere. Georgie was of no interest to him. He'd never really acted like she was. I'd never been jealous before. Not of anyone. But I was now. Because even though it wasn't true, every fiber of my being was screaming that Alex was mine.

It was just getting very, very good when my radio beeped abrasively. I considered, for a second, flinging it across the room until it made a satisfying crunch against the wall.

"This is Jillian. Charlotte Conner, please identify."

Alex's body convulsed with silent laughter as I let a very dirty word fly. I pressed the button, schooling my voice to reveal nothing. "This is Charlotte."

It didn't work. I sounded low and raw. My breathing was strained.

"Charlotte? Are you okay?" she asked.

I licked my lips, trying to push Alex away unsuccessfully. "Yes, I'm fine. What is it?"

Alex's fingers teased the back of my thigh, barely slipping under the hem of my skirt. I strangled another moan, stepping hard on his foot. He laughed again. I sincerely hoped that Jillian couldn't hear him.

"There's a problem at the concierge desk. Can you come up?"

I ran a hand through my ruined hair and searched desperately for the scattered pieces of what had once been my brain. I'd come in with it. It still had to be around here somewhere. "I'll be there in five minutes," I promised, turning off the radio and tucking it into my jacket pocket.

I turned for the door, and Alex grabbed my arm. "This is not done, Charlie."

The words sent another hot wave of violent lust rolling over me. I pushed it away and squared my shoulders. "It is, because it has to be." If only I felt as determined as I sounded.

* * *

It turned out that Jillian really could have handled the problem herself. She'd handled problems like it before. For whatever reason, she'd felt the need to clear comp tickets for a show in Kapa'a with me. I could only be grateful to the universe for breaking up the huge mistake my body desperately wanted to make. I ignored both Georgie and Alex for the rest of the workday, focusing, instead, entirely on the work that needed to be done and on the needs of our many guests. Really, since I'd arrived in June, I'd never seen this many guests, and thankfully, they all seemed to be having a great time.

At every moment the main building's spacious lobby was filled with the giggles of children and the fake, snapping noises of cell phones taking selfies designed to make friends and coworkers jealous. Couples were loving the time together. Children were dreaming of the water park, deep sand, and castles. From large families to extended families to small groups of friends, it was clear that the crisp, sultry Aloha Lagoon air was good for bonding.

At five PM, I headed back to my office to deal with emails that had been getting ignored in favor of luau prep. Alex stepped into my office, and my heart shot into my stomach. He reached for the door. I could tell from his expression that he was here on business, but that didn't matter. I held up a hand. "Don't shut the door."

I couldn't tell what to make of his expression. He stepped closer to my desk, obediently leaving the door open behind him. "Georgie says Christmas used to be your favorite holiday. That you have a good reason now for your special dislike."

Dang Georgie and her "helpful" streak that had her admitting my personal business all over the island. She clearly wanted Alex and me together and was trying to do the work for me. "That's true." I offered no more information.

"Are you going to tell me about it?"

I shook my head. "Most definitely not. Anything else?"

He sat down on the corner of my desk, staring at me for a long second. Then he cocked his head. "Please tell me, Charlie."

The words were like a punch in the gut. Completely unexpected, and even worse, I wanted to do it. Oh, what the heck? What did it hurt?

"Fine. I told you about how I was engaged to a man named Jared. He was a total jerk, but I was just sure we'd be getting married and chugging along happily in our perfect jobs and perfect marriage. We'd been dating since our freshman year of college, and I felt like I'd invested far too much time in him for it to lead anywhere but marriage."

He nodded. "I know about Jared. You and Georgie told me."

I stared at him. "*She* told you?"

He nodded again. "Sure. At the beginning. After you told me about it. I called her on it, and she confirmed what she'd done and then told me why."

I was completely befuddled by the fact she'd admitted to a man that, at the time, she barely knew. I was also really surprised he'd called her on it. I remembered his cold attitude toward her that day, but I hadn't made the connection at the time. "Did she tell you about the wedding? When it was? When she gave me the video?"

He flinched. "Oh man. It was Christmas, wasn't it?"

I nodded. "Jared worked the Christmas card department of a well-known card company. He thought it would be great for business." If bitterness showed through, I was sorry for it, but he hadn't broken my heart. However, he'd ruined my favorite holiday forever. "I was all for it. I loved everything about Christmas. Back then."

Alex shook his head. "Jeez, what a douche."

I nodded. "Truth."

He sighed. "Look, I get where you're coming from. Truly, I do. But we need to replace your negative holiday feelings with positive ones, and the guests will be better off for it. So how can we make your *Kalikimaka* more *Mele*?"

I had to laugh at that. "I have no clue. Especially considering what's going on right now. I can't believe all the poppies were gone!"

He ran a hand through his hair. "No. Although I'm sure Ray was telling the truth. Look, when you finish what you're doing, let's grab Georgie and drive over." He saw my expression of horror. "We're not going down there. I just want to climb up the hill and take a look. Nothing closer. Maybe we'll see something they didn't, since we've seen it before."

There was a long list of ways I didn't want to do that, but he was right. We were in a better position to scope it out than the police had been, since we'd seen every poppy in its full-color glory before being invited to take a swim by our friends at the cove. I nodded, closing my email.

"Okay, let's go."

Maybe the poppies and Mallory's murder didn't relate to each other at all. Maybe it was all a coincidence. However, I wasn't a big fan of leaving anything to chance. If there was a relationship between these things, I wanted to know it. And I wanted her parents to at least know why she had to die, even if we could never figure who had done it.

I was a bit nervous how all of us, scraped up and sprained, would manage to get up the mountain, but we figured it out. It was slow going, and I couldn't help but feel the entire time that we were just sitting up there in the open, asking to be a target. However, since the people in charge of growing in the cove had already taken their drugs, there seemed no reason they'd still be around. I was pretty certain that the drugs that would come from those opium poppies were the reason Mallory had lost her life, though I couldn't seem to make any connection between the two events. We still had no proof of who Mallory's boyfriend was or what, if anything, he had to do with her murder.

We reached the top of the hill and paused to recover before moving forward and reluctantly peering off the side, all of us clearly hesitant. I scanned the rows of brutally chopped plants and shivered, keeping my eyes away from the whirlpool. That was something I could go forever without seeing again.

"Well, all these broken stalks weren't here last time," Georgie said mulishly.

"Uh, guys. That wasn't here last time either."

From Alex's tone of voice, I really didn't even want to look. But I followed the line of his pointing finger anyway, seeing what he did. The single pale, lifeless man, wearing his swim trunks, facedown on the shore, just inches from the ocean.

CHAPTER ELEVEN

——————

We no longer had cell phones. All three of them had been either lost or destroyed in our murder attempt. We had to climb down the hill as fast as our injured feet would carry us and head to the beach next door and hope there was someone out there who had a phone. Luckily, there were several people hanging out on the warm sand, but I had no clue if surfers were normally inclined to bring their phones to catch some waves. We could only hope they did, or it would just be faster to drive down to the police station than to drive into Aloha Lagoon looking for a phone.

Alex honed in on the same three guys we'd seen before. Mo, Big Steve, and the guy whose name Alex didn't know. We'd been to this beach three times, and two of those times, these three guys had been here. I would have loved if that meant something to the case, but it didn't. After six months in Hawaii, as far as I could tell, these people never went home. It was some kind of law people in Hawaii were contractually obligated to spend 75 percent of their lives standing on the beach. This just happened to be these guys' favorite place to stand.

They watched us approach, not particularly curiously. No Name was smoking a cigarette, which struck me as really odd on a beach, though it probably actually wasn't. Mo and Big Steve couldn't have looked more bored if we were Jehovah's Witnesses. They barely glanced up from their perusal of the waves. Didn't look like anything but waves to me, but I had absolutely no doubt they were able to make a lot out of them, like when and where they wanted to drop the boards they were leaning against.

Mo and Big Steve looked like Jack Sprat and his wife—Mo's impressively large girth a foil for Big Steve's skeletal frame. When they realized we weren't going away, they finally sighed in unison, including No Name, and turned our way.

"Hey, do any of you guys have a phone we can borrow?" Georgie purred, and when they noticed her, their demeanor underwent a major change. In her barely there shorts and microscopic, slightly transparent tank top, there wasn't much chance of any man ignoring her.

They scrambled around, each pulling a phone from a pocket or bag. She reached Big Steve first, plucking the phone from his limp fingers and flashing him a smile before stepping back to our side. They watched with undisguised lust as Alex dialed 9-1-1. We'd stepped far enough away that they couldn't hear our conversation, but they'd know soon enough, no question. Detective Ray told Alex he'd be there in ten minutes and to stay away from the cove. Like there was any chance of us going over there again.

Alex brought the phone back to Big Steve, and I followed. Big Steve grabbed at it, never taking his eyes off my sister. His Adam's apple bobbed like a buoy every time he swallowed. His buggy eyes were about popping out of his head with Georgie nearby, and if he got anymore worked up, we'd need to call for him to have medical assistance as well. I felt sorry for him. But he was young. Hopefully, he'd grow into all that...protrudingness.

"Hey, have you guys noticed anything weird around here today?" Alex was all casualness. He was great at making people feel comfortable. As good as Georgie was at making them *uncomfortable*.

All three shook their heads. Then Mo spoke up. "Oh, I saw a helicopter off the mountain this morning."

We already knew about that one.

Big Steve turned to him, and in his squeaky voice said, "Nuh-uh. I would have seen that."

Mo nodded so enthusiastically his hair was all over his face. "Yes, huh. I saw it. Like six AM. It was there for maybe ten minutes. Never landed. I mean, I don't think there's anywhere around here it could land except right where we're standing. But it just flew away."

"Anything else?" Alex encouraged.

Everyone shrugged in unison, looking a little disappointed. They probably thought Georgie was going to leave. All heads turned when a police cruiser pulled up to the beach, lights and siren running. The van from the coroner's office was close behind.

Detective Ray stepped out, and his eyes immediately snapped in our direction. He pointed at all three of us. "You three. Here. Now."

We glanced at each other, and I felt suspiciously like I used to when Georgie and I got in trouble with our mom. And that feeling gave me a highly inappropriate urge to giggle. It must have shown on my face, because Alex raised an eyebrow, and Georgie snorted. We managed to compose ourselves, and I felt bad. There were a million ways this entire situation wasn't remotely funny, but I guess we had to find our amusement where we could when people kept dying and we had no answers, only more questions.

Sufficiently sobered, I glanced at Alex. "I'm sorry I got you into this."

He shook his head. "You didn't drag me. I came on my own, because you don't deserve to have to do this alone."

I pulled in a shaky breath, concentrating on crossing the beach to Detective Ray. Alex was too lethal. He was kind, funny, smart, scorching hot, and I was fairly convinced his kisses should have been a controlled substance. Every single time he proved again what he was really made of, it became harder for me to remember that my life was a transitory one. There was nowhere I stayed for more than a few months. Including Hawaii.

Detective Ray watched us approach, mouth a thin line of disapproval. "I told you to stay out of it."

"We didn't do anything but hike up to the mountain and look over the side," Alex interjected. "You can check us. We have no equipment. We don't even have a phone. We had to borrow one to call you. We just wanted to see how different it was with the flowers gone, that's all. You certainly can't blame us for wanting to see with our own eyes that what almost killed us yesterday is gone today."

Detective Ray's scowl certainly said he could blame us. Rick's helicopter flew by, ruffling all our hair and clothing. It was probably the only way they could really get the body out, though it certainly wasn't what he was normally paid to do. Rick Dawson owned and ran Rick's Air Paradise helicopter tours and normally raked in the dough hauling tourists to look at the jungles, waterfalls, and volcanoes dotting the island. He was one the sponsors of the luau in return for the advertising he'd get. In a little burg like AL, however, there were not a ton of helicopter pilots around for the police to call on.

"Do you know the victim this time?"

There was something very telling about the question, as though Detective Ray viewed us as the Jessica Fletchers of Aloha Lagoon, with dead friends and neighbors trailing in our wake.

I shook my head. "I don't think so. But it was so far down. I can't really say. It was just a man. I think. Though since the body is facedown in the sand…honestly, I guess it could be a woman with short hair who likes swim trunks and going topless."

Ray pointed again, making sure to stare each of us in the eye. "Don't. Go. Anywhere."

Where would we go? Even if we ran, the only place any of us had to go was the resort. Like he couldn't find us there? Even if I *had* committed murder, I wouldn't walk away from such a labor-intensive and important time of year. I would have rather stayed and taken my chances with getting caught than risk anything going wrong with one of my resorts. Which was probably why I would make a terrible murderer.

We spent two hours baking in the sun while Rick and search and rescue volunteers brought the body up and the cops down, and Detective Ray interviewed everyone on the beach. Most of the time we didn't speak. Georgie seemed to have fallen into the same kind of depression that had surfaced the other night when I'd pushed about Marty Gentry, and I wondered if downtime made her think of whatever the problem was between them.

After hour two began to drift away, I started to get twitchy. We needed to get back to the resort in time for dinner, which was barely an hour away. Someone needed to host, and what if something was going wrong right now? There were trustworthy people at the resort, of course, but it was my job to make sure that everything went flawlessly, and the only other person I trusted implicitly was sitting next to me right there, listlessly twirling a stick between his fingers. If something wasn't perfect, I wouldn't have time to fix it before dinner.

I was starting to freak out by the time Detective Ray came back to us. "Okay, you three come with me."

I thought it was odd he kept calling us "you three" like we didn't have identities outside of a unit, even though I knew he and Alex were actually friends. Or they used to be. I wasn't sure how kindly Alex would take to be suspected of murder, even by an old friend like Ray, maybe less so than another situation or a less familiar accuser.

The beach was filled with curious onlookers, and a single officer—I thought his name was Manuel Apodoca and that he had a pregnant wife—was holding back the crowd with his presence. All three of the guys from earlier were still around, along with all their friends and anyone else in the neighborhood who'd gotten curious and hoofed it over to the beach. Detective Ray led us to the back of the coroner's van, where no one could see us, and Dr. Yoshida glanced up at us before pulling the sheet up off the victim's face.

"Do any of you know this man?" she asked in her soft voice.

We all three cocked our heads to the side and stared. He probably hadn't been dead too long. He didn't look too dead. Mostly like he was resting. He was blond, attractive, and his face was friendly and open—the kind of person who was probably a salesman or marketer. I'd honestly figured he'd drowned when I saw him from the cliff, but it was clear this close that the only accident he'd had was falling onto a bullet with his temple.

"He looks familiar," I said at last, though I couldn't place him.

"Really familiar," Alex agreed.

I glanced at Georgie, and she'd gone completely white. She raised a trembling hand to her mouth. "Don't you recognize him, you guys? It's the man from the club. Harry or Henry? Maybe Ned? You know, Eurotrash's brother."

I stared at him and then back at her.

Alex finally spoke. "Niall. Yes. Good Lord. What's he doing here?"

My stomach twisted. "I told him to visit Aloha Lagoon before he left Hawaii. What if this is my fault?"

Detective Ray stared into my eyes. "What is your association with this man?"

I shook my head uselessly. How could this happen?

"We don't have much of one. We met him the other night at a club called Spikers in Kapa'a. He told us he'd just gotten here from Ireland and that his brother, Henry, I think, was a permanent resident of Kauai. He seemed really excited to be in Hawaii." To my horror, my voice broke on the last sentence.

Alex's hand moved to the small of my back, rubbing softly in comfort. I let him. It wasn't even because I was weak like I'd been when we'd found Mallory's body. I was just comforted by him. By his touch and his presence, which was what told me more than anything that I needed to separate myself from him.

"And that was the first time you two had met him as well?" Detective Ray asked Alex and Georgie. Both of them nodded in unison. "So you don't know their last name?"

"Aside from the fact they're from Ireland, so the name is probably Irish, we don't even have a guess," Georgie offered.

Ray sighed and signaled to Dr. Yoshida to cover the body. As she moved to tuck the body in tighter so she could zip the bag, she moved him up slightly, and I caught a glimpse of something on the skin of his shirtless back.

"Wait!"

Every eye behind the van turned my way. I stepped forward. "Could you...could you move him so I can see his back?"

Dr. Yoshida glanced at Detective Ray, and he shrugged. She pulled the body so I could see the mark I'd noticed fleetingly on his shoulder. The tattoo of the Chinese word for opium stared back at me. My voice sounded dead when I said, "Actually, in a manner of speaking, we do know who this man is."

*   *   *

Of all the people I'd pegged to be Mallory's British boyfriend, I certainly wouldn't have picked silly, boyish Niall, with his horrible dance moves. Was it possible he'd been the one to kill her? I couldn't even picture it. Though I had picture proof he was her mysterious boy toy from the beaches. Had he lied about just flying into town, or had he really been gone and just returned? He'd certainly lied about not knowing Mallory. Actually, in retrospect, he most certainly hadn't told me he didn't know Mallory. I'd asked if he did, and he'd vaguely responded that he'd just flown into town. Hardly a denial.

Of all the people in the world I would have pictured as a grower of opium, even a small operation, he wouldn't have even made the list. And if he was part of the opium growing group, was Eurotrash as well? How would the police even find him, since we had no name to give them beyond Henry or Harry—none of us could remember for sure which it was—and the vague description that he was blond and one of the girls at the club called him Eurotrash. Detective Ray had mentioned that Niall had no passport on him, and if he'd never committed a crime, he wouldn't have fingerprints on file.

It wasn't much to go on.

I couldn't concentrate well during the dinner rush back at the resort. I moved from table to table, sometimes with Alex and sometimes without, greeting guests, being friendly, taking Alex's words to heart, and trying my very, very best to be in the proper spirit that people expected for the holiday. I didn't want to be the reason people remembered they didn't have a great time that one Christmas in Aloha Lagoon. I could never be Phillip, but I didn't need to be a jerk either. I'd let Jared sour me completely to a holiday that I'd once loved. He didn't deserve that kind of a presence in my life. I was determined to become jolly if it killed me.

When everyone had moved on to other evening activities, including the show with hula dancers and fire-eaters out on Ramada Pier and a hula-dancing class near the waterfall, Alex, Georgie, and I rejoined each other in the lobby.

"Look, we need to talk about what we know. Lay all of it out," Georgie said. "I'm starting to get confused."

Alex's mouth twisted in wry amusement. "Just starting? I'm well into being confused by this point."

She laughed. "Okay, point conceded. So does anyone think Eurotrash is involved in the drugs or even the murders? Should we go back to the club and find him?"

Alex shook his head. "Absolutely not. If he is involved, we certainly don't want to draw attention to ourselves. At this point, they could still think it was an accident that we stumbled on the drugs. If we seem like we know something, maybe they'll try to attack us again, and when they expect us, they're bound to be much better prepared for us. We don't need that."

Georgie blew out a slow breath. "Right. Okay, let's think. Maybe it will tell us something. Who's the first we talked to about Mallory?"

"Mo, Big Steve, and that dude with no name," Alex filled in.

"And what did they tell us?" I asked, not seeing any way this exercise could hurt.

"That Mallory was there sometimes, sometimes at a beach near Kalihiwai, but if we wanted to know about her we should ask Squid, because they were better friends," Alex answered immediately.

"Okay, so what did Squid say?" Georgie asked. "I wasn't there."

I nodded. "He said that he was friends with Mallory and that she liked to go to the beach, which we already knew, and that she liked to go to Spikers."

"So we went to Spikers." Alex picked up the thread. "And what did we learn there?"

"That Mallory had an English boyfriend, and Niall was sort of close, but no banana, that she liked the club, that she drank and danced a lot, that she hung around sometimes with people from Aloha Lagoon, including Keanu Not Reeves and Poncho," Georgie interjected, getting excited.

"We also learned she was taking surfing lessons, though we have no clue who they were from. We met Eurotrash, otherwise known as Henry or Harry, and Niall, who seemed nice and turned out to maybe be a drug manufacturer, if nothing else, who is now dead. There's no indication either way if he's the one who killed Mallory or if he was responsible for the attack on us." Alex ticked off the names on his fingers. "Also we learned that Squid either can't properly rhyme or can't properly pronounce the name Niall, as it should sound like Neeill, not Nill. So it really rhymes with neither Phil nor Bill."

"So we went to see Poncho and Keanu and learned nothing except that she was friends with Autumn." I filled in the next part. "So we went to Autumn, who gave me the pictures of the boyfriend, if just pictures of some guy's back can be described as pictures of someone."

Alex pointed at me. "Then I took the pictures and checked the symbol, saw it was opium, and recognized the flower as one I'd seen at Strangler's Cove."

"So we all went down there together and got pushed in," Georgie helpfully reminded. "Went to the cops, who sent a copter, who came up with nothing."

"So we went back, and the drugs were gone, but the body was there," I finished. "So what does all of it mean?"

The other two stared at me. Georgie opened her mouth and closed it again. Both of them shrugged.

"Not a clue," Georgie admitted at last.

"Okay, so we have to decide what we want to do at this point," Alex said. "Do we want to keep trying to figure out who killed Mallory and why? Do we want to mind our own business and stay safe? Or do we want to casually ask a few questions here and there and pretend that we aren't investigating?"

"Here's what I want." I touched on the heart of the matter for me and for Mallory's family. "I want to know if Mallory knew. If she was involved in the growing of those drugs. The rest of it, I'm sure the police will figure it out. But I'm also pretty sure that they will assume she was involved in the drug thing, whether she was or not. I don't want her parents having that on their mind forever."

Alex nodded. "So how do we find that out?"

I shook my head. "No clue. We could go through her things. I've been planning to pack them up to send home to her family. But we have to be careful. I don't want this getting around. It might scare the guests or even tip someone off that we're still asking questions."

We agreed that early the next morning, when the security staff was distracted with the personnel change, we would go through Mallory's room, despite the continued presence of police tape on her door. If everyone was busy, it would give us the best chance to get in and out unseen. Until then, all we could do was wait.

*   *   *

I woke up extra early in the morning so I could talk to Seth Peterson again. When I got to the offices, Seth was still in the security pen, filling out reports. I would wait to catch him on his way out. Jonah, the night bellman, was busy packing his things up in the break room across from the security offices. There were three employee break rooms around the building, but this one worked the best for the night staff, and they were frequently here. I poured myself a cup of coffee I wouldn't drink and eyed him.

"I've been thinking of having an employee memorial for Mallory. Were you guys friends?"

He seemed incredibly startled, and I wasn't sure if it was the question, the context of it, or the fact I'd spoken to him casually at all. It could have been any or all of the above.

"Not really. She was social, you know, but we weren't friends. She just liked to talk. And she liked to get drunk." He hurriedly added, "Not while she was on the clock though."

I nodded. "Did you ever hang out with her after the workday?"

He shook his head. "Nah. I'm working two jobs to pay for college. This is my second job, and from here my uncle flies me up to Honolulu for classes. After that, I go home and sleep for maybe four hours. Then I hit my other job. Then another hour of sleep, then back here. I'm not exactly Mr. Good Times." His mouth twisted wryly.

"I'm sure all that work will be worth it in the end," I offered sympathetically.

He blew out a big breath. "I sure hope so. She palled around with Darcy though. You know, from the front desk?"

Right. Darcy of the terrifying fingernails. "Yes, I know Darcy. Maybe she would have ideas for something to memorialize Mallory. Thanks, Jonah." I started to leave and turned back. "Good luck on your degree. Is it in hospitality?"

He nodded it was, and I nodded back. "I'll let the corporate offices know when you're ready to look for a job. We like people who aren't afraid to work hard to get what they want."

He seemed momentarily shocked but then thanked me, quickly agreeing that he would and watching me leave . When I returned to security, Seth was getting ready to leave. I waved awkwardly. "Seth, could we talk for a minute?"

It was clear he wanted to say no, but either way, I was still his boss. Instead he just nodded wordlessly. I took that for assent. "Can you tell me where you were between noon and six on the day Mallory died?"

There was no reason in my mind to be vague or circumspect with Seth at this point. I wasn't asking about the poppies—I was asking about Mallory. Maybe they were really one and the same in this context, but nevertheless, I was asking. I was tired of not knowing what was going on. There were so many avenues that led to places we couldn't yet see. Knowing why Mallory was clutching Seth's card when she died wasn't going to solve everything, but it was something I could concentrate on.

He eyed me for a long moment before speaking. "So you've finally decided to come right out and ask. Sorry, but I'll tell you what I told the detective. I was out of town, on the other side of the island. I have a gas station receipt from around noon. Then an hour later, I arrived at the house of a friend for a barbeque. There were several people there, and all of them spent time with me. I didn't leave until right before opening, since we were all expected to be here. Sorry, but I'm cleared."

He didn't sound angry. In fact, he seemed almost slightly amused. Probably because he had an alibi. I wanted to keep pushing, to find whatever hole there was in his story, but Detective Ray had cleared him, which meant he was probably clean. But he was lying. About the card and his relationship with Mallory. If he was lying, there had to be a reason. I just had no clue what it could be.

I watched him grab his bag and head out of the office toward the security staff morning briefing. I went to the front desk, hoping to catch Darcy before she left. I only had about five minutes before I needed to meet Georgie and Alex at Mallory's room, but I really wanted to see Darcy now, since Jonah had tagged her by name. I caught her in the hallway of the employees' only section of the building, where we kept offices and employee break rooms. She also seemed startled to see me. Either I was really scary, or the staff was really jumpy. I suspected Jonah was just easily startled, living his life on maybe five hours of heavily interrupted sleep a day and a boatload of caffeine. I wasn't sure what Darcy's problem was.

"Darcy, wait."

She stopped, looking decidedly like she was in a hurry and the last thing she wanted to do right now was listen to the boss. She even checked her watch, not particularly surreptitiously.

"I know you're off the clock, but I'm just asking some of the employees who knew her best how you think the resort should memorialize Mallory. Maybe a plaque on the waterfall? Or is that too morbid?"

Her face suggested it was definitely morbid. In fact, she seemed completely appalled. "I think that would be…terrifying. Couldn't you just plant a tree?"

I cocked my head. "Mallory did die, Darcy. There's no pretending she didn't. We should at least acknowledge it."

Darcy's bottom lip trembled. "I know she did. But still. How about something nice that will keep living, you know. Something that will be alive even when she isn't."

I gathered, from her words and behavior, that she and Mallory had been close. "How friendly were you and Mallory?"

She shrugged. "We spent some time together. Like I said, she was really busy with you. But we took surfing lessons together."

Well, that was news. Finally, somebody would know who Mallory had been taking those elusive surfing lessons with. "Where did you take them?"

"Windrock. With Joel Sugarbaker. He was going to be an Olympic surfer before he got hurt."

The name meant absolutely nothing to me, so I just nodded encouragingly. At least it was a name I didn't have before and another person I could interview. I glanced at her. "I'm afraid Detective Ray is going to think Mallory was into drugs because there's some suggestion of drugs surrounding her death. I just don't know anything about her personal life, but I don't want her parents to hear that. It's not…it isn't true, is it?"

She bit her bottom lip, and I knew with a sinking heart that it was at least partially true. Finally, she spoke. "It wasn't true that she was into them. She never took them or sold them or anything. But she did hang around with people who are into drugs. She never took any, I swear. No matter what the cops say."

I knew that much was true. I worked Mallory far too hard when she'd been alive for me not to notice if her performance was impaired. I was heartened by Darcy's proclamation that Mallory didn't sell them either. I wondered if that covered the question of whether or not she raised them. I nodded.

"Thanks. That's good to know. How do you know?"

Darcy appeared startled by the question. "What?"

"How did you know she wasn't taking any drugs or selling them or whatever?"

Darcy blinked at me for a good thirty seconds before answering. "Mallory told me that she was tired of all drama with her drug friends, but she wasn't using. I mean, that would have been obvious. And she wasn't happy with the stuff they were doing. She wouldn't have been a part of that."

I cocked my head. "What kind of drugs were her friends dealing with?"

Darcy blinked at me some more. "I don't know exactly. Not pot. Something harder. She said it was too much. Not good stuff. Maybe, like, I don't know. Cocaine?"

I pushed harder. "Did she say what they did? Buying, selling, supplying? Growing?"

Darcy's lip curled, as though somehow *this* was the question that offended her. "No, she just said they were getting money from drugs. She didn't say how."

If Mallory was annoyed by the drugs, why didn't she do something? Maybe she had. Maybe that was why she'd died in the end.

I nodded. "Thanks for indulging my questions. Have a good day, Darcy."

She nodded at me and turned away, and I watched her practically run from me, her rubber-soled uniform shoes squealing on the freshly polished floor. Once she was gone, I sighed and returned to the lobby, nonchalantly nodding to Alex before getting on the elevator.

The fifth floor was silent and barren, as it always was. My room was empty, since I was here, and Mallory's room was empty, since she was dead. The police had requested a guard be here to watch her room, but we didn't have the kind of staff for that at the moment. The agreement was that someone would come by every half hour to make sure all was well. It would be longer because of the shift change, but once their meeting was over, they'd probably send someone here first.

The elevator dinged, and Alex stepped out. Moments later, the second elevator sounded, and Georgie joined us. With trembling fingers, I used my master key card to open Mallory's room, dreading going inside. Careful to avoid disturbing the tape, we ducked through, closing the door softly behind us.

Alex handed each of us a pair of rubber gloves from the housekeeping closet and glanced at his watch. "The morning security briefing was about in the middle when I peeked. That means we only have, maybe, seven minutes. No time to play. I'll take this room, Georgie gets the bathroom, and, Charlie, you're in charge of the bedroom."

Mallory's room was another manager's suite, smaller than mine but still three separate rooms. Mallory's bedroom smelled like her. Her clothes were still in the closet. I again ignored the urge to cry. Now was definitely not the time. The television was on, no sound. Had it been on all this time? Why hadn't the police turned it off when they'd come through? What a waste of resources. I left it on though. I wanted no indication that anyone had been here.

I sorted through Mallory's dresser drawers, pushing clothes to the side. I even felt underneath each drawer, looking for anything taped beneath. There was nothing. I looked in each bedside table, a search that produced a couple of romance novels, a Gideon Bible, and three pamphlets advertising surfing lessons. Glancing at my watch, I saw there were only two minutes left of Alex's estimated time. Shoot. There was way too much left to check. I was being too slow.

Dropping to the ground, I checked beneath her bed, thrilled when I realized I could feel something fastened to the wooden bed frame. Paper. I stripped it off, pulling it out, and jumped to my feet. I had no idea what it was, but we could look at it in leisure once we were sure we wouldn't be caught by the security staff. I was one hundred percent certain that Detective Ray wasn't going to look on our snooping with tolerant eyes, considering how pissed he'd been about every other move we'd made to investigate.

I ran to the living room, staring around wildly. Alex had a pile of papers from her desk in his hands. Georgie was nowhere to be seen. "We're out of time," I hissed, heading for the bathroom.

As if on cue, Alex's alarm beeped softly. I kind of loved that he'd done that. Set an alarm for our illegal activities. It was so businesslike and yet so bizarre in context. Georgie had her head in the medicine cabinet. "Let's go!"

She nodded and grabbed a makeup bag she had perched on the edge of the sink. Together, we darted out the door and into the hallway. We froze in horror when the unmistakable ding of the elevator sounded. Cursing, we dove for my suite, tumbling inside and closing the door just as the elevator slid open.

My heart was going crazy, but Georgie appeared oddly invigorated, laughing hysterically as soon as the door was closed. I glared at her and dumped our finds on the coffee table. "Come on. We don't have time to look at this stuff now. We'll meet back here at lunch."

We opened the door and came back into the hallway, where Silas was standing, staring at my door in consternation. "Miss. Alex." He glanced at Georgie and raised an eyebrow, giving her only a nod. After the office thing, he probably thought we were the weirdest people on earth. Prone to making loud noises and laughing hysterically for no reason.

"Morning, Silas," Alex said, nodding back. He led us on to the elevator without another word or a backward glance, clearly not feeling the strain of our near miss. It was only two days until Christmas Eve, and we were getting down to the wire, so I didn't see Alex or Georgie all morning, as work took precedence. It took a million touches to make sure every Freemont resort ran like a well-oiled machine, and Aloha Lagoon had some of the highest standards Freemont had set out, since it was one of the highest-grossing resorts the company owned. We started prepping for the big Christmas Eve show weeks, or even months, in advance, but nevertheless, there were always still things to be done.

We broke and joined for lunch at the Loco Moco, since we had to eat something before diving into the things we'd found in Mallory's room.

"I talked to a couple of people this morning, and I did find one thing." I dipped a blue corn tortilla chip into Poncho's famous pineapple salsa. "The name of the man who was giving Mallory, and also Darcy, the night clerk, surfing lessons. He's some kind of professional surfer, maybe Olympic or something like that."

Alex stilled, his hand midreach, chip crushed in his fingers. "Joel Sugarbaker?"

I pointed to him. "Yeah, that's the guy. Do you know him?"

He shook his head. "No. He didn't live in AL But he *is* the one who washed up on the beach three days before Mallory died."

CHAPTER TWELVE

———

After lunch we headed back to my room to take in every detail of what we'd taken from Mallory's room. The balancing of intense resort work and investigation was turning out to be difficult. It was maybe fifteen minutes before someone would start to notice the absence of both Alex and me. We didn't have a lot of time to get this done.

First we went through the papers that Alex found in the desk. Mostly it was practical everyday stuff. Copies of insurance forms, her rental contract for her subleased apartment in Chicago. The contracts she signed every year to continue her employment with Freemont. All of it amounted to nothing that we couldn't have found through public records or that I didn't already know because Mallory and I worked for the same company. A couple of pages were handwritten notes. A grocery list and a list of potential scuba instructors on the island. It was nothing we could use.

The paper I'd pulled from under the bed proved to be just as useless, for all the subterfuge she'd used in hiding it. It was merely a page of rentals in AL that she'd shoved into an envelope. She probably hadn't wanted me to know that she was looking for a place, that she was considering staying on with this resort even when I'd moved on. I was a little sad to know that, but it didn't really change anything.

Georgie finally dumped the contents of the makeup bag on the table, leaving us staring at a mound of mascara and lipstick, as well as a couple of pieces of folded paper. I sorted through the vials and tubes, looking for anything that could be used to conceal something besides under-eye bags, but there was nothing. It was all really just makeup. Georgie grabbed up the papers, and in a second she flipped one out in our direction. "Well, this is interesting."

I took it and discovered that it was indeed interesting, though I had no idea what it meant. "We've seen this before."

I handed Alex another copy of Seth Peterson's customer card, this one folded. Not only had she been holding one when she died, she'd had another copy on hand in her room. Why? What did it mean?

Alex flipped it over. "But we haven't seen this."

On the other side, there was a series of numbers, twenty in all, written in a long line. No spaces. The handwriting wasn't Mallory's.

"What does that mean?" Georgie asked, staring at the number string as though it held the answers to the universe.

Alex shrugged. "I don't know. But as far as I can tell, it's the only useful thing we found today."

The radios we had clipped to our clothes went off simultaneously, causing an angry squeal. It was Ginger from accounting, asking where Alex was. He identified and said he would join her momentarily. Shoving the card into his pocket, he stood. "We'll stare at it later, see if it means anything when we look at it for longer."

When he was gone, Georgie and I glanced at each other. "You want to tell me what's been wrong with you lately? Or do I have to find some way to manipulate it out of you? I know it's related to Alex, so just give over."

She was right. She'd find some way to manipulate it out of me. She always did. I bit my tongue but then blurted out, "I can't stop kissing Alex."

She laughed delightedly. "Ha. I knew it! Man, that does suck."

Scowling, I sat back in my chair. "I'm serious. It's highly inappropriate. Freemont frowns on employee fraternization, even though it isn't outright banned. I'm supposed to be an example. What kind of example goes around tonguing her coworker in every empty room they come across?"

She leaned toward me. "One who recognizes that there are more important things in the world than work and rules?" she suggested gently.

I rubbed my gritty eyes. "I have a job. Then I'll be gone. Just like every other time. To some other resort, in some other town. Maybe in some other country."

She cocked her head. "So now we get to the real reason. Your fear of commitment."

"I'm not afraid of commitment," I argued instantly.

Her hysterical laughter was slightly offensive. She was actually struggling to breathe. She wiped her eyes. "Oh Lord, Charlotte, you're too funny."

"I'm not!" I objected. "I've been working for Freemont over a decade. I'm very committed."

She shook her head. "Charlotte, listen to yourself. You realize that you use your commitment to Freemont to avoid real commitment, right?"

"I…don't…" I actually wasn't sure about that. I'd never even given it thought. I never gave anything thought except resort business. "I don't."

She licked her lips and leaned across my desk. "Take it from someone who has made avoidance an Olympic sport. I've avoided every entanglement in every possible way for my entire life. I've avoided so hard I've spent years landing in a new port every couple of days, let alone every few months like you. I know what running away looks like. However you try to dress it up, you and I are two of a kind."

I wanted to object, but my breath was caught, trapped in my angry lungs.

She continued. "You just wear your reticence as respectability, instead of irresponsibility like me. You were engaged to Jared because you thought that was the responsible and proper thing, and you always do the responsible and proper thing. That was a relationship you could have because he didn't care about you. That meant you were protected from having to care about him. You're Freemont's best little power employee because traveling to every stupid resort on the freaking planet lets you live in your little box."

I opened my mouth and shut it again. I had no clue what to say. I had no desire to face her words. I didn't even want to think about them.

"You know that loving someone, or even needing another person in your life, that doesn't make you codependent."

The words buzzed around my brain. I hated the idea of loving anything. And needing someone—that was totally out of the question.

"You're so far gone that you won't even love objects or places. Loving doesn't always immediately make you weak, and it won't necessarily turn us into Mom. You can be someone's and still be your own. It's really true—I swear."

She stood. "I have to go clean out the lint traps in the linen room before someone misses me. Good times for everyone." She went to the door and turned back while I still stared at her, my brain rejecting any attempt at all to consider her words. "You know we aren't Mom. Neither of us. We won't ever be. And you know not every man is Dad, right? Not every man is Jared either." The door closed softly behind her.

We aren't Mom. Not every man is Dad.

I sat there, stunned for a long time. Could it be true? Could I be just as commitment phobic as Georgie? Did it just wear different pajamas? I stood, grabbing my abandoned clipboard and heading to the South Ballroom, where the Christmas tree would be set up and the guests would be offered special presents on Christmas Eve. The luau would be outside, but Santa would be inside, and everything needed to be perfect for the jolly old man with the bag. I wasn't going to think about Georgie's words. I was just going to work.

I stopped, frozen in my tracks. Even I could read the writing on the wall this time. I was going to avoid Georgie's unpleasant words by working. Dear Lord, she was right. She was right, and I was phobic. I was sick with the knowledge.

I shook my head hard. It didn't matter whether she was right or not. I really did need to work. This was no time to give in to an existential crisis. Christmas Eve was the day after the next, and that was when all the big festivities happened in Hawaii. The real day of Christmas would be spent relaxing on the beach by the majority of the population. Time was fleeting, and my to-do list was long.

I struggled to keep my focus all day, and Georgie's horrible words kept sneaking back. *You're so far gone, you won't even love objects or places.* Every time I pushed the thought away, but progress was slow. When I was done, I headed for the Lava Pot, desperate for Georgie's second-favorite avoidance technique—alcohol, and lots of it. Well, not lots of it for most people. For me two drinks was a lot. Three was way too much.

I slammed my drink, the Lava Pot's specialty, the incredibly potent Lava Flow Cocktail, as a nice alternative to losing my sanity, and ordered up another. Georgie slid onto the stool next to mine, shocking me for a second. "Two," she told the bartender, who was taking my order as she held up two fingers. Then she turned my way. "I'm sorry I'm not nicer, Charlotte. I do try. I'm just not very good at not taking care of business, no matter how rude I seem."

I waved the words away, sipping my new glass. "Really, who cares? Who cares about anything? Let's get drunk."

She stared at me. "You suck at being drunk."

I pointed at her. "Get drunk, or get lost."

She laughed. "Okay, look. Let's get buzzed. You won't be nearly as angry in the morning. And let's call Alex and get him over here with that card."

I lifted my glass. "I'll drink to that." At this point though, I would probably drink to anything.

She saluted me with her glass and glanced out over the gently lapping water. She made a face. "Wow, that's strong."

I shot the entire glass again, gesturing for the return of the bartender.

Like with all hot men, Georgie was immediately interested in him, though I was starting to understand her better. If he responded aggressively, I was honestly suspicious that she'd simply go back to her room. For a long time I'd believed Georgie would sleep with anyone at any time. I'd been wrong. Just like I was about a lot of things.

She put her hand over my glass. "We'll take two orange juices, one tiny shot of vodka. No more of this. And..." She reached up and slid the pen out of his shirt pocket, making sure to stroke his bulging pec underneath his supertight shirt. "Can I borrow your pen?"

He grinned and nodded, leaving to get our new drinks. She pulled a napkin closer and yanked off the pen cap. While she was doodling, I called Alex and told him to bring the card. It was dark in here, and if anyone even bothered to look at us, they wouldn't know what we were doing.

Georgie made a swirl in the corner of the napkin. "Okay, while we wait, let's write down everyone we talked about yesterday."

"Okay." I wanted to be annoyed at her for thwarting my mission to be drunk, but she was right. I'd be sorry tomorrow, the day before the big day, if I was hung over. "Mo, No Name, and Big Steve from Strangler's Cove Beach."

"Got them," she said, scrawling on the napkin.

"Squid. Henry, and Niall. Poncho, Keanu, and Autumn. Darcy Collins with the creepy nails is the one who told me about Joel Sugarbaker, the dead guy on the beach who was also Mallory's surfing instructor. Although she didn't mentioned he was dead, so I'm not sure she even knew. Though you'd think she did, considering everyone in town has been talking about it."

Georgie wrote everyone's name. "Okay, have any of these guys given you any indication they might be involved in drugs?"

I pointed to Niall's name. "Well, he had opium in two forms tattooed on his back, and he ended up dead facedown in a decimated field of opium poppies, so I'm going to say yes on him."

She laughed. "Yes, he's probably a good guess."

I shook my head. "The rest, I don't know. I don't know if they even know each other."

She pointed the pen in my direction. "Well, after we figure out what is written on the back of that card, that's our first order of business. Well, actually, our first order of business is to find out what No Name's name really is. Without that, it won't be real helpful to ask anyone about him."

"Maybe. Maybe not." I waited until the bartender came back and looked at his tag. "Hey, Casey." He had a quick smile and was likely the type who got big tips from men for making great drinks and big tips from women for being a beautiful display of manhood. "Do you know Mo and Big Steve? The surfers who seem to be at Strangler's Cove Beach no matter what time of day it is?"

He nodded. "Sure, yeah. Everyone knows those guys."

"Okay, do you know the name of that third guy? The one who's always with them?"

Casey seemed perplexed by the question, just the same as Alex had been. "We've only spoken once. But he said his name was…Johnny. That's what it was."

"Does he have a last name?"

He shrugged. "I remember the impression it gave me, and I'd know it if I heard it, but it was something improbable like palace. Some kind of big house."

Georgie and I glanced at each other and then back to him. "Castle?" Georgie suggested.

"Hey, yeah. That's it."

"Johnny Castle is Patrick Swayze's character in *Dirty Dancing*," I felt compelled to point out.

Casey shrugged again. "That's what he said. I only remember because I thought it was so weird to have that particular last name."

I nodded. "Okay, thanks. We really appreciate it."

I waited until Casey was gone. "So are we just going to assume that Johnny Castle is a fake name or give this guy the benefit of the doubt?"

"I don't know. It's a weird coincidence. So let's assume that we don't know what No Name's name actually is but refer to him as Johnny Castle when we ask other people."

She drew a sort of bubble diagram like our teachers used to make us use when drawing a map of an essay we planned to write. She circled Big Steve, Mo, and Johnny No Name. "We can be absolutely sure that these guys know each other. We also know they know Squid at least a little because they mentioned him by name. As it were." She drew a dotted line around Squid's name. "We don't know how well they know each other, which is the next thing to check. So tell me who knows everyone in town the best."

I shrugged. "I don't know. I live in my office." It was kind of embarrassing to admit that I didn't know anyone who didn't work directly for me. The problem was, half the staff was either on personal leave for Christmas or just plain out of town for the holidays. The people I could have asked for this kind of information were long gone.

"I hope Alex gets here soon," Georgie mused, chewing on the edge of her pen. "Knowing if these people know each other might help us figure out if there's a drug 'cartel' or three dudes in their mother's basement."

I nodded, my head feeling vaguely like it was rolling around on my neck. Perhaps two of the Lava Pot's strongest drink followed by a couple shots of vodka wasn't the best choice I'd ever made.

It was seven minutes later when Alex finally showed up, clad in a fitted brown V-neck tee and old tattered jeans. Clearly, he hadn't felt the need to dress up for the likes of us. He sat down next to Georgie, eyeing our drinks.

"Did you bring the card?" I asked?

He nodded and slid it across the bar, facing down so only the numbers were showing, in case someone bothered to look. I spent a long moment staring at the numbers, as though I were Sherlock Holmes and could reason it out by doing nothing.

Georgie handed him the napkin. "Hey, we're trying to figure out how all these people know each other. If nothing else, it could only help to know if they're possibly connected, even if it's not drug related."

He slid the napkin across the counter and silently read the names. He circled Niall and Henry and connected them to Mallory. Then he circled Darcy Collins and connected her to Mallory. He didn't darken in Squid's circle but did connect him to Mallory as well. By the time he was finished, everyone but Henry was directly connected to Mallory, and even Henry had a dotted line.

"Well, here's what we do know. Every one of these people is connected to Mallory. So she knew half the town of Aloha Lagoon. What does that mean?"

I had no idea what the answer to that was, but I was nearly certain it didn't mean she was a drug kingpin and the real head of any kind of operation that might have existed here. I refused to believe it. "Look, we know someone is growing drugs. We know that they have at least two friends willing to try to kill us for coming upon those drugs. We know multiple people are dead, though we don't specifically know these people killed them. We know that Mallory dated a man with multiple opium-related tattoos who later showed up dead in a cove where someone was growing opium. To me, that spells out his involvement. He might even have been one of the three who attacked us. He's dead now though, and we still don't know anything. The only solid lead we have is Seth Peterson, and he doesn't seem to have anything to do with anything."

Alex stared at the numbers. "Mallory didn't write this. From the square, cramped appearance, I'd guess a man did. Maybe Seth himself. So let's figure out what it means, and barring that, let's find Seth and just simply ask him."

We spent at least half an hour trying different orders and combinations of the numbers, trying to make them make sense, but none of it meant anything to me. Finally, Georgie gasped and grabbed the card, writing the numbers on our napkin note. She crossed out every other number, until what was left was two very different sequences of ten numbers. She drew a line between the first three numbers, the second three numbers, and the last four, leaving us staring at two potential phone numbers.

Alex grabbed his phone, obviously a replacement for the one he'd lost. "Georgie, you're a genius." He called the first number and held it away from his ear. "Number not in service. Let's try the second one."

He called the next number, and evidently it was answered. He listened in silence, though I wasn't sure how much he could hear with all the noise in the bar. He didn't respond to whatever he was listening to, even with a hello, leaving me to believe he was listening to a recording.

Finally, he hung up the phone. "Let's go. We need to find Seth Peterson. Immediately."

* * *

Seth wasn't at the hotel. The bars and restaurants around the resort were hopping. I was way too drunk to drive with the two cocktails and the vodka orange juices. Alex drove, and I tripped a lot trying to traverse the sandy walks of the buildings. When I asked what the phone number was, Alex handed me the

phone, leaving me to listen in silence to the recorded message
that I had reached the Drug Enforcement Agency and if I knew
the party I wanted to reach, I was free to dial their extension at
any time. Sadly, I didn't know Seth Peterson's extension, but I
was fairly certain I knew why he and Mallory had really been
spending time together.

Our search of the local hot spots, as they were, also
didn't produce Seth Peterson, and I wasn't ready to ask Detective
Ray, in case he wasn't aware that it was very possible Seth was a
DEA agent. And it was very possible Mallory had grabbed his
card to call him, and accidentally grabbed the wrong one, the one
that he gave everyone, not the one with his number coded on the
back. It struck me as unbearably sad she'd planned to reach out
for help, had depended on the card in her hand, and had died
holding it. We really needed to find Seth.

We searched every place we could think of, short of
showing up at Seth Peterson's house, the address of which would
be in his personnel file. It wouldn't be an immediate leap to him
being a federal agent if we showed up at his house, but if
someone in the drug business suspected him already, if they
were watching him, we didn't know what kind of trouble we
could get him in. Our last stop of the night was Ramada Pier,
where Squid sat, smoking pot where anyone could see him,
which I found somewhat mystifying, though maybe I shouldn't
have considering he'd been stoned at lunchtime on the day we'd
talked to him. That required a certain level of commitment.

We headed to approach him, when suddenly Johnny No
Name, Mo, and Big Steve crossed to him, not speaking loudly
enough to be heard over the din of people on vacation making
double meaning of the words *holiday spirits* all over the island.
Alex indicated with his head that we should follow him, and we
approached the group in time to hear Big Steve say, "Where'd
you get those shoes, bra?"

It was certainly not as exciting as I might have hoped.
Alex approached and fist-bumped or shook hands with all four
men. I glanced at Squid's shoes, trying hard to see what was so
special about a pair of neon high-top sneakers that looked a bit
like Nike knockoffs to me.

"Hey, I didn't realize you guys all hung out together." Alex sounded excited, like he wanted to join them, and I applauded his ability to fit in anywhere he went.

The men all glanced at each other. "We don't really. We barely know each other, actually. But those shoes are boss," Big Steve offered.

There was nothing about their conversation that suggested the opposite was true before we'd arrived either. This was all so frustrating.

Alex was undaunted. "I got a pair like that at the pier in Kapa'a."

Squid pointed at him. "Hey, me too, man. That's where I got them. One hundred bucks cash from the trunk of some old Chinese dude's car."

Alex laughed. "Me too."

Big Steve pointed at Squid. "Is that the same guy we bought that knockoff grill from three years ago?"

Squid nodded. "It's right next to that shaved ice stand. You ever go there?"

Johnny No Name, who apparently wasn't a fan of shaved ice, shook his head. Big Steve nodded pointlessly, since no one was looking at him but me. Squid was clearly gravely disappointed.

"You should try it, dude. It's way better than Chinese shoes."

Likely, that was profound wisdom from Squid, but I would pass on both. The conversation proceeded until it petered out, the way conversations do with people you meet at random in a crowded place, and eventually we bid each other good-bye, and the three of us set off in the direction of the resort, while No Name, Mo, and Big Steve headed for the Lava Pot. Squid stayed where he was, sitting on the back of a bench and staring out into the ocean, pot-glazed eyes focused on the reflection of the stars and twinkle lights on the pier.

"Well, that was a pointless conversation," Georgie said, once we got far enough away that we couldn't possibly be overheard.

"No, it wasn't. We got a great tip on shaved ice. And a contact high," Alex argued.

* * *

When we got back to the resort, we tried Seth's coded DEA number again, listening patiently to the list of extensions. None of the names were familiar, though it was unlikely, upon reflection, that Seth Peterson was actually Seth Peterson. He'd been hanging around for months, and now, when we really needed to talk to him, he was nowhere to be found.

He could have filled in blanks, if he was willing. We still had no idea if Henry played any role in his brother's probably growing operation, but none of us was willing to drive all the way back out to Kapa'a on the off chance he might be hanging out at Spiker's despite the death of his brother two days before. I suspected that Seth would know who all the players were, if we could convince him to tell us. And if we could ever find him.

We bid each other good night, and I headed to my room, my mind an endless loop of mysteries I couldn't solve, regrets for the death of Mallory for seemingly no reason, unwanted attraction to Alex, and rumination on Georgie's words earlier about my fear of commitment.

Around four I finally slipped into fitful sleep, and when my alarm went off at five, I nearly threw it out the window. I stumbled through a cold shower, hoping it would get my mind off murder, Seth, Georgie, drugs, and Alex, and three cups of bad coffee in my quarters. One slightly wrinkled outfit, halfhearted makeup job, and another cup of coffee later, I stumbled to the lobby, none too happy.

Darcy seemed startled to see me, and honestly, I didn't blame her. I looked like crap, and I felt even worse. I was exhausted, I was scared and sad, I was sexually frustrated, and I was at the end of my rope. At the start of business hours, I would try the DEA again, though I had no idea who I'd even talk to. The receptionist wouldn't know the false names that agents used, and I didn't know who to ask for. A quick look at the time sheets showed that Seth had not shown up for work.

I picked up the mail and headed back to my office, sorting through it and discovering that Georgie had a package. When I looked at the return address and realized it was a replacement phone, I had to admit I was jealous. Mine hadn't come yet, and I was deprived without a way to constantly check on what the other employees and contractors were doing to get ready for the big day.

I brought her the package into the offices where she was making copies for someone in the accounting department. "New phone."

She grabbed it with obvious glee. "They're so fast. Yay me."

"Physical prep for the luau begins today, so if you could just help whoever seems to need it. They'll be building up the special stoves they use to cook the big, dead pigs. So that's exciting."

"One dead pig. Check."

"Actually, I think it will be three dead pigs. The whole town comes up."

Georgie laughed. "Multiple dead porkers. Check."

"See you later," I said, headed out to check on every single detail.

The time had come. Tomorrow was the big day, and I had no time to be distracted by Georgie, murder, or Alex. As much as I might have wanted to devote myself to the mystery at hand, I was forced to spend all day on the run, checking to ensure every detail was perfect. Caterers were in and out all day, and the kitchen was crazy. Out on the beach, locals were helping to build the *imu*, waiting for the trucks to bring the virgin pig sacrifices. Young men from the town were out on the beach, digging the massive holes where the underground pit would be built and the pigs roasted. Things people never thought of—transportation, manpower, arrangement of chairs—needed to be addressed.

I was headed past the employee break room, and I stepped backward when I spotted Georgie inside. There was no question she was in turmoil. The question was why. I was busy, but not too busy to stop for a moment. I headed through the doorway and waited for her to notice me, which she didn't.

I sat down next to Georgie, who was staring at her phone in bleak desperation. "That's not how I usually look at a brand new phone," I said softly.

She sniffed, blinking hard. "I was just downloading my old photos from the cloud." She shut off her phone and plastered on a trembling smile. It was so fake it hurt me.

I knew she'd probably just get angry with me again, but I couldn't stand to see her hurting this way after we'd finally started to repair our relationship. I knew what was in those pictures, because I'd begun to see what hurt Georgie the most—the only thing I'd ever seen her really care about. Her relationship with Martin Gentry, whatever that might have been.

"Georgie, what happened with you and Marty?"

Her eyes immediately filled with tears, and I looked away while she struggled to contain herself, because I knew she'd want to pretend she was always strong. It was what we did. She was always strong and sassy. I was always professional and efficient. Anything else wasn't acceptable. But it hurt to pretend, especially when I wanted to do something for her so badly.

She didn't speak for a long time, and I wasn't sure if she was simply avoiding the question or if she was just trying to compose herself before speaking. "Remember how I was talking about Alex, and how I knew he was interested because I know men, and I know when they want more than friendship or professional courtesy?"

Of course I did. It had been both welcome and a displeasure to hear it. "Yes."

"Well, I also know when they don't."

Her voice broke at the end, and she turned her back to me again.

I pulled in a deep breath and put my hand on her trembling back. Those seven words explained everything without her having to do it out loud.

She was in love with Marty, and somehow, he was not in love with her.

I couldn't make heads or tails of the information. I couldn't imagine Georgie in love with anyone at all. No matter how hard I tried to imagine. She was just so…remote. Not that I wasn't. But she gave everything physically and held back everything emotional. In every single relationship she had. I'd never seen any indication she was even capable of deep love for a man. And I couldn't imagine Georgie wanting a man and him rejecting her. That didn't even seem like a possibility.

"Does he...does he know how you feel?"

Her shoulders were wracked with the tremors of silent sobbing. I rubbed her back while she cried for a long time. I was in agony. Comforting people wasn't my forte, and she was so desperately in need of comfort. If I hadn't already known at the beach, I knew it now. I'd forgiven Georgie. She made stupid choices, but she hadn't done it to hurt me. She'd done it to stop me from making what she viewed as the worst mistake of my life. It was an act of dumbass desperation. Just like coming here out of nowhere.

"No. He doesn't know anything. We're just friends in his head."

"Well, what did you tell him when you quit?" Wouldn't he have figured it out, considering how emotional she was about it?

"Nothing," she whispered. "I didn't tell him anything. I snuck into his room and left a note on the bed with him telling him I quit, and I ran when the ship was docked. I can't bear it. I can't keep acting like my feelings don't matter or don't exist. It's agony. And I can't hide it either. If I stayed, eventually he was going to know."

"Maybe you should have just told him?" It was a gentle suggestion. Something I thought sounded reasonable. I'd certainly never been in a similar situation, so I had no practical advice to give, but it seemed like the rational thing to do to tell him, and then she wouldn't have been carrying around the secret.

"I can't. I can't bear the idea of him knowing how helpless I am for him. It would be so humiliating, but more than that, it would be the end of our friendship."

A touch of amusement crept in. "And your sudden early morning flight with no notice but a note saying you quit wasn't the end of your friendship?"

She waved her hand. "No, not us. It's not unlike the kind of thing I would do anyway. I've done weirder things before. Chalk it up to my impulsive nature, and move on. I just need a break. I can't handle being on the boat with him anymore. If I have some time away to build up my resistance, I can go back, and I'll be fine."

"Well, how do you know he isn't secretly harboring feelings for you too?"

It seemed like a reasonable question, but I was alarmed by her trembling breath. "Because I know men. I know the signs. I might as well not be a girl, for all he notices me as a potential mate."

I just couldn't believe that. Georgie was way too hot for any man to not see her as a potential mate. At least once in a while. "Okay, well, what *is* his type, then?"

She shrugged. "I don't know. There's nothing in common between the ones I've met except they're all crazy glamorous. I don't really do glamour."

For all her sexiness that I envied, Georgie was right about that. She didn't do glamour. I couldn't even imagine her in an evening gown or wearing some elegant upsweep and our grandmother's jewels.

"Every one of them has been an actress, some celebutant, or a supermodel. Straight down the line. It's clear he doesn't even like these women, but he just keeps dating them." She sighed. "I don't know what the hell he wants. It isn't even clear. He just works all day like a machine, drinks all weekend until he's basically unconscious, and hits the world hard like a linebacker desperate for a scholarship, until he's drained every single possible moment of enjoyment out of every possible experience. He never stays with any girl very long. Maybe if he did, I could move on. I'd be jealous and miserable, but I'd move on, knowing he was committed to someone else. The only thing he's committed to is me and Sapporo, not necessarily in that order. Those girls are just sex for him, or a way to kill time."

"And you don't want to just be sex or a way to kill time," I filled in.

She shook her head, blinking back tears again. "But I'm afraid if he offered even that much, I'd take it, because I'm desperately in love with him."

I would have liked to imagine myself above that kind of desperation, but it wouldn't be true. If I felt like I could survive a relationship with Alex, I would take anything he offered, because I was also desperate. There was no point in lying. And I couldn't even fall back on the excuse that we were great friends that had morphed into something deeper. I was just on fire for him.

I sighed. I was about to do something that was against my very nature with the luau tomorrow. "Why don't you take the rest of the day off and go to the beach or something?"

She stared at me like I was talking crazy. "Seriously?"

I shrugged and nodded. "Sure. Just…don't take the phone."

She wiped her cheeks and laughed. "That's okay. I'm fine. I'll be outside, watching heavily muscled, slick with sweat, half-naked Polynesian dudes dig pig holes. Ciao."

I watched her leave and sighed. If only I was as good at riding the tide. I wasn't. I went back to the conference room where the tables for the Santa visit, as well as the children's activities, would be. From the window, I watched Alex in the lobby. He was so good with the employees. They loved him so much. If we could merge into a single manager, we'd be perfect.

The idea of Alex and I merging in any way wasn't a good one. Actually, it was. Even the idea was incredible. I picked up a coloring sheet from the pile, folded it, and fanned myself, ignoring the employee who was staring at me staring at Alex. Then he turned, and he was staring at me too. Oh, good Lord. I swallowed, struggling for breath. He didn't bother to hide his lust. It was written all over his face.

I couldn't stand it. I couldn't. Not after spending all night drenched in sweat, tossing and turning, fantasizing about this man. When Alex looked at me like that, I become nothing but a quivering mass of hormones, screaming for attention. I licked my lips. I was smarter than this. I was. I knew if I had sex with him, no matter how much I wanted it, I would never get over it. Yet, I still heard my throaty voice carry over the radio without my permission. Apparently, it was a sacrifice I was willing to make.

"There's a problem with the linens, Alex. Can I please see you in the linen room?"

He caught his tongue between his teeth, his lopsided grin punching me straight in the libido. "Ten four, *Boss*."

I'd never called him before. Never asked him to meet me somewhere. He was clearly delighted that I'd caved. I wasn't. It represented a weakness I couldn't seem to do anything about. I tried walking casually to the linen closet, but I couldn't. Within seconds, my clipped steps were nearly a run. When I stepped inside, he was right behind me. He slammed the door hard, and in seconds I was in his arms pushed up against the door, skirt ruched up, legs wrapped around his waist, with Alex kissing me hard.

"*Charlie*. You are slaughtering me. You are so hot. I can't stand it." The words were ripped from his throat.

If he thought he was tortured, he should stand in my shoes. If I hadn't already kicked them off. I didn't even want to do this. I knew I'd never be so sorry as I'd be when I left this place. I just couldn't bear not to do it. We'd done this before, but this was different. This was burning stabs of his tongue, hard bites, tearing at clothing. If I didn't nip this in the bud, I would be having sex with a man I really shouldn't even be with, in the middle of a workday. In a closet. Surrounded by dirty linen.

I wanted it so bad.

"Stop," I murmured, then arched my back when he ripped open my blouse and his hand was in my bra. "We're in a closet."

He felt so good. I couldn't stop shaking. I kissed him until it hurt, tearing at his mouth and tongue with my teeth. His clear lack of control, the trembling of his body underneath his disheveled clothes, the harsh panting of his breath. They were making me crazy, powerful with lust and my control over this man.

"This is a workplace." It was hard to say anything reasonable when he was grinding against me, and it would only take a few very small adjustments to take this exactly where I needed so hard for it to go.

"Meet me tonight at my house," he ordered. It wasn't a request. That was *so* hot.

Now that he was speaking so plainly, the reality of what I was initiating came crashing back, and I couldn't. He was going to hate me. But I couldn't do it. *It would kill me.* I wouldn't survive it. It would be a million times worse than my ruined wedding to walk away from him after this went any further.

Finally I choked out, "I can't. I'll have sex with you."

It sounded better, more reasonable, in my head.

He chuckled, and I felt it all through my body. "I know. That's the point."

I shook my head again. "I can't." I couldn't make sentences. Not ones that would make sense. I had told him this was okay with my every behavior. But sense and panic were overriding lust. I was leaving. *I was leaving.* As soon as I could. I couldn't bear it. I couldn't bear the way it would feel if I let him really touch me and then walked away.

Finally, he paused, hand tickling up my thigh, fingers seconds from teasing into my very unwelcome panties. "Why not?" I heard the dangerous tone to his voice.

"I have to go."

"No one will miss you for a little bit."

I shook my head. "No, I just...I have to go. Aloha Lagoon isn't my permanent assignment. Eventually Freemont is going to call me somewhere else. I don't even know why I'm still here. I can't...I can't have sex with you when I'm leaving. I'm sorry. I really thought I could. But I can't."

He didn't ask me why not, which seemed like the first question a man would normally ask me. That made him dangerous, because then maybe he knew how I felt about him. How much it would hurt to walk away from him. I was trying to minimize the damage, in any way I could. It was already too late. He was far under my skin now. Alex Cho had completely bewitched me. I refused to give my emotions a name, but they were overpowering. If I let him touch me, I wouldn't be able to refuse the name. It would just be there.

He finally stepped away from me slightly, and I slid to the floor. "You're still so eager to leave?"

I struggled to control the ache in my throat that felt a lot like an urgent need to weep. "It's my job, Alex." I blinked against the grainy burn behind my eyelids. It was best to get this over with now. "I'm sorry. Truly, I thought I could do this. But I can't. I'm leaving, and I can't."

"You know they'd give you the manager slot here if you wanted it." He spoke so quietly, his voice even, almost dead. He didn't sound like my Alex at all. *My Alex*. Lord. I was so far gone.

I needed to get out of Hawaii. I did. It wasn't safe for me here. And I didn't want to live forever like this. Aching for a man my own neuroses wouldn't let me be with. Georgie was right. I was controlled by fear. *We aren't Mom. Every man isn't Dad.* But what if I was? What if he was? Then how would I live? My only hope of getting over it was to get away from Alex.

"Being the manager of one resort isn't my job. I work at resorts in flux. You know that. I was never meant to be here even this long."

He stared at me for a long second then licked his lips. "Yeah. Okay. I get it."

He reached around me and opened the door to the room, and I nearly fell out. I would have, if he hadn't grabbed my arm. He released it very quickly, as though it burned. This was a different man than the one I'd had in my arms five minutes before.

I tried to tell myself it was better, while he straightened his disheveled clothing. I tried to tell myself it should have been this way all along, while he nodded in my direction, trying so hard to look like he wasn't something that looked a lot like heartbroken. I tried to convince myself I didn't care, while he walked away down the hall. Then I went to my office and tried to pretend I wasn't crying.

CHAPTER THIRTEEN

———

I spent the rest of the day in a daze, praying that my release from Aloha Lagoon would come soon. I couldn't do this anymore. I had to do what I'd always accused Georgie of doing every time times got tough. I had to run. If I didn't, I'd be sorry. I had to run before I couldn't deny my feelings. And I could not do that. I left multiple messages for both Nadine Rivers and Mr. Kowalski at corporate, begging for a reassignment. I tried to be professional, but heaven only knew if they could hear the agony and desperation in my voice.

I avoided Alex. If I saw he was already in a room, I turned at the door and fled like the coward I was. I got through the rest of the day and the night before Christmas Eve by focusing completely on work. I was really good at using work to squelch my feelings. I would do it now. And when my feelings—sadness, anger with myself, desperation—tried to surface, I pushed them down brutally. Work. It had to be about work.

The DEA was no help when I called them from my desk in the afternoon. They said they didn't know a Seth Peterson. When I asked to talk to a manager, they also told me they didn't know a Seth Peterson. He didn't show up for work at seven, and Detective Ray refused to give me any information on him.

I wanted to stay up late again and scout the town, trying to find Seth. I wanted to do something, anything, to feel like I was moving our investigation forward. But I couldn't do that. Because time was up for resort business, and I knew I had to get some sleep.

I was up at four thirty on Christmas Eve morning, on the beach, checking on the underground ovens roasting pigs, monitoring the dozens of dishes coming in and out of the kitchen, watching Ikaika repair more lights burnt out on the big palm. From taro to turkey, caterers and citizens alike were bringing their dishes to the resort. Because people in Hawaii just couldn't resist one more chance to revel in the spectacular and over the top, every car that rolled up was ridiculously decorated, parading up the drive covered in decorations and blaring Christmas music. Many had thousands of lights draped off their cars, honking their horns at the delighted residents and guests.

To tell the truth, I didn't mind it. A sliver of a nasty urge to love this place was trying to push its way up in my throat, and I wouldn't have it. By noon, guitar and ukulele players wearing Hawaiian shirts and Santa hats had rolled up on the resort, ready to entertain guests. Excitement was in the air, everyone in town was arriving, and the guests were having the time of their lives. I ignored Alex, who was working just as hard as I was. If he was disappointed in my behavior, it wasn't amiss. I was disappointed in me. But that didn't mean I could change.

The outdoor tables began to fill with everything from *haupia*, a coconut and chocolate pie, to the finished pigs, now glazed and sitting on the tables in all their disconcerting giant pigness. Several bowls of a chicken noodle soup–like substance with added raw fish peppered the table. Mashed potatoes and cranberries rested between spring rolls and sushi.

I had to admit I was delighted, and I was doing everything in my power not to be. There was nothing I wanted to love about Hawaii, because apparently Georgie was right. I could call it responsibility, but the truth was I was like a shark emotionally. If I didn't keep moving, I would die.

The party just kept building until I was very sure every single person in AL and possibly in every small burg nearby was on the Aloha Lagoon grounds. I saw Detective Ray, his men, and Silas all roving the beach, keeping an eye on the visitors in between bites. I didn't expect any problems, and it was clear they didn't either, but crowd control was never useless, just in case something went wrong.

Dinner started right on time. Though I felt incredibly awkward with him, Alex and I took the floor and welcomed everyone. Just like the first night, we spoke our holiday sentiments in English and then in Hawaiian. Parents ate and danced. Children darted between tables, laughing and screaming. "Mele Kalikimaka" floated in the air, and my agony pressed at my throat, trying to sneak out as tears.

Mallory would have delighted in this spectacle. The thought was sobering. If only I could have saved her. If only she'd chosen to confide in me. Not that I would have known if she had, because I'd never been listening. Not to her unimportant ramblings nor to anything that might have been an important clue. I simply hadn't cared. That I did now, well, that didn't help anyone. Not Mallory, not me.

I kept busy as long as I could, and when I couldn't anymore, I had no choice. I would have to seek out Alex. I could tell myself it was because we still had to work together, but it wasn't that. I didn't want him to be angry at me, though he had every right to be. The kids watched with delight as Santa arrived on his surfboard, no outrigger or dolphins this time, sadly, and followed him inside like he was the Pied Piper. The parents were close behind, aiming for photo ops. The childless people were hitting the alcohol hard.

I followed Alex into the building. "Can I talk to you for a minute? Please."

I watched a sigh move through his frame. "Do we really need to? You don't have to justify yourself whether you do or don't want me."

I shook my head. "I think we both know me not wanting you is *not* the issue."

He finally looked at me. "Then what is?"

I ran a hand through my hair and then regretted it when it mussed my careful style. Presentation still mattered, no matter how upset I was. "I just...can't. I...really like you, Alex. And no matter what, I still have to go. And if I'm weak and I let this happen the way we want it to happen, later maybe you won't be sorry, but...I will. I'll be sorry in a way that I can't even explain right now. Do you understand what I'm saying?"

Maybe he did, because I wasn't sure I did. At the very least, I wasn't sure I was making sense or doing anything to articulate how I felt at the moment. I couldn't put it in plain words. If I slept with Alex, I'd be a goner. And I couldn't do that. Because I couldn't stay here.

He evaluated me for a long moment under drawn eyebrows. "I don't know. I don't know if I understand you or if I'm trying to read something into your words because I want to hear them."

I swallowed hard. "You aren't reading anything into my words," I whispered, telling the truth cutting me hard. "I'm sure you understand me."

Even if I wasn't capable of properly articulating my feelings, maybe he understood anyway. Hell, he probably understood my feelings better than I did. I was going to leave, because I always left, and when I left, it was going to hurt. And if I let myself fall in love with him, it would hurt even worse.

His slow, deep sigh hurt me. "It doesn't have to be like this, Charlie. We can work something out."

"It does. Please don't be angry or hurt. It isn't you. It's me. Lord knows that's such a cliché, but it's true. It isn't you. It's all me."

He met my eyes. "I know. And I can't change that for you. And for that, I'm sorry too."

I nodded, praying I didn't start trying to tear up again, because I wasn't doing that. Feeling sure he understood what I was trying to say, I turned and sought out Georgie. Who would have guessed a couple of weeks ago that she would ever be a balm for my wounded heart?

She was handing out bags to the kids as they left the door, carefully prepared gift bags full of gift cards for childcentric activities all over the island, not just in AL. I found another employee to replace her and dragged her off to the main lobby.

"Are you enjoying Christmas in Hawaii?"

I hoped she was. It would make up for the fact I really wasn't, even though I enjoyed the elements.

Georgie laughed. "It's insane. I've never seen anything like it. I…"

Her voice trailed off, her expression dropping to total blankness. She stared at the front door. Her eyes turned haunted.

I turned. What else was there to do? There was something in that doorway that had acted as a nuclear bomb to Georgie's brain.

There were only two people in the doorway; a middle-aged dad hauling a screaming toddler back to their room and a man who wasn't too much older than us—mid to late thirties at my best guess. I knew it wasn't doting Dad, because that didn't make sense. So it had to be the other man. He looked innocuous. Actually, he looked a lot like British actor Martin Freeman, with his blondish hair touched with premature gray, tired eyes, and open, approachable face. And that comparison made me think. What if he didn't just look like a man named Martin? Maybe he really *was* a man named Martin. I glanced back to Georgie again.

The agony in her eyes was unmistakable, though she kept her expression indifferent. I was right. There was no one else he could be. This man was Marty Gentry. If I was shocked to see him here, I could only imagine how Georgie felt about his sudden appearance. He saw me first. I could see the short moment of surprise cross his features. It wasn't extreme surprise, so it was clear he'd known of my existence. What wasn't clear was whether he hadn't expected her to join me or he was merely taken aback at how different I could look for being Georgie's identical twin.

His eyes moved from me to Georgie, and she underwent a sudden transformation that I found rather alarming. She went from agony to a flip wave of her hand and an easy smile. How did she do that?

I turned my eyes back to Marty Gentry again, trying to wrap my mind around the fact that this was the man who had finally captured the wild heart of Georgiana Conner, the person who had broken hearts the world over. The one who wouldn't even commit to planning a monthly delivery of a magazine, because that tied her down too much, was now so in love with this man that she couldn't work with him anymore. He wasn't that tall, maybe 5'9", with the body of runner—wiry and graceful but not heavily muscled. Adorably awkward, he looked more like someone's dad that you would have secretly thought was kind of hot in high school, than any kind of heartbreaker.

I remembered Georgie's offhand comment that Marty only dated supermodels and actresses. It might have been his multimillion-dollar Gentry family price tag that brought some of those bleached blondes into his range, but that wouldn't be a motivator for Georgie. I knew that was true. She was flippant and partied hard, but she didn't care about money. If she needed some, she found some. And it couldn't be true of every woman who entered the sphere of Martin Gentry. There was something about this man that encompassed far more than his boyish face, mussed-up hair, rolled-up blue jeans, superhero T-shirt, and green dock shoes without socks. I just didn't know what it was yet.

He crossed to us, returning Georgie's offered fist bump with the impatient twist of his mouth that suggested irritation at having to go through the motions of a customary greeting. He looked so much like a younger Martin Freeman that I sincerely expected him to have an English accent when he spoke, but alas, he didn't. The heavy twang of someone who only could have originated from the deep, deep South didn't fit his appearance at all. I hoped I schooled my expression enough that he couldn't tell how surprising everything about him was to me.

"What the hell, George? You just walk out on me without a word? That's BS."

The no-nonsense tone of voice he used didn't leave a lot of room for her to dodge around the question the way she might have done had I asked. Or anyone else who didn't quite know how to handle the hurricane that was Georgie. I glanced at her, unsure if she was okay with this abrupt way of speaking, like he was challenging her. Not that I had a clue what I could do besides give him the boot if he *was* making her uncomfortable.

She waved him off with a flippant flick of her hand. "You know me, Marty. I knew something I wanted was close by, and so I went for it." She flashed him a smile I could tell was weak around the edges. Honestly, from the body language tells that managed to sneak past her front of indifference, I suspected she was hard pressed not to cry.

He shook his head, lips twisting. "And I would have been totally cool with that. Totally cool, and you know it. Instead I wake up with a crappy note, and you're just gone? It was two words, George." He held up one finger at the first word and then a second for the next word. "I. Quit."

She shrugged, some of her discomfort starting to show through. "You were passed out. What did you want?"

He cocked his head. From his inscrutable expression, I wasn't sure what he'd say next, but he was clearly pissed and not afraid to challenge Georgie like the rest of the world, so who knew. If he got too aggressive though, I'd make sure someone saw him out.

"I wanted you to give me the respect I deserve. You and I are way beyond that piece-of-crap note. If you wanted to visit your sister, you didn't have to quit. You know I don't care what you do. And if there's any advantage to being best friends with the boss, it's that I won't even make you kiss my ass to get all the time off you want."

I was beginning to see why Georgie and Marty were two of a kind. And I was also starting to like him. There was something about his frank honesty and up-front dialogue that was hugely refreshing. I glanced at Georgie again, monitoring her unconscious tells, trying to gauge when I'd need to push the conversation to an ending. I frankly wasn't sure what Georgie would do at this point. She was so hard to read when the subject was Marty.

"I'm sorry." She didn't sound completely sorry, but there was an edge of repentance in her words. "I just didn't want to have a huge discussion about it, and anyway, we were about to leave the dock. It was then or never."

I noticed Alex approaching, sensing there was some kind of problem. When he got close enough, I held up a hand behind Georgie's back, hinting he shouldn't get involved. Not yet anyway. I didn't know where this was going, but I was pretty sure they just needed to work it out.

Marty ran a hand through his already badly disheveled hair. "Are you seriously going to quit on me?" There was desperation behind the question, but I didn't see barely restrained passion or secret love.

It seemed that Georgie was right. Marty Gentry clearly loved Georgie, but maybe he didn't view her as a potential partner. Maybe not even as a woman at all. I wasn't sure how I'd feel about being the one with an unrequited passion for my boss, but I was fairly certain it wasn't an experience I'd enjoy. I was badly mussing up a completely requited passion for my equal around the office. It must have been so difficult for her.

She swallowed. "I don't know." I could barely hear the words right next to her. I wasn't sure Marty could at all. "I'm not ready to leave. I want to be with Charlotte. For a long time. Maybe years. That's a lot of vacation time." The second half was spoken with more force, like she regaining herself from the surprise of his arrival.

He stared her down for a long minute, eyebrows pulled together, mouth tight. So long I started to feel uncomfortable, so heaven only knew how she felt. His tongue darted out, licking his lips.

Then he looked at me. I was shocked by the sudden eye contact, feeling slightly electrocuted, though I wasn't the one with feelings for him. There was a bizarre intensity about meeting his eyes that had nothing to do with my feelings for him as a stranger and everything to do with his personal electricity, the force of his...aliveness. I understood it, then. Why Georgie loved him. He came off like a little boy, but he was clearly a man, maybe too much for anyone who wasn't as full of sass and attitude as Georgie.

He offered a hand, flashing a dimpled smile that was completely, disarmingly charming. "Hi. I'm Martin Gentry, of the Mississippi Gentrys. I don't have a résumé on hand, but I've been working at hotels, motels, yachts, dinghies, and rental shacks since I was old enough to toddle. Now I run an entire cruise line, though that could be blatant nepotism as much as it's a sign of my proficiency in the hospitality field. George should vouch for me, considering that I've saved her ass from being thrown in prison in just about every continent in this world, but given she isn't in for doing that, I can write you up a list of references. I'm particularly good at tending bar, throwing out annoying people, and delivering mail, although I know about everything about hospitality. Are you hiring?"

I stared at him, completely flummoxed. A request for a job from a man worth dozens of times my material wealth wasn't something I'd expected. I blinked at him for a couple of awkward seconds, until Alex stepped forward, shaking Marty's hand too.

"Hi. I'm Alex Cho, one of the managers here. I take it you're a friend of Georgiana?"

Marty snorted, either at the appellation of "friend" after Georgie's sudden departure, or at the use of her full name. "Guilty as charged, of that and so many other things that might, or might not, be illegal in our last port of call."

Alex smiled. "So you want a job?"

He shrugged. "If George is here, I guess I'm here, too. I'm really good at hospitality, and I'm also a very hard worker. To let you know up front, I like to spend my weekends drunk off my ass, so something Monday to Friday would definitely be best."

It was the frank way he said it, as though it was simply a given, the way another person might say they left town on weekends to care for an ailing parent, that surprised a laugh out of me.

He pointed at me. "By the way, I'm also really honest. This is either my best or worst personality trait, depending on who you ask."

Alex was clearly completely delighted. "As far as I'm concerned, you're hired."

I couldn't tell too much from Georgie's body language, so when both men turned to me, I held up a finger. "Hang on for just a minute, will you?"

I pulled Georgie off to the side and pulled out the hiring log, burying both our faces behind it. "We don't have to do this. Just because he wants to be here doesn't mean we have to allow him to be."

A shuddering sigh passed through Georgie. "The thing is, he knows I want to be around him. He wouldn't have followed me if he'd believed I was no longer willing to be his friend. He believes I just left because I wanted to be with you. Unless I'm willing to tell him why I really don't want to be with him, there's no smooth way out of this."

"So let it not be smooth. Do you want him or not?"

I hated the pure pain in her eyes. "I always want him. That's the problem."

Time for proper clarification. "Should I hire him or not?"

She shook her head, but then said, "Yes, go ahead."

I wasn't completely moved by her conviction, but I didn't know quite what else to do. I lowered the log and pasted on a smile, crossing back toward them. "We have a single position available in the bar, but we only want licensed bartenders. We also have a position in security, one in housekeeping, and two for bellboys."

"As it happens, I'm a licensed bartender. But I think I'm most interested in security."

I nodded. "Our real head of security is not around right now. He may want to interview you when he gets back in January, and he may find you're a better fit in a different position, but for right now, let me page Silas."

I stepped slightly away and got on the radio, paging Silas to come to the lobby. I let them work it out and went back to work, debating Marty's appearance the entire time. I wanted to be that person. The one who wasn't afraid to take what I wanted. It was the thing I'd always envied the most about Georgie, though the time had come I could see there was one risk she wouldn't take. I'd spent my entire life avoiding risk, while people like Georgie and Marty took risks like vitamins, swallowing life whole.

After everyone was gone into town for the big candle-lighting ceremony, the employees in charge of cleaning up had begun their work, and I couldn't avoid seeing other employees again. I went to the Lava Pot and found Alex, Marty, and Georgie already there. I collapsed in a chair and put my head on the bar. Alex reached out a hand and rubbed my back, and I let him because I was a horrible person.

Marty and Georgie were in the midst of a conversation. Alex was silent and slouched in his seat. Georgie had come alive. The old sister I remembered was back, as though some of Marty's incredibly electric energy was the thing that animated her. Her depression must have been acute, though it had taken me days to notice it.

"Oh yeah. And we got that snakehead coffee cup from the dude with the hammer nose at that market in Nepal, and then we'd have some stupid-ass bet every weekend to see who got to keep the cup in their cabin for the week," Georgie recalled, joining Marty in hysterical laughter that told me they'd already had plenty to drink, they were simply high on being back together, or the bets they'd undertaken really were painfully stupid, and I didn't want to even know what they were.

I chanced a peek at Alex, who shrugged, looking as befuddled as I was. Either by their shared humor, by what a snakehead coffee cup was, or by what a hammer nose was. It really could have been any or all of the above.

Missing my phone, I snatched Georgie's off the counter and scrolled through, prepared to find Candy Crush or something like it, desperate for a moment of escape from reality. But Georgie had the camera open. She'd been taking selfies again. I scrolled through Georgie's photograph history, taking in hundreds of pictures of the planet she'd been exploring for the last two years.

Almost every one of them had Martin Gentry in them. From silly, playful selfies with the two of them to pictures that he clearly didn't know were being taken, on high mountains and in front of Chinese temples. Grinning friends, drinking foreign beers, eating food I'd never be brave enough to eat, climbing mountains, jumping from planes, and conquering the world. There was something so poignant about this travelogue captured through images.

I'd never been so close to anyone, not even Georgie, my own twin. The closeness and chemistry between them couldn't have been more obvious, even on film. They had these smiles for each other that I'd only ever seen on people deeply in love. People who were so happy to be together that they just couldn't contain it. Except there was nothing in his behavior that suggested he was in love with her. She was right. He was in it for the friendship, and there was no question it was the closest friendship I'd ever seen. No wonder she'd felt the need to flee. My heart hurt for her. It must have been agony to be with or without him. I couldn't imagine which was worse.

I closed her phone and laid it down, games forgotten. I sighed, exhaustion moving through my frame until I was considering lying on the floor and going to sleep right there.

"You should go to bed." The tender words were spoken by Alex, and my heart welled, and I hated myself again. For being so weak that I wanted to be with Alex. For being a coward and not taking that chance. For so many things.

I forced a smile. "What, and miss the potential of hearing what they did to keep possession of the mug? Never."

He laughed, but I stilled.

He cocked his head. "What's the matter?"

"On the pier." Maybe it didn't matter. Maybe I was way off.

"What?"

"How do we find property ownership records?"

He blinked, clearly thrown by my apparent sudden change of topics, but it wasn't at all. "I don't know. Why?"

"On the pier, when Squid and Big Steve were talking to us."

He nodded. Marty and Georgie stopped talking and turned toward me. I ignored them. "When you guys were talking about your shoes, they were telling you about the guy who sells Chinese shoes out of his trunk, and they were saying they barely knew each other."

"Yes, I remember."

"But then one of them said to the other that they got a grill from the same guy years ago. I was just listening to Marty and Georgie talk to each other, and it was reminding me of them. People who hardly know each other don't talk like that. People with shared history do. And they don't buy a single grill without arguing about who gets it."

"They live in the same house," Alex finished.

"How do we find out where they live, and what does it even mean?"

Alex shook his head. "I don't know what it means, but I know they're lying for a reason. You don't lie about not really knowing someone and secretly live with them for no reason."

He headed behind the bar and dug behind the counter. The bartender, a young man with bleached hair named Raph, just watched Alex in silence, not even bothering to ask why Alex was behind the counter. He just went down the bar to serve another exhausted resort employee. Alex leapt over the counter and started scouring the small Aloha Lagoon phone book.

"Who are you looking for though? We don't know either of their real names."

Alex shook his head. "I'm not calling them."

He grabbed the bar line and dialed quickly, greeting whoever answered the phone in what I suspected was Korean. The conversation was quick, and the only part I understood was "Johnny Castle." He thanked the person in English, then again in Korean before hanging up.

He glanced at the three of us. "That was a woman named Mama Leoni. My parents like me to visit her because they're heartily afraid I'll suddenly forget how to speak Korean. She's ancient. Probably the oldest person in Aloha Lagoon. She knows everyone. She says that she doesn't know Johnny Castle's real name, but Squid's name is Peter Eldridge. He was raised around here, but he took off years ago. He only showed up about two years ago. At the same time as Johnny Castle, the dead surfing coach, and the same time when Henry told me he first moved to Hawaii. They must have all come together to grow those drugs."

Peter Eldridge seemed like such a run-of-the-mill name for a guy like Squid. Someone who spent all his time vaguely high, but not so high he couldn't find it in himself to possibly run an opium ring off an abandoned beach. Alex flipped through the book, scanning for an address for Peter Eldridge.

I grabbed his hand. "Wait. The envelope Mallory had taped under her bed. Where is it?"

Georgie pulled a plastic baggie from her purse that contained everything of evidentiary value that we'd found at Mallory's place. Sadly, it contained only the torn piece of newspaper from the envelope and Seth's coded card. I flipped it so I could read the paper clipping again. "Look, this house she circled. It's in the lower-rent part of town, and you can see the house next door in the corner of the ad. I thought maybe she was looking for a new place to live when I left, but what if she wasn't? Look in the window of the house next door."

Alex took the ad and stared. Georgie snorted. "Seriously? The curtains are decorated with pot leaves. If that isn't Squid's decorating taste, I can't guess what is. They came here together and made friends, pretended not to know each other. Maybe this isn't Squid's house, but I sure bet it is. The only way to avoid giving away potential information about what they were up to was to blend in with the locals."

Alex pointed at Georgie. "Call the police and have Detective Ray meet us at the Na Kukui O Ka Mana`Olana. I have no doubt they'll be there. If they're playing locals, they'll be missed if they don't go to the ceremony, and that would be noticed."

Georgie shook her head. "What's a Na Kuku whatever?"

"Candle-lighting ceremony. It's in the town square." He grabbed my hand. "Come on. Let's get downtown. If we don't find him there, we try the home address."

I scrambled after him, blood finally pumping back to my numb brain and limbs, returning me to life after the day we'd had. We took his car, because it was parked closest, and headed for downtown, exceeding the speed limit. If we got pulled over, that would be still better. Then we'd have a police escort. But like Alex, I was sure everyone was at the candle-lighting ceremony. No one would be patrolling tonight.

Normally, as I understood it, the ceremony would take place in a church. There was no church in AL that could accommodate a group this big. Every single person in town would come to light a candle for peace. It was simply expected. And they would do it on the lawn of city hall where long rows of wooden blocks had been set up to receive the candles.

We couldn't get in close. It almost would have been faster to just run over from the resort. We parked at the rear of an endless line of cars, and Alex ran, pulling me clumsily behind him. "What do we do if we find him?" I asked as we approached the square, yelling to be heard over the din of the crowd and the singing of a children's choir.

I stopped dead in my tracks when we got close enough to see the ceremony. The night was lit by thousands of candles. The vision was breathtaking. The candles rested in the wood holders, making long rows of flame-lit paths. The grass was filled with candles, more in hands.

"Wow."

Alex hesitated too, both of us overcome by such an unexpected sight when our minds had solely been on Squid. Then he shook his head. "Come on. Ray must be here."

He grabbed my hand, and we plunged into the crowd, finding two men in uniforms, but one was officer Apodoca and the other was an unfamiliar officer, possibly from a nearby town, who was either here for the ceremony or a resident I simply didn't know. Ray was nowhere to be found. We could only hope that Georgie had gotten through. "What do we do now?" I asked, trying to fight our way out of the crowd.

"I don't know. I guess we go back to the resort, and we wait for Ray. We don't want to go to Squid's house without calling Ray first. At least someone would know where we were. It seems crazy to show up without anyone knowing we'd gone."

My breath caught brutally in my lungs when a face appeared in front of me. Still reeking of pot, for once Squid didn't appear to be high, and I frankly wasn't sure he'd ever actually been. "Why would you want to go to my house?" he requested intently. "See, I've just been following you around, and I couldn't help but to hear my name. You know how that is when someone says your name, even in a crowd."

I restrained a scream, swallowing the noise brutally. Alex grabbed my arm stepping in front of me partially, blocking Squid from access to me. "Merry Christmas, Squid. Let's talk."

I felt something cold and hard jam into my back. "Yes, let's."

CHAPTER FOURTEEN

————

It took me a moment to realize the object was a gun and the speaker was Big Steve. I glanced at Alex, who flashed me a warning look. I knew what he was saying. I was to do nothing and let him handle it. I might. Or I might run for it, if I thought I had a clear shot. Unfortunately, I wasn't the one with a clear shot. Big Steve was.

We started walking slowly and casually towards the edges of the crowd. I scanned the throng but still didn't see Detective Ray. At this point I would have taken any officer. Or even that off-duty guy. But they were nowhere to be found.

"You guys are the biggest pains in my ass ever," Big Steve said, almost conversationally. Belatedly, I realized that Squid was deferring to Big Steve, which befuddled me. Big Steve clearly couldn't be the man in charge of an operation like this, even if I was kind and free with the appellation of *man*. He was, like, twelve years old!

"I had to kill my best bagman. And three other people I really didn't want to kill. Now I have to move my operation somewhere else, and I'm going to kill you two as well. And maybe your hot sister," Big Steve complained, waving the gun in my direction. "You're really pissing me off. I shouldn't have to do this."

His best bagman? Really? *Big Steve?* Big Steve was in charge of the opium ring? I just seriously couldn't wrap my brain around it. I could imagine anyone before I could imagine Big Steve.

"Stop."

The word came from in front of us, and it took a minute before I could tell who the speaker was. I was shocked, though I really shouldn't have been, to see Darcy emerge from the tree line and block our path. "This has gone on long enough, Big Steve. I get that you killed Mallory as a message to me. Because she followed me to the cove and saw the field, and then she talked to Sugarbaker. If only she'd have kept her mouth shut, like I told her."

I really didn't want to draw attention my way, but nevertheless, I had to ask. "Mallory didn't even know what you guys were doing until she found out, what, maybe a week before you killed her, did she?" The truth was shocking. She'd had literally nothing to do with that scene. "She followed you because she thought you'd be surfing. She probably heard about the challenge there, and maybe she thought you were ready to take on a bigger challenge and trying to hide the best waves in town from her. Maybe she just thought she missed you, and she was trying to catch up with you."

Darcy sighed. "She didn't. She knew nothing. Mallory was a sweet girl, but she wasn't that smart. Usually, she believed whatever she was told. I made the mistake of introducing her to Niall when he dropped by the resort one night. I didn't expect them to fall in love. He was Big Steve's bagman, and Mallory was innocent. I told him to stay away from her, but he didn't. She believed he was a businessman though. She would have continued to believe anything if we'd told her. It wasn't until she saw it that she knew."

It must have been about that time that Seth Peterson had approached Mallory, done something to make her understand that he was there for the people she'd just discovered were growing opium just outside of town. Maybe he'd asked her to get him information. Maybe he'd simply advised her to call him if she needed help. Either way, he hadn't come through for her.

Darcy swerved her gun to our right when she likely saw Big Steve move out of the corner of her eye. "You stay put. You and I are through. And don't move another step, or I will kill you."

She raised her arm and gun number two, or maybe even number three, depending on whether or not Squid was armed. Alex and I glanced at each other. Squid proved he was indeed armed, by pulling out his gun. Behind us, the ceremony was still going strong.

"Darcy, you stupid bitch. You can't overthrow me, and you know it. One gun isn't enough."

"How about two?" The question came from the bushes before I saw Eurotrash step out, looking one hundred percent deadly with his European assault rifle. "You killed my brother. Did you think I'd just be okay with that?"

Big Steve shifted, and I guessed he was uncomfortable. Or his mother hadn't told him to use the potty before leaving the house. But I was guessing from the big gun that he was afraid he'd lost his advantage. "The idiot tried to kill me when he found out I killed Mal when he was out of town. I couldn't let that go."

"You killed my brother. I can't just let *that* go," Henry countered.

I couldn't deal. They could shoot each other to pieces, but not here. Not at a peace candle-lighting ceremony. "There are innocent people behind you. Hundreds of them. Please, let's just move away from the crowd."

It was stupid, practically signing our death sentence to leave this location where there was safety in numbers, and we might run into Detective Ray at some point, and I couldn't imagine letting them have a drug turf war, however small, right here where innocent people could die.

Alex shot me a look, and I could see it was a combination of exasperation and admiration. I often felt that way about him. I could only hope that something happened and we were able to escape this. I refused to consider anything else.

Darcy looked at us. "I'm sorry Ms. Conner and Mr. Cho. You guys have been really nice to me. It's a shame it had to come to this. And I'm really sorry about Mallory." She really did look sorry. "I trusted Big Steve, and I loved him."

I glanced at Big Steve again, barely restraining a shudder. Good Lord. The thought was nauseating.

Darcy continued. "I was wrong. And I'm sorry. He shoved Mallory up in the waterfall because he knew the entire staff would be present for the opening-night ceremonies, and he wanted me to know what happens when you talk, just in case I was getting ideas. Well, here's what happens, you douchebag." She touched her gun to the side of his head. "You die."

She turned back to us. "Go. Get in your car, and go straight back to the resort. Don't talk to anyone. I'll take care of these two, but if you don't give me time to get out of town, they won't be the only ones who end being taken care of."

I stared at Darcy, then the others, and shuddered. She had my guarantee. I just wanted to go home. Unsure if they were going to seriously let us go, I glanced at Alex, and he stared back for a long second before grabbing my hand and darting straight into the bushes. I cursed, tripping and banging my way through the prickly bushes, strangling on low-hanging branches. I got it. He wanted them not to have an open view in case someone changed their mind, but he was killing me.

"We've got to help them," he hissed behind him as he dragged me.

"Help the people who wanted to kill us?" I just needed to clarify that one.

"Look—regardless of what they did, we can't just leave Darcy there to kill them. But since we're not armed, there's not a lot we can do except call for help."

We emerged on the other side of the bushes within seconds, and I struggled to keep up, letting him pull me until we reached the nearest open shop, the local bakery, normally closed at this hour. It was probably open in celebration of the festivities, or merely because Aiden, the baker, had come here after enjoying the lighting ceremony and left the door unlocked.

We stumbled inside, dirty and covered in scratches, me wearing a single shoe. We looked almost as bad as when we'd come out from Strangler's Cove.

"I need to use your phone," Alex gasped out when Aiden, standing near the counter, continued staring at us, eyes open wide in horror.

I didn't blame him. We were pretty alarming.

Alex dialed 9-1-1, and this time he was patched through to Detective Ray's mobile, explaining the entire situation in scrambled words. However, when we saw flashlights disappear into the jungle, I figured that the message had been received and understood. We apologized profusely to Aiden, who hadn't yet spoken, and stumbled to the car.

*   *   *

Detective Ray arrived two hours later to tell us that the candle-lighting ceremony had gone off without a hitch. The criminals had never returned closer to the crowd. Big Steve had been found dead on the beach. I was almost one hundred percent certain that could be attributed to Darcy, though Henry had certainly been ready enough to murder the guy. Squid, Johnny Castle, and two other men, including Mo, turned themselves in to Detective Ray when they were discovered trying to drag Big Steve's body off the beach.

Darcy and Henry were gone. Ray saw evidence that a helicopter had approached the beach, and it was very likely we'd never see either one of them again, but I had an inkling that Big Steve's opium-growing operation wouldn't be dying the way he did. Somewhere, Darcy would be running that machine with an iron fist tipped with hideous nails.

Seth Peterson had come out of the woodwork right after he wasn't of any use anymore, and he and Detective Ray contacted the ATF, FBI, and a number of other acronyms, and they were confident they would track Darcy down. I wasn't so sure. She was wily. With the help of Squid and Mo, Detective Ray was sure that there were no other members of the drug group, and peace had been restored to Aloha Lagoon, with most people none the wiser.

Big Steve's operation wasn't that big. Not a massive cartel. Just a small danger to Aloha Lagoon, but I was still glad it was gone. I wasn't certain it would stay that way. I had an inkling Darcy and Henry had resources and bigger ideas. At least they'd be having them someplace else.

*   *   *

I slept until nearly noon. No one woke me up. I shot up in alarm, scrambling for the ringing hotel phone, heart thudding when I saw the time. The call was probably someone saying the whole place was burning down, and I'd slept right through it. Instead it was Alex. "Hello, what's going on?"

His low, throaty laugh shot straight through me. "Merry Christmas, Charlie."

"You...let me sleep in?"

"I figured you needed it. Juan is going to come up with breakfast in about thirty seconds. Enjoy."

"Alex..."

But all I heard was dial tone. I wasn't fast enough. I took a couple of slow, deep breaths and dialed my mother. I gave her a rundown of Mallory's murder, of what had really happened. That Mallory had stumbled on to an ugly truth and tried to do her best to rectify it, and then died for her efforts. I wanted her parents to know that their daughter had left the earth for something, at least. She'd tried to keep others safe, to the extent she'd failed to save herself. It seemed important that they know. Mom said she would pass the information on, and I truly felt hearing it from her would soften everything much more than hearing it from me.

As soon as I hung up, the phone rang again. I snatched it back up, expecting Alex on the other end. Instead, it was the breathless, shrill voice of the VP of Freemont, Nadine. She was one of the two I'd begged to leave town yesterday. Hearing her voice today made my stomach sink.

"Charlotte, darling, I guess you still want to leave Aloha Lagoon?"

Did I want to leave? My stomach twisted brutally. "Yes." The word barely existed. I was ashamed of myself, but my fear was bigger than anything else. I just needed to accept it. The way Georgie accepted who she was. I couldn't shake it, so maybe embracing it was the ticket to breaking out of my self-made prison. At least it had to be a step in the right direction.

"Well, Merry Christmas. You're out of there. There's one flight out of Kapa'a to the big island tomorrow morning. Be on it. Your flight to Chicago will leave the big island two hours later. Take the rest of the year off. We'll see you at corporate on the second."

The words were not a pleasant kind of shock. I wanted out, I reminded myself. *I wanted out.*

"Tomorrow?" I couldn't stop the way my voice shook when I spoke.

"Yes, you'll have to catch a taxi up to the airstrip in Kapa'a tonight, or you'll never make the six AM flight. Better get packing."

We spoke about flight details, and I hung up the phone in a daze. I sat in silence for a long time, maybe hours, before Juan knocked on the door. I took the tray of food and thanked him as sanely as possible. I put the tray on the dresser and grasped for my motivations that were driving me away. I was feeling curiously heartbroken right now. I was very sure I was risking my sanity either staying or going. There was no winning in a situation like this.

Loving something doesn't make you Mom.

I stared at my brunch for a moment and turned away when my stomach heaved. I rubbed my eyebrow and reminded myself that I didn't cry. Not for anything. If I had cried for Mallory, and because of Alex, in the last few weeks, well, these were extreme times, and this was what I wanted, not a reason to mourn.

I took a deep breath, plastered on a happy face, and went to find Georgie. She and Marty were on the pier, talking quietly, standing too close for me to still believe their "just friends" story in my heart of hearts. Maybe they both believed he wasn't into her, but from the outside looking in, I didn't.

"Hey, sorry to break up the Christmas party, but I got a call from corporate."

Georgie's eyebrows rose. "Corporate? You're being relocated?"

"Yeah." I struggled to sound excited or at the very least not completely miserable. "I'm supposed to fly out tomorrow."

Marty was clearly unsure how he was supposed to greet this news. "Is that a good thing?"

I shrugged. *No! It wasn't.* It was. I knew it was. I just had to keep believing that I knew what was best. "Of course. It's my job to move from resort to resort. I'm an interim manager. I shouldn't have been here even this long."

"Charlotte…"

I cut Georgie off. Whatever she was going to say, I didn't want to hear it. I couldn't stand to hear it. "No worries about your jobs. As long as you guys want to stay, you're welcome here."

Georgie shook her head and glanced at Marty. "Can you excuse us for just a second?"

He nodded and moved down the pier, watching the ocean with a still contentment that I deeply envied. I didn't know Marty Gentry, but I wanted to. It was too bad I never really would.

"I wasn't kidding about wanting to be with you," she said grimly.

"Oh, come on. You came to ditch Marty."

Her mouth twisted. "I could have ditched Marty in Colombia, in Puerto Rico, in Milan, or in a thousand other ports of call. I left in Hawaii because I wanted to see you. I don't actually need money. I never did, because I'm Marty's assistant, and he pays me grotesquely well. Even I can't possibly spend it all. I just didn't have a better excuse to stay. I wanted to be with you. I just…I miss you, and I'm sorry, and I wanted my sister back."

I took a deep breath, fighting back another layer of crushing emotion. If people didn't stop, I would never make it out of here alive. "I missed you too," I whispered, giving her a quick hug. "But I can't. I can't stay here. I can't."

"Why don't you just give yourself a chance, Charlotte? Why don't you just try?"

At least she focused in on what was really driving me away. Not my fear of what Alex would turn out to be but my fear of what *I* would.

"I'm sorry, Georgie. For so many things. I can't. I'll see you again, I promise. I…I have to go."

I pasted on my brightest smile, though I had no idea who the presentation was for. Georgie knew I didn't want to go, and no one else was here. Maybe it was just to try to convince myself. I had to go and pack.

I kept my back straight as I packed up everything I'd brought. It wasn't much. Just a few suitcases. I was moments from falling completely apart, and I had to hold it together with all that was in me. If I cracked, it would all come pouring out. Then I would break. I couldn't afford that. Not any of it.

The lobby was empty when I brought my bags down. It was Christmas day. Our staff was a skeleton crew. Everyone in Aloha Lagoon was partaking in another Hawaiian holiday tradition—hanging out at the beach. The other employees had their radios. They weren't otherwise required to be present.

Alex came out of the back office behind the front desk, stopping in his tracks when he saw me. He didn't ask me why I had my suitcases. He'd either already known, or it wasn't hard to guess. He didn't say anything for a long time.

His eyes were like lasers, burning my flesh wherever they touched. I just couldn't handle it. I looked away, staring at the bag at my feet.

"Please see me in your office for one minute before you leave, Charlie." The words were spoken softly. It was begging. Or as close to it as Alex ever got.

I shut my eyes hard, willing myself not to cry. "I can't," I whispered. He had no idea how much I couldn't. I couldn't do anything but concentrate on getting out of town, because I was barely holding on already.

"Please," he whispered back. If I went into that office with him, it wouldn't matter what he said or did. I wanted so desperately to cave, to find some excuse to stay here when we had no real future together. And we didn't have a future because of me. Because I couldn't bear to own my feelings.

I shook my head. "I can't." It came out stronger this time.

He took one long, slow breath, then nodded at me. He turned and left, headed in the direction of the grand ballroom. This hurt so bad. I could barely breathe. It wasn't supposed to be like this. I was supposed to be gone before this ever happened. I was supposed to be gone before I ever lost my heart. Because moving before I cared was how I kept my sanity.

The desk phone rang. There was no one around to answer it. I considered, for a wild second, just ignoring it, but I couldn't do that. "Aloha Lagoon Resort and Spa, Charlotte Conner speaking."

"Oh thank goodness I caught you." I recognized the voice as Nadine's. I watched a group of employees return, practically glowing from happiness and sunshine. Nadine continued, but I could barely pay attention. "Can you please reconsider? I know that Alex said you could go, but there's no one to take your place, and Juls is in Florida for another month. I really need you there, at least until everyone else gets back from the holiday and someone can take over."

It took a moment for the words to really sink in. Not that she was trying to torture me and wanted me to stay another month. The ones before that. "Alex…said I could go?" What did Alex have to do with anything?

"Oh yeah, you know. Or maybe you don't. We were going to pull you out of there four months ago. He said if we pulled you, he was going to quit. Aloha Lagoon just won't run right without him. He's too important to that particular operation. So we did what we had to do."

The words were like rushing in my ears. Alex. Alex had threatened to quit if they sent me on to a new assignment. Alex was the reason I was still in Hawaii after almost seven months. He was the reason I'd had such a regrettably long time to fall in love with him.

Rage warred with the pain of leaving, and thankfully, rage won. I could handle anger. It was a safe place in a sea of agony. I absently hung up the phone without responding.

I put down my suitcase and grabbed the radio from the desk. "Alex Cho, I need to speak to you this instant. Please meet me in your office."

My voice sounded as sharp and hard as every atom inside me felt. He didn't come back to the lobby, and it was a long moment before he responded at all. Even then it was only a single word.

"No."

I pressed my eyes closed. Depression was trying to creep back in when I heard his voice. I needed the anger to stay with me. It would keep me sane. "I need you to come see me, now."

There was a short, harsh laugh from Alex on the other end of the line. Across the room, the returning employees paused, staring at their radios. Even Georgie did as she entered the front door. "I don't think so," he returned, voice hard. "You're not my boss anymore, Charlotte."

Charlotte. My stomach lurched. He'd betrayed me. Kept me somewhere he knew very well I didn't want to be. For what? Just to torture me? And still I had a soft spot for him a mile wide. "You need to come and talk to me now, or we're going to have this discussion right here on this open line. And assuming you don't want the entire staff to know about your behind-the-scenes manipulations, you're going to want to come. Now."

The anger was finally back. *There you are, my old friend.* I needed it to keep me sane.

He appeared in the doorway of the ballroom but didn't come any closer. "Your taxi is going to leave," he pointed out, his tone as lifeless as his expression.

"Corporate just called me. They asked me to stay a little longer, even though *you said it was okay if I left.* Then they told me all about what you said to them. Your demands. Did you seriously do that? Did you seriously threaten them to keep me here even when you knew how badly I wanted to leave?"

There was absolutely no guilt in his expression. There was nothing. He crossed his arms over his chest, the radio held loosely in his right hand. "Yes."

He didn't even try to excuse it. He didn't try to pretend it had never happened or justify his actions. He didn't do anything. Tears threatened again. Anger wasn't enough. Nothing would be.

"Why? Why would you do that?"

He rubbed a hand over his eyebrow. "Because I'm a dumbass. That's why."

It was no answer. At least not one I could understand. Every employee was now completely still. Several more had wandered into the lobby. A few had their radios out, probably to hear this hot mess all the better. I couldn't bring myself to care.

"That's not an answer, and you know it."

"Go catch your plane, Charlotte. We can handle it alone until Juls comes back."

It threw me off, confused me, because it was so unexpected. "What? What the hell, Alex? Why did you do this to me? There are dozens of people who would have killed to come down here from corporate if you wanted help."

I realized I was raising my voice, and I tried to keep it down. There was no reason any stray guest needed to hear this, even though every employee was listening.

"I didn't want help, Charlie. I wanted you."

The words were a hard shock, and they kept me immobilized for a long moment. Then the practical reality of what he must mean finally sunk in. He wanted me to help him. He wanted someone who already knew this business. He wanted to keep the person Freemont qualified as the best.

He snorted, and then suddenly he smiled, though it wasn't one of his familiar grins. It was bitter and hard. "I wanted more time."

"More time for what?"

"More time to make you understand…" His voice trailed off. "You need to go."

I blinked slowly, the words sinking in. Make me understand what? Now I desperately needed to know. "Alex," I repeated softly, the anger draining out, no matter how much I might be relying on it to help me not give in. "Please come and see me in your office."

He stopped, and for a long second I thought he might say no. He looked like he was going to. His slow, shuddering breath hurt my heart. He looked like a man defeated, and nothing ever defeated Alex Cho. It was one of the things I loved most about him. And I loved a lot. I loved him. I was in love with Alex Cho. My stomach twisted hard. It didn't matter what I said to myself or how many lies I told. It was already too late. I loved Alex, and I loved Aloha Lagoon.

I would never tell him, even if I were to stay, but it was too late.

Then he slowly nodded and started walking toward the offices. I followed behind, insanely, embarrassingly aware of every eye on us. I was always professional at work. Every moment of every day. If I stayed until Juls came back, if I stayed for longer, they would probably never look at me with respect again. I couldn't think about it.

He held the door for me, gesturing wide that I should come inside. I swallowed hard, then walked past him. He shut the door behind us with a quiet snick. His arms crossed over his chest, blocking me out with his unmistakable body language.

I had no idea what I was going to say, but it had to be something. I couldn't let this sit. I needed clarification. I needed answers, from myself. So first I needed answers from him.

"What did you want me to understand?"

His jaw clenched. "Does it matter?"

I shook my head, befuddled that he even had to ask. "Of course, it matters. I…I care about you. About what happens to you. And now it's too late. I *need* to know."

He didn't ask me why it was too late or what I meant. I was glad, since I couldn't give him the answer. It was too late because I was already in love. With him and with Hawaii. He was quiet for so long I didn't know if he'd ever answer.

"Charlie, no matter what I meant, could you ever actually see yourself with me? I mean, honestly. Don't you think you're a little…"

He trailed off, but I knew what he was going to say. Anal retentive. Unfriendly. Maybe inhuman. Tears pricked. I shook my head, looking for anything I could grasp on to that wasn't pain.

"A little out of my league."

The words surprised a combination of laughter and tears out of me. Really? That's what he was thinking? "Is there anyone who's out of your league, Alex?" I wiped at my eyes, trying to do damage control before it got any worse.

He stepped closer to me, head cocked. Slowly, he raised a hand, cupping my cheek, wiping an errant tear with his thumb. I was trying so hard to control myself. "I wasn't aware you cried outside of death," he whispered.

I shook my head just slightly. "I don't," I lied. Not when it signified a weakness for him and he'd know what it meant. Not when I might get scared tomorrow and try to run again. He deserved better.

His nostrils flared, and for a second he seemed angry, but then he stepped farther forward and pulled me in, wrapping his arms tighter around me. I couldn't help it. I buried my face in his shoulder, taking in the scent of his detergent, sun-warmed skin, and the organic scent of Alex—the ocean, hot sand, subtle soap. I burst into tears. All the agony of leaving, all the pain of his words, all of the things I'd been holding on to so tightly.

He held me tightly, letting me cry it out for a long time. When it faded to mere hysterical gasps for breath and sniffles, he used a finger to lift my face.

"Charlie, things haven't gone so well between us. It's been…difficult. Sometimes it's been awkward. We stretch each other in the places we don't know how to stretch. But that doesn't mean we can't try."

Maybe I *could* do this. Maybe he was right. Maybe loving someone and not being my mother was something I could do, and a relationship with him was like that hot yoga class everyone else was so wild about. I was too stiff. Too unyielding. My soul was like my body at that class. It didn't want to stretch in the ways the instructor wanted it to. It hurt to move in ways that my body didn't understand. Alex made me move in ways I didn't understand. Ways that hurt because I was too unyielding and too afraid to let go.

He pushed my wildly undone hair away from my face. "Can you tell Nadine you changed your mind? Would you?"

He was asking me to stay. There was no question. My motivation to get out of Aloha Lagoon had been purely centered on trying to avoid falling for Alex and for the magic of Hawaii. It was too late now. I was a goner. The urge to run was momentarily squelched. I had nothing to run from now.

"I…yes." The word made me a dreadful combination of terrified and ecstatic. I nearly passed out, my heart thudded so hard against my ribs.

He grinned. "There you go, baby. That's my favorite word."

"How do you always make everything sound dirty," I sniffed.

"It's a gift."

I was still too terrified to tell him the extent of my feelings. How incredibly hard I had fallen in just seven months. There would be time for that later if I ever got that far. We needed to have a long conversation about my parents, about my fears, about my urges to never be codependent driving me to a fear of ever loving anything too much at all. But for now, the easiest thing to concentrate on was the pedantic, the daily work issue.

"You know I still can't date a coworker. It's wildly unprofessional, and it's completely inappropriate."

He raised an eyebrow. "You're going to stay here and not date me? Is that what you're saying?"

"Yes. No. I don't know. I mean, maybe, you know. Not in public. We can date...alone." I was making a mess of this. But I couldn't be a bad example. It was against everything that was in me. I was already taking a chance staying at all. I could only sacrifice so much before the urge to panic and run would be back.

"You want to have a relationship with me, but you don't want anyone else to know," he clarified.

"Yes. Well, the other employees. I don't care about the people in town. Except, they'd just tell the other employees. So yes."

He nodded. "That's just stupid, Charlie. They heard our conversation anyway, and granted it was very vague, but at least a few of them are going to read between the lines."

For a second anger flared, but then died. *Stretching.* "Take it or leave it, Cho. I am the boss."

He grinned, stepping forward, pulling the lapels of my jacket until we were only a fraction of an inch apart. "That is very hot, when you get all bossy with me. It's one of my favorite things about you."

I couldn't even begin to make a list of my favorite things about him. His never-ending humor. His endless enthusiasm. His keen intelligence. Everything. I loved everything about him. Even the stuff that made me crazy.

"Take it or leave it," I repeated.

He pulled me closer, a wolfish, predatory smile sending chills across my skin and calling every single inch of my body to attention. "Oh, you can bet I'm going to take it," he growled, and there was no mistaking his meaning.

I grabbed his tie, pulling his mouth down over mine. The radio beeped. "This is Eve. Charlotte Conner, please identify."

I ripped my lips from his, head dropping to his chest. With a sigh I couldn't control, I searched for my radio and found it on the desk. Eve was one of the daytime desk clerks, and there might be a problem, despite the quiet day.

"This is Charlotte," I said, watching Alex standing there and being sexy.

"Nadine Rivers is on line three. She says the last call was lost. She needs to speak with you."

I closed my eyes and then opened them again. This is what it would mean to be here and to try to have a relationship with Alex without anyone knowing. It would be this. Over and over again. Stretching. We were just stretching. "Thank you, Eve. Tell her I'll take it my office."

"Your office, ma'am? Does that mean…you're staying?"

The hope in her voice was unmistakable. At some point I'd forgotten what flux did to a program. They needed stability. "Yes, I'm staying. Thank you, Eve," I repeated.

I tucked the radio into my pocket and headed for the door. Alex caught my arm and then pressed a quick, burning kiss against my open mouth. "This is not over," he whispered, echoing the last time we'd been interrupted by the radio.

"Better not be," I whispered back, ducking out of the room, grinning at the sound of his laughter behind the door.

ABOUT THE AUTHOR

Aimee Gilchrist lives in New Mexico with her husband and three children. She writes mysteries for both teens and adults. She calls her lifetime of jumping from one job to another 'experience' for her books and not an inability to settle down. Aimee loves mysteries and a good, happy romance. She also loves to laugh. Sometimes she likes all of them together.

A fan of quirky movies and indie books, Aimee likes to be with her family, is socially inept, and fears strangers and small yippy dogs. She alternates between writing and being a mom and wife. She tries to do both at the same time but her kids don't appreciate being served lunch and told, "This is the hot dog of your discontent." So mostly she writes when everyone else is in bed.

Aimee also writes YA and Inspirational Romantic Comedies under the name Amber Gilchrist.

Visit the official

website!

Trouble in paradise...
Welcome to Aloha Lagoon, one of Hawaii's hidden treasures. A little bit of tropical paradise nestled along the coast of Kauai, this resort town boasts luxurious accommodation, friendly island atmosphere...and only a slightly higher than normal murder rate. While mysterious circumstances may be the norm on our corner of the island, we're certain that our staff and Lagoon natives will make your stay in Aloha Lagoon one you will never forget!

www.alohalagoonmysteries.com

If you enjoyed *Mele Kalikimaka Murder*, be sure to pick up these other Aloha Lagoon Mysteries!

www.GemmaHallidayPublishing.com

Made in the USA
San Bernardino, CA
18 December 2016